Praise for the short story writing c

About *Small Regrets*

"Margoshes has a fine ear for dialogue, and his characters communicate with razor-sharp exchanges reminiscent of those found in Raymond Carver's work." — *The Globe and Mail*

"His stories capture those poignant moments in life when mistakes, inadequacies or emotional cowardice dog every human relationship....These stories are thoughtful indictments of a world where people have forgotten how to love each other. Dave Margoshes is a perceptive observer of the world and a talented storyteller." —*The Register Guard*

"Margoshes' style is simple, clean, precise and powerful. No word is wasted; no word is vague.... Margoshes is an artist whose strokes demand close examination." —*Prairie Fire*

"Whether living in New York, Vancouver, Reno or San Francisco, a typical Margoshes hero seeks sex and violence as a release from boredom and frustration; standing at the edge of a void, he looks for answers to questions, but waits in vain for vision in darkness. The reader is left shuddering with the sinister feeling that some of the agonies beneath everyday life have been exposed." —*Event*

About *Nine Lives*

"This collection is wonderfully subversive and funny and bursting with Prairie wisdom and Margoshes's own unique vision of the unusual and seductive....He is truly one of Canada's finest poets and storytellers." —*Michael Coren*

"Margoshes weaves a strange spell with these stories. You laugh a little, you wince a little, but you can't turn away. Like them all or – as I did – feel the odd shiver of revulsion, you can't help but appreciate the bare-bones writing." —*The StarPhoenix*

"Margoshes' imagination is fervid and eclectic..." —*The Vancouver Sun*

DAVE MARGOSHES

■

Long
Distance
Calls

COTEAU BOOKS

Long Distance Calls

Edited by Geoffrey Ursell.
Cover painting by Alex Colville, "To Prince Edward Island," 61.9 x 92.5 cm, acrylic emulsion on masonite, 1965.
Cover design by Bradbury Design Inc.
Book design and typesetting by Val Jakubowski.
Printed and bound in Canada.
Author photo by Don Hall.

The publisher gratefully acknowledges the financial assistance of the Saskatchewan Arts Board, the Canada Council, the Department of Canadian Heritage, and the City of Regina Arts Commission.

Canadian Cataloguing in Publication Data
Margoshes, Dave, 1941-
    Long distance calls / by Dave Margoshes
    ISBN: 1-55050-104-6
I. Title.
PR199.3.M374L65 1996   C813!.54   C96-920068-4
PS8576.A647L65 1996

COTEAU BOOKS
401-2206 Dewdney Avenue
Regina, Saskatchewan
S4R 1H3

This book is dedicated to the memory of my father.

Contents

These are the days of miracle and wonder
This is the long distance call
— Paul Simon, "The Boy in the Bubble"

The past is never dead. It's not even past.
— William Faulkner

From the Burns Family Table

WHEN MY UNCLE Woody died in 1977, a grand old man of ninety-two, I went back to Ontario for the funeral filled with mixed feelings.

I hadn't been home for five years, and I hadn't seen my "uncle" – he was actually a third cousin but uncle was the word always used – for probably another two, so my mood, on the long flight from Vancouver and on the interminable automobile rides – airport to my parents' house, where my wife and I would be staying the night, then to Aunt Vera's, the massive old house strangely still, then to the funeral home, church, cemetery – was one of sadness, regret, even guilt. There was so much I should have done, I knew, a visit, letters in the years since I'd left home, more kindness – at least *attention* – to repay all that he'd given me; there should have been more things said to compensate for all that which had been left unspoken during the years when our lives were only a half hour's drive apart.

But it's hard for a child or a teenager to be anything more than what he is, and it would be wrong, I told myself, for an adult to attempt to force the kind of familiarity, almost intimacy, he'd had with certain people when he was a child beyond their natural boundaries. Uncle Woody had his own life – and it was a big one – that I had been a casual inhabitant of when it was still possible for him – for the *family* – to have certain hopes for me. Once those hopes began to fade, there hadn't been much point in trying to keep breathing life into a friendship that probably had no other reason to be. Woody would have understood that, at least I hoped he had. He was a *user* of people, not in the malignant sense the word has come to have, but someone who was able to grasp and develop a person's best possibilities. When those possibilities were exhausted, it was better to turn one's attention elsewhere.

Beyond that, and I admitted to myself the triteness of the thought, Woody was not the kind of man one could easily imagine dying; he seemed to have the sort of permanence, despite his age and the arthritis that had made his later years almost always painful, of history itself.

By the time the funeral party migrated again to the Thamesford Road estate, where Uncle Woody had presided for so long, most of these feelings had evaporated, much the way the perfect little puffs of smoke that erupted over the heads of the smartly uniformed soldiers who fired the salute at the graveside had slowly dissipated into the sharp blue air. There had been hundreds at the church – over five hundred, I read in *The Globe and Mail* the next day, a number befitting the funeral of a former premier – taking up every space in the pews and spilling out onto the steps and lawn in front, where they'd stood like anxious retainers, straining to hear every word of the tedious sermon broadcast from a tinny speaker set above the door, and almost as many in the solemn-faced throng that stood in polite, observant rows at the cemetary, where there was a better view of the widow and assembled members of the Burns and Barnett clans, and it was easy to convince myself that there had been plenty of love and attentiveness filling the Old Saddlemaker's moments in his last years to excuse the absence of mine. By contrast, the reception at Aunt Vera's, to which only the family and closest of friends had been invited, seemed intimate, with fewer than a hundred in the collection of faces and names for my storehouse of memory to juggle.

"Bob, who's the man with the basset hound eyes?" Anne whispered, raising her chin in the direction of a well-dressed, silver-haired man of average height and build but possessed of the most melancholy gaze. "He looks like a professional mourner."

"I don't know, not a member of the family, that's for sure," I said. I had noticed the man she indicated several times at the cemetery, dolefully gazing in my direction as if uncertain as to my identity and unhappy at the possibilities. "Must be one of Uncle Woody's old cronies. There were dozens of them close enough to be here today."

The white-haired man, who seemed to have noticed us returning his gaze, turned away with a self-conscious shrug and busied himself with staring at the ice in his drink, swirling it slowly around in the glass, but, as we watched, looked our way again and seemed to be considering approaching us.

My father drifted by, eyes bright from tears and drink, a vague smile flickering on his softly defined mouth. I touched his arm, which seemed thin and bony beneath the dark wool suit jacket.

"This must be tough on you kids," he said, "especially you, Annie." Although they'd met only a few times, a real warmth had developed between my father and my wife, the empathy of two outsiders, and they smiled at each other.

"Dad, who's that over there in the corner, the white-haired gent with the hound-dog eyes pretending he's not looking at us? Don't look over too fast or you'll spook him."

My father said hello to a red-faced woman who had strayed within chatting distance and let his head swivel around to follow her wobbly progress past us. "Ah, that's old Dolan, Richard T. Dolan and don't forget the T., thank you. I didn't realize that old bird was still alive."

"He's the *saddest* looking man I think I've ever seen," Anne said.

"Oh, sure, he would be. Woody made him. Without Woody...." My father let the words trail off and his shoulders rose in a shrug that seemed to mingle resignation with defeat. "Like so many others." He paused and smiled at Anne before adding: "And this husband of yours, *he* didn't help." He patted my arm and headed across the crowded room toward the bar, his mouth setting itself into an expression of determination.

Anne turned to me, to ask the inevitable question, but Dolan was already heading our way. "I wasn't sure who you were until I saw you talking with Al Barnett," he said, extending his hand. "The beard hides the family resemblance. Richard T. Dolan. My condolences on your great-uncle's death." He tilted his head slightly toward Anne and produced a courtly smile. "I hope you'll forgive my staring."

"I was just telling my wife about you. You were social services minister, weren't you?"

Dolan smiled with childlike pleasure, but even with his face open, his eyes retained their disconsolate quality, as if they'd been touched by a sadness they alone could never forget. They were the flat, dull grey of an aging battleship. "First labour, then social services, yes. You have a good memory. You were only a little boy."

"I paid attention. And you ran for the leadership, too."

Dolan's lips turned the smile into something else. "Fifty votes, that's what I lost by." He lowered his head, as if there was something in his glass he needed to consult. "I never blamed your uncle – no one ever did. He was above that sort of thing."

"What about me?"

The question seemed to surprise him. The grey eyes fastened themselves on me, examining me as if I were an object of some considerable curiosity. Then they shifted to Anne. Dolan looked at her appraisingly, but it was hard to tell if he was appraising her or, through her, me. "You haven't introduced me to your charming wife."

"I'm sorry, I thought I had." I made the introductions.

"Ah, I'm delighted," Dolan said, nodding his head slightly. "I must tell you, I owe your husband a great debt."

Anne smiled. "How's that?"

"He freed me from the yoke of leadership, what his uncle Woodrow used to call 'the magnificent burden.'"

"How did he do that?"

For some reason, as if she had sensed something fearful,

her hand slipped into mine, and we were still young enough, still married a short enough time, that it thrilled me.

"Ah," Dolan said, smiling and nodding his head. "He was only a little boy. But, as he just said, he paid attention."

He put a hand on my arm, as if to console me for some old hurt, but his eyes said it was I who would never be forgiven.

Our family was prominent in Western Ontario for several generations before Uncle Woody became premier, but during the thirty or forty years of his prime, he was the undisputed head of the family, and his approach to government and the party was not dissimilar to the way he ruled the family. There was fairness, even-handedness, with each affected member in a dispute given his turn to speak, but Woody's word was law, and, once he had pronounced it, there was no argument, no recourse, no appeal.

The family had made its fortune and name in commerce – at one time, a Barnett had been the owner of a factory, the richest and most powerful industrialist in London, while a Burns had been the owner of the largest block of land in the district and the operator of the area's most popular brewery – and, over the generations, the two clans had become inter-twined, with the leadership often alternating between the two. They were hard-nosed, pragmatic Anglicans of the old school – smart, shrewd, righteous and without mercy, at times, al-though they had their weaknesses, like any family does. A great-great Barnett uncle had sullied the family's good name with a divorce and the incident simply ceased to be: the wife, it was said, had "passed away," the uncle had been "ill, for a long time," and the story told so often that the tellers had probably come to believe it themselves, forgetting the truth. Even my own fall to the left and marriage to a Catholic, in times when tolerance had come into vogue and notions of family fallen on hard times, was enough to cause embarrassment for my parents and a great silence to emanate my way from London and its outports.

The two distinct strands of the family had begun as competitors – a bit of family lore that adults liked to suppress but a mischievous aunt was always likely to leak to thrill-hungry children was that Great-great-great-grandfather Barnett, the industrialist, and Great-great-great-grandfather Burns, the landowner, had once come close to fighting a duel, pistols at dawn, but had settled for settling their differences instead in a less dangerous, if more visceral, way by battering each other senseless with their fists in one of Great-great-great-grandfather Burns' barns, while a crowd of onlookers cheered.

There was a marriage of a Barnett daughter to a Burns son less than a year later – Uncle Woody was a direct descendent – and this auspicious beginning has always seemed to me an appropriate symbol for the history of the family itself: there were rivalries between the two branches but they were better resolved through a coming-together than combat.

Often these rivalries erupted into open hostilities – "Don't forget, you're a Barnett," my mother used to sniff to me when I was a child and she was suffering under yet another perceived insult to my father, who, after a promising start, had resigned from the race for influence within the family – but always there was the transcendent notion of the unity of the family itself to pull opponents together, to heal wounds, and always implicit in my mother's reminder was the knowledge that I was a Burns too, for better or for worse.

This was the state of the world as I grew increasingly conscious of it during my boyhood in the late forties and through all of the decade of the fifties: Uncle Woody was in the premier's office in Queen's Park and the family, like the party, was prospering – even my father, who, to the disappointment of the family, had become a pharmacist, not a doctor, was doing well, within his own smaller sphere.

On Sundays during most of that period – every Sunday when the Legislature was out of session, every other Sunday when it was in – there was open house at the rambling old stone and white clapboard mansion where Uncle Woody and Aunt Vera had lived all their married life, just outside London, on the old road to Thamesford. The estate had been in the Burns family for three generations already – Uncle Woody's grandfather, the brewer's son, had built it – but it showed little sign of wear. There was room after room after room, with unexpected nooks and a perplexing locked door leading to the attic, and it was crammed with alluring objects, like the slim silver cigarette box I once stole and later returned; it was the kind of house which, with its graceful, well-lit arches, replicas of Greek statues and expensive, not-always-comfortable furniture, was hospitable to adults but intriguing to children. Outside, there were several acres of trees, a stream crowded with glistening stones, a pack of goofy and playful dogs, a stable with two dignified old Morgan horses and two agreeable ponies, and, of course, the lake, not big enough to make Uncle Woody open to charges of ostentation, but big enough just the same to float a small rowboat. It was stocked with trout, and it was his greatest pleasure.

I guess I was about nine when I fell under the grace of Uncle Woody's eye and became his favourite. His own children were grown by then, but had yet to present him with grandchildren, so it seemed natural that he should choose someone from the flock of nephews, nieces and cousins who crowded into the house, spilling out onto the grounds, on Sundays. It was well known – everyone said it, that is – that Uncle Woody loved kids, and there was evidence to back that up that my younger brother and I and the troop of cousins we played with on those weekend visits could appreciate: little cellophane-wrapped hard candies came in an endless, multicoloured stream from the pockets of the leather and corduroy hunting jacket he wore when he was taking the air at home, and there was always a friendly word, a little joke and an energetic tousling of hair, delivered with the same sort of even-handed cheerfulness that, as I got older, I noticed him applying to many of the adults he encountered as well.

We had the run of the house and grounds, the dogs to play with, the lake to swim in or skate on, and the ponies to ride – under the guidance of old Peter, the gardener and handyman who made sure neither we nor the ponies came to any harm. The one place we weren't allowed, a place reserved for adults – and only male adults at that – was the study, the book-lined, leather-and-tobacco-smelling room where Uncle Woody would hold court, dispensing liquor and politics in equal doses.

My great-uncle never discussed the thinking of his government with his kin, "but he sure as hell lets everybody within earshot know what he thinks of the opposition, there's no confidentiality about that," my father used to report as he drove our old cream-coloured Plymouth toward home Sunday evenings, and he would sometimes – not always – regale us with some of Uncle Woody's observations, suitably laundered, I suppose: the Opposition leader, a sour-faced man with white hair, was referred to by the premier as "that mouldy lemon," my father said as my brother and I roared with laughter, and it was easy to imagine Uncle Woody making this pronouncement, curved pipe in mouth, caterpillar brows furrowed, as the other men in the family, whisky glasses in their hands, chuckled and nodded their heads appreciatively.

My father was not completely comfortable in those Sunday trips to the Thamesford Road estate, and probably even less so when the door to the inner sanctum of the study closed behind him, sequestering him in with the cigar smoke, whisky fumes and the dust of family history and tradition, and I suspect he would have liked to have kept us at as great a distance as possible if he could have, but he couldn't. Uncle Woody and my Grandfather Barnett, who I never knew, had been close, and the head of the family took a proprietary interest in his cousin's war-widowed wife and her offspring that made it all but impossible, without an actual rupture of relations, to escape his attention. And, perhaps because my father had been such a disappointment (Uncle Woody paid his way through university and would have paid for medical school as well, if my father hadn't faltered at the last minute), perhaps because of the solemn, thoughtful manner I adopted in those years to mask my shyness, I fell beneficiary to that interest.

Our relationship as something more than that shared by the jolly old uncle and the rest of the children in his wake began with fishing. I loved to fish, as he did, and while the rest of the cousins were engaged in shrieking games on the broad, shaded lawns, I would often spend my springtime and summer Sunday afternoons on the dock or under the ancient oak growing on the bank where the stream poured noisily into the lake, trying to induce the shimmering shadows flickering beneath the water to grace me with their favour. He'd seen me there, had watched me, I suppose, made inquiries, considered, with the same deliberateness he brought to the most difficult and serious decisions of state.

"Boy, let's me 'n you go fishing," he said to me one Sunday in early May, the year I was nine. His voice combined in one smooth flow of fluid, reassuring sound a countrified ease of diction with a precision that he'd learned during his two years at Oxford. It was a comfortable voice, comfortable and well fitting as a slipper from the expensive men's shop in Toronto where Aunt Vera bought his accessories.

In the boat, he rowed while I let my line dangle and he coaxed me gently into the chatter that was always bursting within me, just below the surface, with questions of fishing.

"This look like a good spot to you? It certainly does to me. What do you say?"

"Sure. This is fine."

He looked at me, letting the smile fade from his sensual mouth to be replaced by something that was as close to severity as I'd ever seen on his face. "Let's get this straight between us right now, shall we? I want us to get off to a good start. I'm your great-uncle, and I have an important job. I don't make it my custom to tell lies, but I do, on occasion, find it to my advantage to leave things out. Do you follow me, boy?"

I was frightened by the sudden change in his mood, but, inexplicably, impressed by the words themselves. I liked that he'd said he had an important job, not that he was an important man. It was something I'd heard my father say about him. "Yes sir," I said, trying to keep my voice level.

"And I'm not accustomed to surrounding myself with people who tell lies – or leave things out. *I* have to do that, sometimes, but I never like doing it, and I won't tolerate other people doing it to me." The smile came flooding back

9

into his round face and the small, pig-like eyes of startling blue danced over his small, snub nose. "That's a little luxury I allow myself, that double standard. Some people might say I'm a hypocrite because of it – do you know what that is, boy? A hypocrite?"

"I think so, sir. My dad told me."

"Good. Your dad is giving you a vocabulary. Good. You might hear that, that I'm a hypocrite, but I figure I need that double standard not because of anything about myself but because of the job I have. That always has to come first. Do you understand what I'm saying, boy?"

"Yes sir."

"Fine. I believe you do. You seem like a bright boy, and I like you. We're going to get along fine, as long as the fish and the bait hold out. But there has to be one thing straight between us, and that's what I've been *attempting*, in my somewhat long-winded way, to get at. There can't be any subterfuge between us. Did your dad teach you that word, boy?"

"No sir," I said, though I was tempted to say yes, to impress him.

"Subterfuge, that means little deceptions, where you say one thing but mean another, or you twist things around."

"Lying, you mean, sir?"

"Well, yes, but more than just lying. Trying to fool somebody else, I think that's it. We'll make this little agreement: I won't lie to you or try to fool you, *ever*, and you won't lie to me or try to fool me, *ever*. Do you understand?"

"Yes sir."

"And you agree?"

"Yes sir. I do." I could barely contain the wonder I felt at that moment, or the love, and my hands trembled on my fishing pole, something Uncle Woody's sharp eyes didn't miss.

"Okay, then, fine. Now, how about this spot? Does it look okay to you or would you like to go someplace else?"

"I saw one jump a minute ago, sir, over there." I pointed over his shoulder toward the bank on the other side of the lake.

Uncle Woody grinned and pulled at one long, slipper-shaped ear with his stubby fingers. "Okay, boy, let's go on over there, then, and catch some of 'em." He began to row, looking like a man at ease with himself and the world.

Woodrow Dyson Burns was fifty-four years old, just a few years older than the century, the summer he became premier of the province of Ontario. He was a King's Counsel, had been a Rhodes Scholar, had made a considerable amount of money. He'd been a member of the Legislature for seven years, four of them as attorney-general, and his influence within the party was impressive, enough to assure him an easy capture of the leadership on the second ballot; his popularity with the people was immense, enough to bring his government a sixty-seven seat majority in the election he called almost immediately after the convention. "People may be reluctant to buy saddles for horses they may never have use for," he said, explaining that his government lacked a mandate to do anything until it had been blessed at the polls, and inspiring the nickname "Saddlemaker" the press gleefully attached to him and that was to stick for the rest of his time in office.

He was in his second term when our weekly fishing trips began, and would lead the party in one more election before, unexpectedly, he announced his retirement the autumn I was thirteen and he was sixty-five, as many years between us as there are cards in a deck. I say unexpectedly because the press and public, even the party, had no idea it was coming. His health was excellent and his popularity undiminished, the skin of his government bright with that well-fed lustre of contentment and ease that good management and a strong economy produce. There had been some blunders, even a few small scandals – the gold-capped walking stick of Arthur McConnell was the most notorious – but he had managed to let precious little of that mud fall on his shoes, and there was little thought of challenging his leadership, even among the restless ministers close to him, like Dolan and Royce, and no thought that he would lead the party to anything but another majority in the next election.

The reasons for his departure had more to do with Aunt

Vera than political problems or any loss of relish for the work, and he had mentioned this to me, as he'd come to do with many of the things weighing on his mind, months before he actually made the decision.

"Think I'm going to have to pack 'er in, Bobby," he said one lovely April morning.

We'd been on the lake less than half an hour so I looked up with surprise, disappointment flooding into my throat. "Sir?"

He laughed at my face. "I don't mean the fishing, boy, I mean the *other* puddle I dangle my line in."

Uncle Woody was fond of rural imagery, convinced as he was that that was where the majority of the voters' hearts were, even if earning a living had led them elsewhere, and I knew what he meant.

"You're not in any trouble, sir," I said. "Dempsey is all bluster. If he had what he pretends he has, he would have trotted it out already, isn't that so?" The Liberals, now led by red-faced Richard Dempsey ("Carrot-Face," Uncle Woody called him privately), had been pounding the government over the budget for weeks but they'd so far made as much impression as a child plucking at its father's pantslegs.

Uncle Woody looked at me shrewdly. "You think so, eh?" He laughed, leaning back in the boat and puffing on his pipe with that contented expression I'd come to associate with our fishing but little else. He'd begun talking to me about things on his mind almost as soon as our relationship began, talking with the kind of careless, intimate abandon one does sometimes with a dog or an infant. I guess, at nine, that I was not far removed from that – at any rate, I'm sure I had no idea what most of the things he said meant, though I listened with fascinated, adoring intensity. Then, as my trustfulness became proven, his trust in me increased, the circle spinning itself out with the same logic and determination as the life cycle of the insects our lures imitated.

I don't think it ever occurred to me to repeat any of what I heard, even if I could have made sense of it ("Just stuff," is what I told my parents when they pressed me on what Woody and I talked about during those long mornings on the lake). It was something special and private just between him and me – "our little secret," he called it, when he was thinking seriously about the election date and it struck him suddenly that his ramblings to me could become a liability, but those were the words that I had been thinking to myself all along. "Our secrets" – there was no more chance that, before or after my pledge, I would have revealed any of them, to mother or father, my brother, a playmate or anyone else, than that we'd land Old Brownie, the huge brown trout that lurked beneath a sunken tree stump along the edge of the lake, surfacing briefly to sample the mayflies and tempt and frustrate our efforts.

I was a quick study – then as I am now – and was an avid reader by the time I was nine, turning to the newspaper for the kind of glimpses into the world of adults the books I had available to me couldn't provide, so even by the time of Uncle Woody's third election I was a fairly intelligent audience for the kind of political musings he allowed himself on the lake, and, at thirteen, when he told me he would be calling it quits, I flattered myself that I was as shrewd and knowledgeable a political observer as any of the parties or press could provide, and Uncle Woody was no longer afforded the indulgence of a monologue – we *talked*.

"Aunt Vera's getting no better?" I asked on one of our last times on the lake that autumn, when Uncle Woody seemed particularly preoccupied.

"She's getting no worse, but it's only because she's intuited what's on my mind," he said, flicking his line with a graceful arch of the wrists that I'd long copied but still hadn't completely duplicated.

"So she'll be OK?" I asked hopefully, really more concerned with my uncle's career than my aunt's health.

"Don't know, but it would be nice if we old horses could spend some time in the pasture, wouldn't you say?"

As it would turn out, Aunt Vera's ailment – he never told me exactly what it was, and the family was certainly too secretive to acknowledge the mastectomy I now believe she had that year, certainly not to a thirteen-year-old boy – cleared up, and she went on to outlive him. But her health was the chief thing on his mind that morning in the boat and two weeks later, when he dropped his bombshell, first to cabinet, then later in the day to caucus and, still later, to a press conference packed by the rumours circulating around Queen's Park.

Royce was the first one in the race, less than twenty-four hours after the announcement, and some people said that would hurt him, that so much eagerness on the part of the attorney-general was indecent. Morgan, the treasurer and early favourite, came in next, then Dolan, Richard T., the social services minister, who was solid, respected, had made no serious enemies but was somewhat colourless, lacking in, well, *something*. These were my own observations, bolstered somewhat by the views of the press. Despite Uncle Woody's openness with me on any number of matters of party and government, he kept his opinions of the men vying for his job to himself, and the last thing in the world I would have expected him to tell me was who, among the half a dozen who finally entered the race, was his favourite.

The convention was held in late April in Toronto, some two thousand delegates from across the province cramming into the massive hall in the basement of the Royal York Hotel. But the highlight, at least as far as I was concerned – and probably for thousands of others, people who didn't care as much for the possible new as the tangible old – was Woodrow Burns Night, the lavish outpouring of love and respect the party paid to its long-time leader on the first night of the convention, a few blocks from the hotel at Maple Leaf Gardens, with bands, speeches and the presentation of an automobile as a going away gift.

It seemed to me there was a full house – though that would have meant that for every actual delegate there were another nine people who were just Burns fans – with open-faced admirers hanging from the balconies and cheering their lungs out, just as if it were Glenn Hall down there in the spotlight rather than the large, beaming man with the greying hair rolling the smooth bowl of his pipe in his cupped hand like a talisman, a man who had dominated their headlines for years but, with the exception of a campaign

14

handshake or wink, most of them didn't really know. There were speeches, of course, testimonials from cabinet members past and present, the mayor, even Dief was there, drawing applause and whistles loud as those for Uncle Woody, and the two of them stood for a long moment with hands clasped together above their heads in a sort of upside down v that seemed to be providing a shelter for us all: beneath the strong hands of these men, within their strong arms, their gesture seemed to say, no harm can come to you.

The night climaxed with the presentation of the car. Uncle Woody had always been partial to Chryslers and this one was an Imperial, snow white, with a big v8 engine, creamy leather upholstery, air conditioning, power windows, the works. It was a beautiful car, and when it was pushed out into the middle of the Gardens, to where the stage had been set up just over where the blue line would have been, I was sitting in the driver's seat, a grin plastered across my face, my heart beating louder than the engine of that car ever would.

The band was playing something brassy and a spotlight was shining on the car as it was rolled toward the stage, where Uncle Woody and Aunt Vera and a group of men were standing in the sudden dark. There was a drum roll, the door clicked open and the dry, electric voice of the speakers was hissing: "Woody, we asked your nephew Bobby what he thought you might like as a going away present and he suggested a new fly rod... said some of the snap is going out of your old one (laughter)... but, and begging your pardon, Bobby, that just didn't make much sense to us, so we settled on letting you keep your old fly rod and giving you something to get you *to* the fishing hole. And, no, it's not a horse and saddle. Bobby, would you do the honours?"

That was my cue to scramble out of the car, climb the stairs to the stage and hand Uncle Woody the dangling, gleaming keys. The lights came back on and the band was playing again, and Woody looked sort of stricken, almost shy, a man who made his living talking to people suddenly without anything to say. His eyes were big with pleasure, bigger than I'd ever seen them, and he gave me a hug and said something to me – I think it was "I'll get you for this, boy," but I couldn't be sure, the cheering was so loud and my heart was pounding so violently.

A funny thing happened afterwards. We were all going to a party at the hotel – since I was sort of a guest of honour, there hadn't been any thought of excluding me – but well-wishers were swamping Uncle Woody and it was taking forever getting out of the crush of the Gardens. I found myself out in the arcade area and I stopped at a stand to get a pop.

"Hey, you're the nephew, eh? Burns' nephew?"

Standing next to me was a bright-looking young man with longish, slicked-back hair wearing a checkered jacket and brown knit tie on a rumpled white shirt. There was a tape recorder slung from his shoulder and I could see from its markings he was from CHUM, the big rock 'n' roll station.

"Sure. How're ya doin'?"

"Great. Hey, that must've really been somethin', eh, ridin' out into that crowd in that car? It's a beauty, too."

"Yeah, it was wild."

The reporter took a swig from his Coke and looked at me much the way Uncle Woody sometimes did. "I guess you and the premier are real buddies, eh? Fishing pals?"

I grinned and shrugged. "I guess."

"He tells you things? I mean, he talks about what's goin' on with the government, cabinet meetings, that sort of thing?"

I was glowing, my blood racing again. "Sure, he tells me all sorts of stuff."

"But I guess he swears you to secrecy, though, eh?" The reporter winked.

"Sort of."

"I don't suppose he's, you know, mentioned anythin' about who he's backing, has he?" He put his paper cup down on the stand and looked at me closely, his hand straying to the tape recorder, resting on it.

"Naw, he don't talk about *that*." I looked at the tape recorder. "That thing on?"

"The tape? Naw. This isn't an interview, we're just

talkin'." He brightened suddenly. "Say, though, how'd you *like* to be on the air? Who do *you* think is gonna win? I mean, you must pay pretty close attention to this sort of stuff, eh? Know a little bit about politics? I bet you're thinkin' about goin' into politics yourself, eh?"

He had me then, though I guess there wasn't any doubt about it from the beginning. His finger pressed a button on the recorder and a small red light went on and a minute later I was telling him that Royce looked like the best bet to me. The A-G's eagerness was a good sign, I said, showing that he'd thought a lot about the job and the things he could bring to it, not a bad one indicating indecent ambition. He was the best man for the job, and delegates would realize that after the second ballot, when Morgan, who was still leading in the polls, started to slip.

"You think that'll happen, Bobby?"

"Sure." The treasurer couldn't make it because he already had all the support he was likely to get, and it wasn't enough.

"And Dolan?"

He was overrated and wouldn't make it past the second ballot. The others didn't count.

That was the way I had figured it, on my own, pretty much from the same sources of information – the newspapers – everybody else had, and, I guess, the bit more I knew about each of the leading players from things Uncle Woody had said about them over the years, that Morgan was shrewd, methodical, a good right hand, Royce brilliant and headstrong, Dolan cranky and loyal, things that anybody who paid attention might have known, should have known. I didn't think I was breaking a trust.

But on the morning broadcast, and the successive airings it had through the day, when the speeches were being given and the delegates were making up their minds for the next day's voting, what I'd told the reporter the night before was being called "tidbits from the Burns family dinner table."

"It looks like James Royce, Woody Burns' attorney-general, has his boss's blessing, at least privately," the voice of the newscaster said. "The premier has refused to say anything *publicly* about who he's supporting, but one of Mr. Burns' closest confidantes told our Jim Bittersly that Royce is the chosen one."

Then there was my taped voice, sounding wise and pompous for about fifteen seconds, saying Royce was "the best man for the job" and Morgan's support "wasn't enough," Dolan was "overrated."

Then the young reporter's voice: "Admittedly, young Bobby Barnett is only thirteen years old and he's not on the premier's payroll, but the bright young lad, who had the honour of presenting his great-uncle with the keys to the spanking new Chrysler Imperial a grateful Conservative party gave him last night, does have the premier's ear. The two are constant fishing companions and, as young Bobby readily admits" – and here my voice could be heard again – "'he tells me all sorts of stuff.'"

Then the reporter again: "So, while it may not have the ring of authenticity it would have coming from Burns himself, this young man's prediction sure sounds like a tasty little tidbit from the Burns family dinner table. I'm Jim Bittersly."

"Very funny," my father said. There'd been a telephone call to our room at the hotel from one of the young fellows in Uncle Woody's office to warn us to listen to the next newscast.

"That dirty guy," I said. "He *did* have that recorder on all the time."

Through the day, the corridor talk among delegates was that it was a joke, not to be taken seriously, but by late afternoon Uncle Woody's office put out a press release re-emphasizing that he had made no endorsement, and wouldn't, publicly or privately. "There are no tidbits," the press release said, but that just made it possible for the other radio stations and the papers to repeat the original story. And the next afternoon, Royce was surprisingly strong on the first ballot, with about fifty more votes than the *Globe*'s informal delegate count had shown, but still way behind Morgan, whose strength didn't slip on the second ballot, as I had thought it would. As it turned out, Royce never was a real threat, but he was strong enough that Dolan, who began to falter on the third ballot, seemed to have no choice but to drop out, going to Morgan, who won handily on the next vote.

I often wondered who Uncle Woody wanted to win – certainly Morgan turned out to be a good leader and premier – but we never talked about it. I lived in dread those two days, but Uncle Woody was busy throughout it and if there was something he wanted to say to me he didn't take the time to say it. Immediately after the convention, he and Aunt Vera went off for a week's holiday, then there was the busy time of the transition, though Morgan, unlike the Old Saddlemaker, wasn't all that eager for an election and he didn't go to the polls until the fall. So there was a series of Sundays that, for one reason or another, Uncle Woody wasn't at home and my parents took the opportunity to spend some time on themselves, as my father liked to say, "rather than the damned family." That summer, with high school coming up after it, my parents thought it might be good to send me to camp to give me some of the socializing skills I still didn't have, at least that's what my mother said.

I still saw a lot of Uncle Woody, though more and more he and Aunt Vera would spend time in the Bahamas, where they had bought a little place, or with their growing grandchildren, and as I got older I always seemed to be too busy with my friends or sports to join my parents on Sundays at the Thamesford Road estate. At any rate, while the affection between us seemed undiminished, at least on the surface, the fishing mornings never resumed.

Uncle Woody was a great man, as I told Anne, one of the greatest premiers in Ontario's history, serving for fourteen years and presiding over the enactment of some of the province's most worthwhile and enduring legislation. He wasn't the sort of man who would be angry at a kid for being no more than a kid can be. I had lived up to my end of the bargain, I felt sure of that. I had never lied to him, never held anything back, within the narrow sphere of intelligence through which we moved, and I hadn't betrayed any trust, hadn't told any secrets. I hadn't done any more, in fact, than what he had always encouraged me to do: "Think things through clearly, state your mind, stand your ground." I had done that – although maybe, just maybe, there was a part of it I hadn't thought through clearly enough – and if there was any disappointment, it was more likely mine than his.

When I graduated from high school, Uncle Woody gave me a new fly rod and reel – though it had been some time since I'd done any fishing – and a beautifully printed, limited edition of Isaac Walton's *The Compleat Angler*, a book he was fond of and often used to quote to me. On the title page, in his large, flowing hand, he'd inscribed this message: "To my favourite nephew" and this quote from Walton: "Good company, and good discourse are the very sinews of virtue." There was a nice cheque, too, "a little something to help get you started in university," the note with it, signed by both Woody and Vera, said, but it was the book I valued most, though the inscription troubled me. It was nice – reassuring, I guess – to know I was still his "favourite nephew," but I was a little unsure what he meant by the line from Walton, if anything. At any rate, it made me feel a little better about what had become of Woody and me, about what I had done, not so much to him as to us. And it made it hurt so much more, then, when I graduated from university, where I'd distinguished myself at sit-ins and rallies, politics of a sort Uncle Woody would never have dreamed of, and only got a cheque and an impersonal sounding card from him, and the same when Anne and I married.

I guess the thing I regretted most – just a small thing really – was never getting around to asking him what he'd said that night on the stage when I gave him the car keys and his eyes were big with pleasure in his stricken face, the words torn away in the ringing heat of applause.

A Book of Great Worth

M
Y FATHER WAS there when the Hindenburg went
down, killing thirty-six people.

He was a reporter on one of the Yiddish papers
of the day in New York, and, though labour was his specialty
and he rarely covered regular news, had been assigned, because of a staffing problem, to cover the dirigible's arrival in
New Jersey, after its trans-Atlantic flight from Germany. It
was only his fourth day back at work after having been off
for more than a week for an appendectomy and he was still
sore, and after the long train ride to Lakehurst he was feeling
quite a bit of discomfort. Gritting his teeth, he interviewed
officials and some of the people in the large crowd that had
come to watch, then found a chair where he could ease
himself while he waited.

Ropes had been set up to keep the crowd at some distance, but that was more for the safety and convenience of
the passengers than the sightseers, so he was no more than a
hundred metres from where burning debris began to fall
immediately after the explosion. Like everyone else there, my
father was stunned by what happened. Heat blasted into his
face as if he had opened the door to an oven and peered in
to check the roast. His eyes flooded with tears, an automatic
response of the body, he supposed, to protect them from the
heat. Standing up to get a better view of the arrival in the
moments just before the explosion, he was just a few steps
from the radio man, chattering into his microphone, "Here

it comes ladies and gentlemen, and what a sight it is, a thrilling one, a marvelous sight," then continuing to broadcast after the eruption of fire, which seemed, my father used to say when he told the story, to literally split the sky with dazzling colour, and, except in patches where bursts of explosion obliterated his voice, my father could hear him clearly:

"It burst into flames, get out of the way, get out of the way, get this Johnny, get this Johnny, it's fire and it's flashing, flashing, it's flashing terribly ... this is terrible, this is one of the worst catastrophes in the world ... oh, the humanity and all the friends just screaming around here... I don't believe, I can't even talk to people whose friends are on there, it, it's, ah, I, I can't talk, ladies and gentlemen, honest it's a mass of smoking wreckage and everybody can hardly breathe and talk and screaming, lady, I, I'm sorry."

Everyone was running and, after a moment in which he was frozen in place, transfixed, my father was too. His notebook and pen were in his hands, and his mouth, he remembered, was open, and he ran, thinking not of his story or even of helping people – those in the dirigible or directly below it seemed beyond help, he said – but of his own safety, something which, when he would tell this story to us children, years later, he conveyed without any discernible sense of shame but rather a small pride for his prudence. But when he had reached higher ground and stopped to catch his breath and, scribbling in his pad in that illegible shorthand of his that used to fascinate me so much, begun to record the sights and sounds billowing in front of him like a film running haywire through a projector, only then did he feel the pain and wetness in his side and, holding open his suit jacket, see the spreading blossom of blood soaking his shirt.

His first thought was that he had been injured by a flying piece of debris, like the shrapnel or flak in the war he had heard so much about, but then he realized it was nothing that romantic or dangerous, that the stitches closing his incision had merely given way under stress and that, like a corroded bathroom fixture, he had begun to leak.

At that time, my father and mother were living in a small third-floor apartment in Coney Island with my two sisters;

my birth was still four years away, but my mother was pregnant with a child which, had it lived, would have been my brother or, perhaps, rendered my conception unnecessary. In addition to the four of them, there was a fifth person crammed into the small set of rooms: a living room with the apartment's one partial view of the ocean, jammed with an overstuffed sofa, upon which the guest slept, and two frayed easy chairs, rough bookshelves, a coffee table, lamps, and my mother's piano, at which she instructed several wooden-fingered neighbourhood children; a kitchen so small that two people could barely stand at the sink to wash and dry the dishes; one small bedroom which was my parents'; and an even tinier room, not much bigger than a large closet but described as a den, in which my sisters slept, the eldest in a small bed, the younger on a folding cot permanently unfolded. This guest was a young woman my father had met a few weeks earlier and invited home with him. She had come from Montreal in search of a man she described as her brother, a poet who my father knew slightly. She had, on a slip of grimy, much-folded paper, the name and address of Fushgo's bookshop, through which the brother had told her he could always be reached. There, standing in one of the narrow aisles sandwiched in among the groaning walls of second hand books my father loved to browse through, he'd met her.

"Morgenstern, I'm glad you stepped in," Fushgo said, beckoning him over. "A damsel in distress. Just the ticket, you are." He indicated the tiny woman standing beside the cash drawer so drably dressed and standing in so unimposing a posture my father had at first failed to notice her. "This is Anna," Fushgo said, winking in the sly way he affected when he was trying to interest my father in a book beyond his means. "She is that rarest of women. She cannot speak."

My father was presented with a woman of indeterminate youthful age – she could have been sixteen, so smooth and clear was her skin, or thirty, so severe was the expression of her cloud-grey eyes – whose dirty yellow hair coiled like a tangle of unruly wool down the back of her tattered shawl, which at one time had been maroon. Everything about her was in disarray – the buttons of her white blouse askew, the hem of a slip showing beneath that of her pleated grey wool skirt, even the laces of her high shoes undone – but her clothing and hair, even the nails on the fingers of the small white hand she extended to my father, were clean; and she smelled of the sea, not the rank, oily waters of the East River that often shouldered its way on the back of fog along the Lower East Side, where he worked, or the flat, hotdoggy smell of the beach at Coney Island, but the bracing salt spray of the pounding surf at Far Rockaway, where he and my mother would sometimes go walking with the girls on Sunday afternoons. "Show, show," Fushgo grunted, prodding her with a sharp, tobacco-stained finger.

The woman offered my father a small sheet of paper obviously torn from a pad, and freshly so judging by the clean ragged edge, and already scribbled on with a sharp pointed pencil. He took it from her, noticing that her delicately veined hand trembled. On the paper, in a handwriting that was both clear and immature, was written in Yiddish: "My name is Anna Fishbine, from Montreal, in Canada. I am seeking my brother, Abraham Diamond, the poet, who receives his mail at this shop. Can you assist me?"

My father had several small weaknesses – *schnapps* and cigarettes among them – but only one great one, and that was his love of books, not merely reading them, a love which in itself could have been satisfied by the public library, but of possessing them, feeling their weight on his knee and the rough texture of their bindings on his fingers as he read, seeing the satisfying substance of them on the shelves he had constructed in the living room, the heavy dusty aroma wafting off their old, roughly cut pages as they lay open on the kitchen table. New books, with their crisp, clean jackets and unsoiled pages, failed to impress him the way a book with a life and a history behind it did, so he was an addict to Fushgo's constantly replenishing stock and devoted to the man himself, his irritating mannerisms, come from a lifetime of communing with dead authors at the expense of living readers, notwithstanding. But my father, who had from time to time seen the poet at the Café Royale and had exchanged words with him on one or two occasions, had never encountered Diamond at the shop.

"Diamond gets his mail here?" my father asked, raising his eyes to Fushgo, who, despite his stoop, was a tall man.

"Only invisible letters," Fushgo said, raising his brows, "delivered by invisible mailmen."

The two men exchanged glances redolent of the comfort with which they felt in each other's presence. Both were shy men but they had a mutual love, they'd known each other for over a dozen years and, over that time, my father had contributed to Fushgo's upkeep with the same regularity and consistency of a Christian tithing to his church. Fushgo shrugged his rounded shoulders, raggedly incised by the frayed stripes of his suspenders, and made a comical face with his eyes and blue-lipped mouth that suggested despair over the antics of women.

"How long since you heard from your brother?" my father asked.

At the woman's feet there was a brown cardboard suitcase. In her hands she clutched a blue leather purse from which she produced a pad and pencil, laying the purse awkwardly on the suitcase. She scribbled, looked up, scribbled again, then tore the page loose and handed it to my father.

"Six months without a word." Here was where she had hesitated. Then: "Our parents are frantic with worry."

My father nodded his head as he read. "Your brother often goes to the Café Royale. Do you know it?"

The woman shook her head, a look of mild fright briefly passing over her eyes.

"I'm on my way there now for a bite," my father said. "I'll escort you. Maybe you'll be lucky and he'll be there. Or someone will know where he might be found."

The woman seemed so grateful my father was infused with a feeling of well-being that propelled them both out of Fushgo's shop onto East Broadway with the gentle force of a summer breeze. My father carried Anna's suitcase, which seemed so light as to be almost empty, while she clutched her purse to her chest. Because of her silence – he didn't know at this point whether she was an actual mute or merely too frightened to speak – there was no need to chat, but my father grew expansive and rattled on, describing the scenery through which they passed and, occasionally forgetting, asking her questions she could not – or would not – answer without stopping to write on her pad. "That's all right," my father said. "Forget it." Or: "That was only a rhetorical question. There's no need to reply."

She paused several times, hindering their progress, to gaze into a shop window or down the length of a street they were crossing, and one of the rhetorical questions my father asked concerned the nature of Montreal, for the woman gave the appearance of having stepped directly from the boat or the countryside.

At the Café Royale, there was no sign of Diamond nor any of the men who my father thought he might have seen with the poet. Nevertheless, after he had placed the order – a corned beef sandwich with coleslaw and a pickle and coffee for him, strong tea for Anna – he inquired of the waiter, who asked several others. Most didn't know Diamond, but one who did said he hadn't seen him for several days. Perhaps this evening. Mendel and Solarterefsky, two playwrights my father knew, were at their usual table in a rear corner and he inquired of them as well. Both knew Diamond, and Mendel said he thought he'd seen him in the company of Ishavis Lazen, the actor, who was sure to be at the café that evening, after his performance. My father had a meeting to cover so he introduced Anna to the two men, spared her the effort of the notes by explaining her situation, entrusted her to their attention and left her there, promising to look in later. "Hopefully, you'll have found him, you'll be gone and happily ensconced in his apartment," he told her. "I'm sure all will be well."

My father went to his meeting, where he listened, took notes and afterwards talked to people in attendance. He went back to his office and sat at a heavy oak desk where he wrote an account of the meeting on a standard Royal machine with Yiddish characters. He and another man who was working late had a drink from a bottle of Canadian whisky my father kept in the lower drawer of his desk. He gave his story to Lubin, the assistant city editor, and he put on his raincoat before stepping out into the light drizzle that was falling in the darkness of East Broadway. He walked past Fushgo's shop, dark as an alley, and the Automat, closed but its lights still shining, and toward the café, from which, as he approached, he could see light and hear noise spilling. Anna was sitting at the table where he had left her, an island of mute and painful isolation in the midst of the tables crowded with loud men. Mendel and Solarterefsky were gone, there was no sign of Lazen, though the theatres had let out more than an hour earlier, and, of course, there was no sign of Diamond.

My father sat down and ordered a coffee. "I'm delighted to see you again, my dear," he said, "but sorry to find you alone. Was there no news?"

Anna wrote this note: "No. Mr. Mendel was most kind. He and the other gentleman introduced me to several men who know Abraham, but no one has seen him for several weeks. There is a possibility he has a job with a touring company. Someone promised to inquire."

My father frowned and looked around the cafe, raising his hand to several men he knew. "Have you eaten?"

Anna nodded vigourously, but he was struck again by the emaciated quality of her small, smooth face he found so appealing, the cheekbones high, the skin tight and without lines except for the sheerest hint beside her nose where, though he had yet to see her display the ability, surely she must occasionally smile.

"Are you sure? The cheesecake here is very good. I wouldn't mind one myself but I couldn't manage the whole thing. Would you help me?"

She agreed and, when it came, ate all but the few forkfuls my father took to put her at ease.

She looked down at the plate, as if ashamed at the weakness her hunger had revealed.

"You have a room?" my father asked. "Someplace where you're staying? Perhaps I should take you there."

Anna looked up, then down again. On her pad she wrote: "I had hoped I would find Abraham."

"So you have no place?"

She shook her head and they sat in silence while my father smoked a cigarette and finished his coffee. "I want you to understand," he said presently, "that I'm a married man, with two wonderful children and a third on the way. So please don't construe my intentions as anything but the most honourable."

Anna wrote: "Surely your wife will object."

My father smiled. "Bertie would never turn someone away from her door."

Again he carried the suitcase, extending the elbow of his other arm to her on the dark street and, after a moment's hesitation, she took it. On the long subway ride home he wondered if what he'd said was true, but my mother, of course, was asleep, and if she did object, he knew, it wouldn't be until afterwards. Not once, as the subway car lurched through its velvety tunnels or as he made up the bed for her on the sofa in the tiny living room, did he question his motives, not once did he long to heal her wounded tongue with his own.

My mother did have a generous heart, and patience which, after three weeks, was beginning to grow thin. She was four months pregnant and suffering greatly, her body wracked by cramps at all times and swept by waves of dizziness and nausea when she moved with anything but the most deliberate slowness. False calms would arise during which it appeared the worst was over, then the pain and sickness would come crashing back without warning. Inside her, the baby seemed to be warring with the notion of its own life. There was no question but that Anna could be useful. My oldest sister was six and already in school, but the younger one was only three and needed care and attention, and diversion during my mother's worst times. My father, who always worked into the evenings and often later, saw to the children in the mornings, getting the eldest off to school, while my mother stayed in bed preparing herself for the day ahead, but in the afternoons, after he'd gone, the little one often grated on her nerves, the older one was soon home demanding to be heard, and there was a meal to prepare, then bathing. As the pregnancy deepened and the nature of the ailment became more clear, a plan had taken shape to have my mother's younger sister join the household to help her; Anna's presence made that unnecessary. She immediately took charge; at the same time, her presence grated on my mother, aggravating her already stripped nerves. By day, Anna helped in the apartment, relieving my father of some of his morning duties, but, more importantly, being there in the afternoon, playing with the younger one, keeping her quite and amused while my mother lay propped up against pillows on her bed reading detective novels and feeling the muscles in her legs slowly turn to jelly. Sometimes, rising to go to the bathroom, my mother would open the bedroom door and find Anna and my sister sitting side by side on the piano bench, the little girl enthralled as Anna's fingers silently raced over the keys my mother hadn't touched in weeks, just above them, producing a music only the two of them could hear.

In the evenings, she took the subway to Manhattan and the Café Royale where, like an urchin awaiting her drunken father, she sat at a table by herself and passed notes to people asking: "Have you seen Abraham Diamond?" My father often dropped in on her there and, if his work kept him late, would stop at the café on his way home to give her company on the long subway ride, which still frightened her. My mother, without accusing him of anything, clearly resented the attention he paid to the girl.

"Three weeks and still no sign of that *brother*," she said on a Saturday. Anna had taken the girls for a stroll on the boardwalk, and she and my father were alone at the breakfast table.

My father shrugged. "It appears he's gone with a company on a road trip. No one seems to know for sure where they are or when they'll be back. What do you mean *brother*?"

"Oh, Harry, it's as clear as the nose on your face that the man is her husband. Or her lover. God knows if there really are worried parents in Montreal. The woman has been *abandoned*."

"You really think so?"

My mother rolled her eyes upward, as if to seek support from the angel of the ceiling. "Men are so blind."

"All the more reason to give her sympathy and support," my father said after a moment.

"You think so?" my mother said sharply.

At times like these my father would often retreat to his books, forming his own private library wherever he was sitting, the world shut out by an invisible, sound-proof barrier as he pored over the pages of his latest acquisition. Although he had gone no further in school than the fifth grade before he'd been required to begin to help support his family, and English was his second language, he was partial to Shakespeare and – inexplicably – the American Civil War, but his deepest passion was for the classics, and his most treasured possession was a richly illustrated edition of Caesar's *Wars* in Latin that he had taught himself to read. He had paid Fushgo ten dollars for the Caesar, more than four times the portion of his weekly allowance that he allotted to himself for books and, with the interest Fushgo charged, it had taken more than a month for him to pay it off. In later years, he would acquire huge volumes of Dante rich with Blake engravings, and, though he wasn't religious, a variety of Bibles, in several languages, their oiled leather bindings giving off a smoky aroma of history, damnation, and salvation. At this particular time, he was engrossed in a book that appeared to have been hand-written, in the manner of monks, in a language he had not been able to identify. The handwriting was skilful and consistent through the several hundred pages, the unintelligible words clearly scripted in a faded blue ink, the capitals at the beginning of each new paragraph shadowed in a red the shade of dried blood. There was no date, no publisher's name or city, no illustrations that might serve as clues as to the book's origin, and the title and author were just as indecipherable as the text itself. The leather of the binding was so thick – more like a slab of oxblood hide used for making shoes than the soft black grainy cloth publishers used – and the spine so warped, the book could not be fully closed and when it lay on a table it seemed like a head whose jaws have sprung open, eager to share the untapped wisdom within it. "For you, Morgenstern," Fushgo had said when he produced the book for my father. "Read this and you'll learn much the same wisdom you acquire conversing with your Anna." And he laughed, Fushgo, spraying the dark air of his shop with tobacco-scented breath.

For hours at a time my father would sit poring over the book, comparing the strange script with works from his collection in Latin, Greek, Russian, Hebrew, not that he thought this language could be any of those, but hoping for some clue, some similarity of characters that would provide a hook, an opening through which he might shoulder to some dim understanding of the message the old pages indifferently held. One night when he had come home early, he was sitting at the kitchen table engrossed in the magic letters, my mother asleep in their room, when Anna returned from the café, her small shoulders rising in their inevitable shrug to my father's raised eyes. She came and sat beside him and he poured them both drinks. She sipped hers, then wrote this note: "I fear I may never find Abraham."

"Surely not," my father said. Then, after a long silence: "But you should give some thought to what you'll do, just in case. Have you written to your parents?"

Anna hesitated, then wrote: "Neither can read."

"And the neighbours? A friend or *landsman* who could read a letter to them."

Anna shook her head. "There is only me," she wrote. "I must return to them soon."

My father nodded. "You know you're welcome to stay here as long as you want. Bertie is irritable, I know, but it's the baby, not you." He put his hand on hers, marveling at its smallness, the way her entire hand, even the slender fingers, disappeared beneath the cup of his palm.

Anna smiled and wrote: "You're very kind."

She gestured toward the book and my father slid it to her. "This is a book of great worth," he said.

She bent over it, puzzled, then raised her head, her cheeks and mouth and eyes moulded into a quizzical smile of such sweetness it pierced my father like an arrow fashioned of the finest, purest gold.

"Eskimo?" she wrote.

As my father's one indulgence was his books, my mother's was her piano. It was an upright Baldwin of indeterminate age, the ivory of its keys yellowed like Fushgo's ancient teeth. It had been purchased at a second hand shop on the Bowery with a hundred dollars it took her three years to save and had been lifted by rope and tackle along the outside wall of the building and brought into the apartment through a window. My mother had studied the piano as a child, and music for two years of college. She'd long since given up any ambitions of the concert stage, but her greatest delight was to sit at the piano in the evening, the music students of the afternoon just an unpleasant taste in her mouth, the children in bed and my father not yet home from work or, perhaps, enveloped in one of the overstuffed chairs reading, one ear cocked, and play the concerti and sonatas of Mozart, which was her passion, and Chopin, which my father preferred. Since the third month of the pregnancy, the lessons had been cancelled and my mother, her head light, stomach lurching, legs and fingers aching, had sat not once at the piano, and the apartment resonated in the evening with a silence that seemed more like a presence than an absence.

Into this silence, where one would have thought she would be comfortable, Anna intruded, passing this note to my mother one evening: "When you are out and I won't disturb you, may I play the piano?"

"Of course," my mother said with irritation. She rarely left the apartment, but when she did she could care less what happened in her absence. "You play?"

Anna nodded, smiling shyly.

"Let me hear."

"Won't your head hurt?" Anna wrote.

"My head's fine today. I'd play myself, but my fingers have rubber bands around them."

Anna sat at the bench and raised the cover, exposing the Baldwin's soiled smile. She raised her chin, facing the window which looked out – past the roof of the hat factory across the street – at the ocean, stretching with calm indifference toward the horizon and the old world beyond it. After a moment, she began to play. Chopin. The Fifth Concerto. My father, who had been in the bathroom shaving, came to the door with a broad smile on his lathered face, saying "That's wonderful, Bertie," then filled the doorway in confusion, looking from my mother, who stood by the window, to Anna at the piano and back again.

"I'm sorry, my head *is* hurting," my mother said after awhile.

My father's appendicitis attack came completely without warning. At dinnertime, he had a sandwich, salad, coffee and piece of cheese danish at the Automat, then went for a short walk to allow the food to settle before stopping at Fushgo's for a chat and a drink from the bottle the bookseller kept behind his counter. He began to feel ill immediately after downing the shot and Fushgo had to help him back to the newspaper office where he sat at his desk taking deep gasps, his face drained of all colour, until the ambulance arrived. My mother was telephoned from the hospital and she came at once, leaving the children with Anna, who had been just about to leave for her nightly visit to the Café Royale. The appendix was removed that night and when my father awoke from the ether the next morning, my mother was sitting on a straight chair beside his bed, his hand in hers. She'd been there all night and her face was etched with pain and exhaustion.

"Who's the patient?" my father said. "I should get up, you should get into this bed, the way you look. Or better yet, we should both be in it. The way you look." He squeezed her hand.

"It's too narrow," my mother said, smiling.

"Too narrow?" my father said. "According to who?"

She told him what the doctors had said. He asked for a cigarette and she told him they were forbidden. He told her about the drink he'd had with Fushgo. "It's the first time liquor's ever hurt me," he said. They laughed and gazed at each other fondly.

"Anna's with the children?" he asked after a while.

"Yes."

"Thank God we have her. Especially now."

My mother didn't say anything right away. Then: "She'll be a great help while you're here, yes. But when you're home I'd like to have Sarah come."

My father was silent.

"It's been over a month. We can't be responsible for the woman forever. She's taking advantage of your kindness."

My father nodded slowly. "After I'm home," he said.

He was in hospital for four days and was under strict orders to rest and not go back to work for a week after he went home. The attack had come on a Friday, and he was released on the following Tuesday. By the doctor's orders, he shouldn't have gone back to work until the following Wednesday, but the city editor phoned and he went on the Monday. He felt fine, just a little tired, the incision, already beginning to scar over with bright pink flesh shiny as fingernails, just a little tender. On Thursday afternoon, feeling completely fit, he went by train to Lakehurst.

It was well after midnight when he came home, my mother asleep, the living room dark. He'd served his editor as well as he could, though he'd retreated from the scene of the carnage soon after he began to bleed and was unable to attract the attention of any of the medical people who rushed to the airfield. In the town itself, he found a small hospital and, while he was waiting, telephoned in his story. After several hours, a nurse whose hair had slipped out of its careful bun into shreds of haphazard grey cleaned his wound of the coagulated blood crusting it and bound him securely in bandages wrapped around his lower chest and belly. No doctor was available, though, so no stitches were taken, and it was this delay – the opening required seven stitches the following day, when he reported to the hospital where he'd originally been treated – that caused the odd shape and thickness of the scar he carried the rest of his life.

My father went to the kitchen and poured himself a whisky, drank it quickly and poured another. The ceiling light spilled through the doorway into the living room and he could see there was no one sleeping on the sofa. He went into the bedroom and sat down heavily on the bed and took off his shoes. My mother, who had been sleeping lightly, rolled over and opened her eyes, reaching out her hand to touch his arm.

"Harry? What time is it?"

"Almost one. Go back to sleep." He bent over her and kissed her head.

"How was it?"

"You didn't hear?"

"No, I didn't play the radio."

"I'll tell you in the morning."

"Okay." She rolled over.

"Anna's not back from the café?" my father asked.

"She's gone."

"I thought not till next week."

"We had an argument," my mother said. "I asked her to go."

"I see," my father said. He tried to imagine what such an argument would have been like, the flurry of notes being scribbled, torn from the pad, crumpled, thrown to the floor.

"I'll tell you in the morning. Sarah's coming tomorrow evening."

He took off his shirt and went out of the room, closing the door quietly behind him. He stepped into the small room where my sisters slept and gazed down at them, muffled in darkness, but glowing halos around their heads formed by the streetlight from the window drawn to their hair. He bent over each head and kissed it. In the kitchen, he slowly drank the whisky he'd poured. A dull red stain the size and shape of a strawberry had gathered on the bandage just below and to the left of where, he believed, his heart lay. His body was exhausted but his mind raced, filled with the dazzle of flame, its surprisingly loud roar, the plaintive voice of the radio man, "get out of the way, get out of the way, get this Johnny, get this Johnny." He walked across the living room to the shelf and found the book written in the mysterious language and took it back to the kitchen. He sat at the table, the open book in front of him, and looked first at its inscrutable script, then up at the icebox, standing silent and white against the wall. From the living room, he thought he heard the tinkling of piano keys, the first tentative notes of a Chopin concerto, but it was only the sound of an automobile passing on the street below, rising through the warm night air and the open window. His side ached, just beneath the strawberry stain by his heart, and he didn't know if it was the incision, or something else.

River Rats

U NCLE BOB PIKE came home from the university one afternoon in November when the sky was blue as a Miro canvas and heat pressed down on the shimmering streets like a cruel hand. A letter from Clim awaited him on the kitchen counter, but he didn't know that. He parked the humming Celica in the driveway and hesitated for a moment, frowning at the coarse, browning grass, his hand on the key.

At the age of thirty-three, Uncle Bob was beginning a career at long last. With a family, too, already complete. And in Yuma, Arizona, of all places. It wasn't what he had wanted, but he was happy enough.

When he turned the ignition off, the purr of the air conditioner and the syrupy strains of the Carpenters on the radio disappeared abruptly, leaving an empty silence. He made a dash for the house through the stifling heat.

"Letter from Clim," Myrna said as Bob slammed the porch door, letting the air conditioning wash over him with its cool breath. She was sitting at the kitchen island peeling apples for one of her famous pies. Ordinarily, she would have greeted him with a "Hello, darling, how was your day? Beer's in the fridge. Get me one too, would you?" but she knew Bob would be excited by the letter. They'd been married less than a year, and Climinhaga had sent a telegram on their wedding day – "Don't sell that cow," it said, some kind of a private joke that Bob had been reluctant to explain, "just something from a movie" – but there had been nothing from him since. Bob had written once, before they came to Yuma, to say that was where they were going, and once after, to say what it was like. But there had been no replies.

"Hmmmmm. Beer?" Uncle Bob said. He snapped the caps off two bottles and placed one in front of Myrna, next to the plastic bowl. He glanced at the Vancouver postmark, smiled at the austere image of the Queen on the fourteen-cent stamp, and opened the envelope with a steak knife, immediately absorbing himself in the sheet of triply folded paper. Myrna lit a cigarette – the third of the five a day she allowed herself – and watched the animation in his eyes. She was three years his elder, a divorcee with three children, two of them already in their teens. She had a silly putty face and there wasn't any expression she couldn't satisfactorily reproduce, but the pained clowns of Charlie Chaplin were her favourites. When Bob looked up and said, "Hey, he's coming, he's coming to visit at Christmas," she said, "Hey, that's great," and twisted her face into a happy, joyful smile. But inside she was pulling a Chaplin face, the ripe lower lip completely covering the top one, trembling and rich with sorrow.

Myrna had never met her husband's great friend, but she had read his books and some of his old letters Bob had saved, and heard Bob's boisterous stories of him, and, for no reason she could identify, she didn't like him. "Jesus," Uncle Bob said, misinterpreting the look she couldn't keep from creeping into her eyes, "we're going to have to buy that sofa bed after all."

Uncle Bob was no one's uncle – in fact, his only sibling, a younger brother named Duane, had drowned while surf-boarding in Hawaii seven years earlier, while still a student at McGill – but the nickname, bestowed almost a dozen years earlier by his friend Paul Climinhaga, the famous Canadian novelist, poet and river rat, had stuck with him. He hadn't seen Clim for a decade, their friendship sustained only by sporadic letters, but he bore his stamp, like a faded watermark on a ceiling.

Bob Pike was a tall, skinny man with acne scars on his bony face and a well trimmed reddish beard designed to hide them. His auburn hair was not as long as it had been when he was a student, though it still partially covered his ears, and it was thinning at the top of his head. His hands were long, bony-fingered and always cold, as if they had an existence apart from the chemistry of his body, though Myrna said it was a sign he had a warm heart. He spoke with the flat, slightly nasal twang invariably produced by growing up in the Lakehead, or other places in northern Ontario, for that matter. In Uncle Bob's case, it was the Lakehead, where his father had been the superintendent of schools in Port Arthur, where the family had lived for three generations.

Bob's Ontario accent made him stand out in Yuma, where most people talked as if they were asleep, mumbling with pleasure as they turned over beneath the covers. Except for the occasionally chilly nights, everything was warm in Yuma, *hot*, and he tried to arrange his life so that he went from the air-conditioned adobe bungalow, with its shuttered windows and red-tiled roof, directly to his air-conditioned Celica, and directly to his cluttered office in the air-conditioned Language Arts Building on the university campus, where he taught his classes in magazine writing and feature reporting, conducted his office hours, and occasionally chipped away at a magazine article himself, like the one on sky diving he'd been working on that day. It was an insular life, he knew that, but the hot air made his lungs ache with a stale longing that brought boyhood river days flooding across his mind. That and Clim, whose face always seemed to float in rivers.

Uncle Bob Pike, Ph.D., author, journalist and university instructor, had been a student twenty-five of his thirty-three years. He'd wanted to be a writer – not what he was now, but a *real* writer – and was good enough, after his English degree at U of T, to get into the Writers Workshop at Iowa, where a year of the unrelenting criticism of the instructors and other students was enough to make him realize he'd made a mistake. The only good thing to have come out of that year was his friendship with Clim. Then came two years of law school, at Dalhousie. Somewhere between contract law and torts, he lost interest – perhaps it was the exercise they did in defamation, where the Halifax lawyer who played the part of the judge kept cutting him off while he was examining his witnesses. "I believe we've heard enough of *that*, Mr. Pike." He took a year off after that.

Travelling through Europe, a red maple leaf insignia on his backpack so he wouldn't be taken as an American, he visited relatives he hadn't known he had in England, and had an affair with a German girl in Greece, living in a cave on the beach for over a week. When he came home, he took his father's advice and went back to school, at Western, to get his teacher's certificate, graduating right at the peak of the cyclical glut, when teachers suddenly became plentiful as Japanese calculators. The only job he was able to find was teaching boy's shop at a country school north of the Soo. He still had a letter from Clim, who was on the Vancouver docks, scolding him: "Shop? That is really too much, man – the one man I know who burns himself manipulating a cigarette lighter and puts his car into reverse in passing lanes, teaching innocent little boys about tools. That *is* child abuse." But he'd taken a course in guidance counselling, because his father told him there was a shortage, and the next year he had a better job, with an office of his own, the word "Counsellor" on the oak veneer door students rarely knocked on. He had time on his hands and a typewriter in his office, so he took to writing little things, first an article on counselling jargon for the Ontario Teachers' Federation newsletter, then an expanded version of the same piece for the national publication. He tried a slightly wittier version for *Saturday Night* and came close, the rejection slip said.

Uncle Bob Pike, who had slunk away from Iowa's writers and critics with his tail between his legs, started augmenting his income by writing! When his maternal grandmother died, leaving him her house near London, he quit his job, moved in with the musty furniture and family portraits and set up a workroom with two typewriters – including a brand new, correcting IBM Selectric – on long tables made from second hand doors. He did pieces on pool players and bowlers for the *Billiards and Bowling Journal*, one on a local hardwareman who had developed a new kind of nail for the *Hardware Retailer*, and half a dozen different versions of the same story about a popular ice cream store for as many magazines, most of them in the States, where he was finding most of his markets. He bought a used VW camper and went around the Midwest looking at student films, then all the rage, for a series of articles in one of the men's mags that became a book published by a small house in New Jersey. It sold five hundred copies, then went into remainder and sold another couple hundred. No big deal, he wrote Clim, who was still looking for a publisher for *his* book, the first novel, but Uncle Bob had it in his blood. He was a writer!

Climinhaga was not impressed, not amused. He was a big, round-shouldered man with a face like Dylan Thomas and no trace of ears or neck beneath his tangled hair. There was a scar on the very tip of his broken nose that he claimed had been left by a woman's bite. He'd been the one supporter Bob had at Iowa, where most people had sneered at the prosaic quality of his prose. "What I like about it," Clim would say, warming his beer between his big hands, "is that it says what it wants to say. It doesn't fuck around with similes, images, not even goddamn adjectives. It *says* it. Like Hemingway." Bob Pike was no Hemingway, and he knew it, but he had appreciated Clim's saying that. But Clim didn't have anything good to say about the stuff Bob was writing now, even though it was making good use of those clean, uncluttered qualities Clim had once professed to admire. "Jesus, Uncle Bob," he wrote from Prince George, where he was lumberjacking that year, "is this any way to pay back society for having invented the printing press? Gutenberg is rolling over in his fucking grave. McLuhan is triumphant!" This was after the film book had come out and Bob's ego was soaring like a balloon. It came crashing down like the Hindenburg.

Maybe it was that blow, or maybe it was a changing market, but articles started coming back from the magazines that had been regulars, and the publisher in New Jersey didn't like the next idea Uncle Bob came up with, a thing on CB radios, which Bob figured was the coming thing. He sold his grandmother's jewelry and signed up at Syracuse for the master's program in journalism. "I know I'm not a great writer," he wrote Clim that first cold, snow-bound winter, "and I don't even think I have the discipline to be a good journalist – Jesus, they've got us working on the student newspaper, and the deadlines make me break out into a sweat – but I *can* write, that is to say I know how to put one word after another and make a sentence that *means* something, which is more than a lot of people can do, and if I can learn some of the tricks of the trade, maybe I can even learn how to practice it. A man's got to work."

"Amen to that," Clim wrote back. He was all for the work ethic, as long as the work was physical, the dirtier the better.

Clim arrived four days before Christmas, in the late morning after a flight from Denver. He was hung over, or perhaps still drunk, and his bear face was pale, the pouches beneath the eyes dark and pronounced. "Unca Bob," he said as he came through the arrivals door. "Yuma? *You* never had a sense of Yuma."

Uncle Bob grinned. "Well, you know," he said. As they drove home, the Celica purring with cool contentment, he kept saying that. That and "Clim Kadiddlehoffer, what'd'ya know?"

Climinhaga had grown up on a wheat farm somewhere in Saskatchewan, and had gone back to Canada after Iowa, working as a lumberjack in northern B.C. and a stevedore on the Vancouver docks. Along the way, he'd published two novels and a slim volume of poetry, all to good reviews. The second novel had been a finalist for the G-Gs, and he had a Canada Council grant now that was letting him work on a big novel, he explained as they flashed through the shining suburbs, the palm trees laden with Christmas lights and cut-out reindeer. Some of the money was for travel, he went on, and he was making a round of some of his old Iowa friends, hoping to give his juices a jolt.

"Jesus," Bob said. "Does that mean they're dry?"

"Now, now, Uncle Bob," Clim said. "No, it don't mean nothin' like that a'tall. You know well an' good that after you come a few times you got to eat some oysters afore you can come again."

They drove past a roadhouse where Bob and Myrna sometimes went. "Hey, see that place? Was in there a couple weeks back, sittin' at the bar listenin' to the good country music, and there was this fellow at the bar there, big fella with a beard streaked with grey and eyes could see tomorrow, and I kept thinkin', hey, this dude looks just a little like he might be Willie Nelson – except no ponytail."

"No ponytail," Clim said.

"But this old geezer," Uncle Bob went on, "he's drinkin' a Lone Star beer, I should tell ya, he's just the spittin' image of old Willie. I'm starin' at him, I guess, and he spots it and gives me a smile, nods his head, then he finishes off his beer and ambles up to the stage. And the next thing I know, the music's stopped and they're saying on the mike, 'Hey, folks, got a little surprise for ya'll tonight, got a good old boy here you might like to hear.' Can you beat that?"

Beneath his beard, Clim's lips were just barely visible. "So, who was it?"

"Willie Nelson, of course. Jesus, Clim Kadiddlehoffer. I told you he was the spittin' image."

"Well, who the blue fuck hell is Willie Nelson?" Clim said.

"Willie Nel … man, you are putting me *on*. Now that Elvis is dead, Willy's the king, everyone knows that."

"Elvis is dead?" Clim asked innocently.

Myrna came through the kitchen door to greet them, wiping her hands on a towel, as the Celica pulled into the driveway. Uncle Bob felt himself glowing over her prettiness, her lustrous black hair, her high breasts. "This here is a feller claims he never heard of Willie Nelson," he said as Clim fiddled with a shopping bag filled with gift-wrapped boxes. "Biggest damn fool in the western world. Come to the desert lookin' for oysters."

. . .

When Bob Pike was growing up, the family used to spend their summers at his grandmother's, and his days were focussed on the breath-warm water of the Thames River, a thick brown worm that lazied its way around the country-side outside London. Bob swam in the river, fished in it, skipped stones over it, learned to canoe on it, roasted hotdogs and corn over fires with his pals on its grassy banks, felt a girl's wondrous breast for the first time on a raft floating on it. The Thames, goofy, nothin'-much-to-talk-about river though it was, twined its slow lapping way through his memory like some sinister Freudian theme, except there wasn't anything sinister about it, it was just there, part of him.

In Iowa City, Bob used to take a yellow pad and a ball-point pen down to the banks of the Iowa River beneath the art building and try to write. It made him feel at home, being able to look up and across that big-shouldered muddy river and downstream to where the water got mad and roared across the power plant dam like a cat hissing at the neigh-bour's dog. He ran into Climinhaga down there, one afternoon in late September. They'd met at the Workshop already and acknowledged each other as fellow Canadians but hadn't gone beyond that. Clim was walking along the path beside the river, his face toward the water, and he would have stumbled over Bob if Bob, at the last moment, hadn't said something, which was "Hey."

Clim teetered with surprise, looked down. "Don't ever sneak up on me like that again, man," he said. "I've got reflexes like a cat. Killed a man in Abilene who said good mornin' to the preacher's wife on a Monday. See what I mean?" He flopped down beside Bob, glanced at the yellow pad and pen and took a worn paper copy of *Huckleberry Finn* from his back pocket. "This is it, man, this is the truth. I mean, the great American novel? This is it, already done. Whatever you're doin', it just won't make it, it's already done."

44

"Second place," Bob said, shading his eyes with his hand.

Clim's hair came down to his shoulders, and when he snapped his head back, the way he did then, Bob could see the flash of one gold earring, in his right ear. But there wasn't any mistaking him for a girl, not even from behind, not with those shoulders. "Yeah, that's good," he said. "Second place. That's what it's all about, isn't it? The race for second."

Where Climinhaga came from, God hadn't made many rivers and the only water he was intimate with was the small creek that ran nearby the farm and the weedy, mosquito-spotted sloughs the rain his father prayed for caused if there was enough of it. But he had read Twain and fallen in love with the notion of the river – that's what had made him a writer, he said, and he'd come to Iowa, he said, as much because the Mississippi was only a hundred miles away as for the Workshop. He wanted, he said, to get a job on a riverboat, stoking coal or dealing five-card stud.

Bob Pike leaned back, his head in grass, and blinked up at a cloud that had wafted across the sun. "Been there yet?"

"Been where?"

"Ol' Man Ribber. Squished your toes in the mud, swam in it?"

"Drove across," Climinhaga said defensively, "in a bus, on a piece of concrete they call a bridge."

"That's no way to see a river you love, man. You gotta put your feet in the mud to hear what it's saying. Hey, you ever eat a catfish?"

"Those guys with the whiskers?"

"Them's the numbers. Say." Bob sat up. "Tomorrow's Friday. Don't know it for a fact, but there's bound to be some fish fries on that river. Somewhere. What'd'ya say we go find some?"

Climinhaga had a gold cap on one tooth, and it flashed when he smiled. "You have got yourself one hell of a date, Uncle Bob," Clim said. It was the first time anyone had ever called him that.

The next day, while most of the writers from the Workshop were attending an antiwar rally on campus, they took Bob's beatup old Ford – Clim didn't have a car – to Moline, then drove upriver till they came to a leafy village with a view of the water below and an ancient looking tavern set off behind a spreading oak on which they found carved "W-F-Cody." Inside, the tavern was dark and smelled of beer and frying fish. "Yep, tha's him, Buffalo Bill," the bartender told them. "He was born here, just up the road aways." They gorged themselves on fish, got drunk on draught beer colder and sweeter, Clim swore, than any he'd ever tasted, got silly with the old-timers who crowded the tavern after sunset, and Clim told him gravely: "Uncle Bob, you won't ever be Mark Twain, mind, and you can't have second place, either, damn it, but maybe you can get third, if you don't mind standing behind me."

At dinner, Myrna eventually gave up trying to keep order and let things fall where they may. Her boys showed off and Brenda flirted. Even after a year with Bob in the household, the boys were still making up for six years without a father, and that was what was pushing Brenda too. At nine, she was the youngest, the lone girl against the two bully boys, the only one who had no memory at all of her father, the only one of the three who had cried at leaving Syracuse, where Myrna had been working as a secretary at the J school after the divorce. Life was hell for her, Myrna knew that, and she let her make her own way.

"So I hunched down, you know how you do at the beginning of the play, and I put my hand right in it," Little Bob said. He was thirteen, almost fourteen, and nothing about him was little, but he'd picked the nickname up when Uncle Bob came into their lives. The kids didn't call him Uncle Bob, of course; he was Big Bob, and little Bob was Little Bob, even though he was heavier than Big Bob now, broader in the shoulder, and would be stronger soon, if he wasn't already. "*Dog shit*. This great big pile of it, right there on the field, right under my nose, and my hand right in it."

"Little Bob!" Myrna snapped. "Can't you wait till *after* dinner to be disgusting?"

"No, Mom, you know I'm disgustin' all the time."

"Tell me about it," Shawn said. He was in the middle, twelve and almost thirteen, blond and too good looking for his own good. "He's just naturally disgusting, he can't help himself." He looked sideways to Clim, who winked at him. "It's a real talent."

"I guess you didn't wash your hand for a week, eh?" Clim asked Little Bob. "Like shaking hands with the president."

Brenda giggled and squirmed in her seat. Her bangs were freshly cut and she looked pretty. Beneath the cuffs of her shorts, her knees were gravelled raw.

"You're a lucky man, Uncle Bob," Clim said, pushing back his plate and looking downtable toward Myrna. "She produces monsters, and can cook, too."

"You're too kind," Uncle Bob said. "You'll spoil her, flattering her like that. *Monsters* is a compliment."

"It's *you* I was complimenting, not her. For your good taste and shrewdness in making a bargain. *You* got her and him and him and her." Clim pointed out the grinning children. "All *she* got is you, eh? *Her* taste is maybe not so hot." He grinned back at the kids and turned to Myrna again, the gold of his tooth flashing. Every way you look at him, she thought, he glitters – the tooth, the earring, even the scar on his nose is shiny. She didn't like him any better now that she'd seen him close up.

"Tell us about your new book, Clim," she said boldly, almost certain he wouldn't want to.

"It's not a *book*, ma'am, it's a *novel*. Only flacks, excuse me, *journalists*, like your good husband can be certain that what they write will turn out to be books."

Myrna made a Charlie Chaplin face and Brenda giggled, peering at him from under her bangs. The boys guffawed, and Little Bob took the opportunity to lean over the table and give Shawn the whack on the ear he'd been saving.

"Mom!" Shawn yelled.

"Don't I wish!" Uncle Bob said. "It's not that simple, really, it isn't."

"Nothing ever is," Clim said. "Not on the river, not in

this here pie, neither, ma'am." He wolfed another forkful of Myrna's special apple-pumpkin, winking at Brenda.

"But, hey, speaking of books," Uncle Bob said, "have I told you yet about Reno? Been up there three or four times already, with a, ahem, *book* in mind, *if* I can find a publisher. Crazy place. Gambling fever, it colours everything, the whole town's tainted, not just the strip. Everybody writes about Vegas, but Reno's more interesting, more *real*. You can't imagine what it's like."

"No, I can't," Clim said. Behind his beard, his lips were setting. "You're right, I just can't imagine."

After dinner, they went into the living room, where a tree had been set up next to the fireplace. It wasn't trimmed yet, but the presents Clim had brought were piled up beneath it. "There's that party I mentioned, I ought to, you know, sort of show my face at," Uncle Bob said. "Faculty thing. Want some eggnog?"

"Sure. But maybe the kids should open their presents first."

"Shouldn't they wait till Christmas?" Myrna asked.

"Oh, Mom," the boys groaned in unison.

"Won't be around that long," Clim said.

"That right?" Bob said. "Well, go ahead, kids."

"Yay," the boys shouted, and even Brenda came around from behind Myrna's chair, eyes bright. They tore the ribbons and gift wrap, letting the glitter and crinkle fall to the cool hardwood floor in puddles. Uncle Bob perched on the arm of Myrna's chair.

Little Bob got an old boot. Shawn got a tangle of fish line, with a broken bobber at its heart. For Brenda, there was half a dozen pari-mutuel tickets, each one neatly torn in half.

"Weird," Little Bob said.

"People must remember it's better to give than to receive," Clim said gravely. "These are *your* gifts to *me*. Life's what you make of it. Ain't that so, Unca Bob? S'cuse me, *Big* Bob."

Myrna got an old pot holder, greasy, one corner singed. "I've already got one of these," she said, her lower lip going Stan Laurel.

"Oh, good," Clim said. "Now you've got a pair."

For Uncle Bob, there was the broken expansion bracelet of a Timex watch, with a card bearing this message: "To Uncle Bob, you'll do to float the river with."

At the party, the hostess, a tall woman with a piercing gaze and curls tight as fists, made everyone put *something* on the tree, and tossing a handful of tinsel wasn't sufficient.

"Grown-ups are just like children," she explained to Uncle Bob and Clim. "They have to be coaxed into everything. You don't know what you miss if you don't try things."

"That's what the Romans told the Sabine women," Clim said. Uncle Bob rolled his eyes and picked up an ornament.

The hostess glared at Clim. Her husband, a dry-witted man who had turned the science of asking trivial questions into a high art, was the chairman of Bob's department and she was accustomed to dealing with rude young men. "This is a *tree*-trimming party," she said with cold precision. "Just pretend this is a bar and those ornaments are legal tender. *Buy* your drinks."

Clim hung a candy cane on a green bough and retired to the kitchen for another glass of mercifully well-spiked nog. "Are you a student?" a slim woman with a sexy mouth asked him. "I don't recall seeing you before."

"Aren't we all?" he said, showing his gold tooth, but he turned his back on her because he knew that mouth wasn't for him.

"They don't *grow* tinsel," the chairman of the department was telling the wife of a statistics professor. "They *mine* it. In *mines*. In Bolivia."

"Oh, come *on*," the woman said. She was tiny, with an oversized face that was all smile and wonder.

"No, he's right," Clim interjected. "A special kind of geologist finds the mines, flying overhead in planes set up with radar." He gestured with his hands in a big arc, to show how the planes look. "Beep, beep, beep." His hand dove down to the woman's bare knee. "Tinsel mine at eight o'clock." Across the room, Uncle Bob twisted his mouth

Myrna style, made a slashing gesture across his throat and turned to a very fat man in a red wool jacket. "Seriously, it takes a dozen highly trained men three months, working round the clock, to mine a pound of tinsel. That's why it's so expensive. They use u*tin*sels."

The others laughed, but the chairman snorted through a big nose flecked with veins, looking at Clim suspiciously.

"Boogie," a woman with grey hair and a child's face said. She moved her shoulders in time to the music on the record player, Fleetwood Mac. Clim moved away.

"Maybe we can go to *Superman* tomorrow, after we wallpaper," a man called Alan said to a man called Duncan. Alan had eyebrows that blended together, giving him a beetle scowl. Duncan had fine, fine features, a thin, fragile nose, long lashes, a faint mustache. One of them was Uncle Bob's office mate, the other was across the hall. Both wore pastel slacks with flared bottoms.

"I heard that at the beginning, when the curtain opens, the first thing you see is a curtain opening," Duncan said.

"Is that right?"

"Yeah, and then a big hand turning a page."

"Is *that* right?"

"I hope so. That's the way *I* would have done it."

They laughed, and Clim moved toward the kitchen. The woman with the sexy mouth was by the door, as if she'd been waiting for him. "In this department?"

"Biblical studies," he said. "That's why I'm here tonight. Studying the rituals." She arched her brows, pursed those wondrous lips, took a sip of eggnog and turned away without a word. "Touché," Clim said.

Uncle Bob and Myrna were now in a group clustered around the fat man, who was manipulating a loose-jointed duck on puppeteer's strings. Clim grinned at Uncle Bob, who arched an eyebrow back and drank thirstily from his third glass. He was getting drunk but he didn't give a fuck. Myrna sat on the floor beside him, her elbow on his knee. There weren't enough chairs to go around and the men and women took turns in them. Except, he had noticed, Clim, who hadn't sat down once.

They drove home through the incredible Yuma darkness with the windows open, the desert's heat still clinging to their skin, though it had finally become bearable. It was always summer here, even when plastic Santas peered shyly from the palms.

"You have to have a real sense of the desert to live in a place like this," Uncle Bob said.

"If you say so, Unca Bob," Clim agreed. He was smoking a cigar someone at the party had given him, with a blue ribbon wrapped around it, and his head was wreathed in smoke. He was in the passenger seat, with Myrna in the back, her knees curled, practicing a W.C. Fields sneer. "But I don't get the joke."

Late at night, when everyone else had been put away like broken toys and the house was still, Uncle Bob and Clim, the river rat, sat up, talking and drinking beer in the extra bedroom made over into a study, like children waiting up for Santa Claus.

"Who're yer friends?" Clim asked. He wiped his wet mouth with the back of one big callused hand.

Uncle Bob shrugged. "Just some creeps I work with, uh, excuse me, work *for*, in the case of the one particular creep."

"And what about those Bobbsey twins, Alan and whatshisname?"

"Duncan? He's not a bad guy. They're not bad guys."

"*Duncan*," Clim said, as if it were a Latin word he was trying to master. "Alan and Duncan. Very nice."

"Hey, take it easy, those guys are friends," Uncle Bob said.

"See? What I say, bro?"

Uncle Bob went to the bathroom to let the eggnog out, and when he came back Clim was on the phone, changing his reservation.

"I thought you'd be here a couple of days," Bob complained. "There were things I wanted to show you. If I'd known, we didn't have to waste our evening at that stupid party."

"Sorry, Unca Bob. I really gotta get to California. You know how it is."

"No, I don't," Bob said. "Or maybe I do. Maybe my friends *are* creeps. You have to understand the way they make their living."

"Same way you do," Clim said. At least there wasn't any smugness in his voice, and what he said was true.

"It was that stupid party, wasn't it? I know exactly what you mean. Elsie Rossman and her Christmas balls! *Another glass of eggnog, dear? Have you done your duty to the tree?* Shit. A bunch of overgrown teenyboppers, wearing their parents' clothes." Uncle Bob shrugged, feeling cold, a sensation that was alien to his life in Yuma. *Cold.* "It made me feel *old.*"

Clim's look was steady, cool, his eyes dark and sunken. At least he had opened another beer, as sort of a gesture. "No, man, that isn't it all. And, hey, shit, no offence, but look at you, man. You don't need a party to make you feel old."

Uncle Bob made a chagrined face and Clim hunched his shoulders back against the chair, retreating into it. His feet, in socks, were up on an ottoman. "I mean, you know, man: wife, kids, this house." He made an airy motion with one big hand. "Everything, you know, man," he said softly. "It's a different life. It's not *you*, Unca Bob, it's me, I just don't fit here."

"Sure, sure," Uncle Bob said. "You *say* that, and thanks for it, but I know what you *mean*. When you say, 'It's not *you*,' you mean *this*, this isn't me, the real me. I've gone square, soft in the centre. I know man, I know it. I don't need you to tell me things I already know."

Clim swung a leg off the ottoman and leaned forward. "Hey, don't lay your self-pity trip on me, Unca Bob. Something wrong with your life, that's got to do with *you*, man, not me. I mean, you know, man, you keep saying, 'Hey, it's me, me, me,' but the way it comes out of your mouth, it sounds like 'you, you, you.'"

They glared at each other, the sound of the labouring air conditioner invading the silence like the singing of locusts. "What the fuck are we talking about?" Uncle Bob said.

"Damned if I know," Clim said. "You and your fucking Ph.D., you gotta make a big deal outta everything. I get a fucking itch, and you're the one insists on scratching."

They laughed and pulled at their beer cans. "Like the man says," Climinhaga said, "'You'll do to ride the river with.'" He put his big poet's hand on Bob's shoulder. "Uncle Bob, Uncle Bob, old Unca Bob. Now, le's us get drunk."

"You mean drunker," Uncle Bob said. He was grinning, but he wasn't happy.

It was still dark when Uncle Bob went upstairs, weaving, but the cool desert air coming through the partially opened bedroom windows had the smell of morning in it. He stopped by the boys' room, leaning over their sleeping heads. Little Bob was smiling, Shawn was frowning, as if, even in sleep, they must always be opposed. He straightened the covers, sighing. In Brenda's room, he paused longer, gazing down at her face, marvelling at the way her mouth and nose were twisted into the pillow, as if sniffing at the source of life. Myrna had warned him not to let one of the children become a favourite, but he had already lapsed and he was afraid they all knew it. He'd learned to love the boys, too, though, somewhat to his surprise. They weren't *really* his, but in a way they were. He tousled Brenda's hair, whispering her name.

He sat on the foot of his own bed in the darkness and undressed. Myrna stirred when he crawled in beside her. "Hi, hon," she said. He was so tense, she knew something was wrong.

"Clim's leaving later today," Uncle Bob said.

In the darkness, she made a Charlie Chaplin face. "I thought he might."

Uncle Bob stared at the dark ceiling. "Why'd you think that?" He sounded annoyed, like he was getting around to accusing her of planning it all, of *doing* something, and Myrna made her hands into fists, pressed them against her thighs. Once, years ago, she had promised herself she'd never get married again; she'd thought of that, once in a while, this past year. But only once in a while.

"I don't know. He just seemed restless. Fidgety. Like that dopey duck at the party. Jerking."

"That party! Everybody seemed so ... *middle-aged*," Uncle Bob said, his voice rising. "Children playing at being adults."

Myrna opened her hand and entwined her fingers around his. "They *are* adults. And so are we. So are *you*."

"I know it," Uncle Bob said. "I know it. I don't even mind. I just wish people wouldn't rub it in."

Before falling asleep, he thought, for the first time in many months, of his brother, Duane, drowned almost seven years before, to the day. He'd gone to Hawaii for Christmas vacation. He was three years younger than Uncle Bob, with a clear complexion, blond hair and eyes that saw right through clouds to the reflecting sky. In his magazine writing class, Uncle Bob had a student who reminded him, just a bit, of Duane, in the expression of his wry mouth, the easy, athletic roll of his shoulders. He couldn't think of the boy's name, and he realized, with a sudden shock, that he couldn't remember – not *really* remember – Duane's face. He saw his brother sitting across from him at the dinner table when they were boys, swinging on the backyard swing, his feet high in the air, he saw his brother taking off his shirt in the bedroom they'd shared, and he could see the funny little way the muscle just above his collar bone used to jump, but he couldn't see his face. That was blank.

He squeezed Myrna's hand, but she was asleep, far away. In his mind, he rose and tiptoed to the children's bedrooms. His eyes tightened, but it was too late and he felt moisture on his cheek. He would never, he thought, be an uncle. And, at the age that most men are just beginning the rest-of-their-lifetimes as uncles, Bob Pike took a red pencil and drew an editor's line through that part of his name forever.

Night Is Coming

I NEVER REALLY forgot her, not through war, two marriages, kids, even grandchildren – a whole life – but when I got to be seventy-two she came flying back into my mind like a boulder in one of those disaster movies, smashing away everything in front of it.

I was watching CBS Sunday Morning, which we get here in Winnipeg on cable from Detroit, and Charles Kuralt ended the show with a quote: "I must hurry, for the night is coming." He said who it was from, some poet, I think – Robert Frost, maybe? – but I was so stunned by the line everything else just faded. I must hurry, for the night is coming. That was me in a nutshell: seventy-two, divorced from one wife and separated from the other, in relatively good health but two heart attacks under the bridge already and the third one likely to be the backbreaker, as we kids in Milwaukee used to say, two or three centuries ago or whenever it was I was growing up. I had been putting old age out of my mind – the only time I thought of myself as a "senior" (ugh) was when I was queued up at the movies feeling smug as hell – and suddenly here it was, coming crashing down on me through the voicebox of the TV, just like those old Victrola ads had prophesied: my master's voice, breaking the goddamn news.

And with it, with that bombshell, had come the memory of Ardis, fresh as a daisy, if you'll forgive an old man an occasional lapse into dog-eared writing. I've been making my living at it long enough to qualify.

I guess I should fess up that it wasn't really that simple. I've been working on my autobiography – oh, it's really more about the oddball characters I've known over the years, from ex-cons to astronauts, than about myself – and that week I'd been making notes on the Iowa days. On an index card, I had typed this line: "Also, I have had numerous love affairs, after being engaged to a Catholic girl (Irish) when I was twenty-one. We broke it off fifty-one years ago, but the flame is still there." I was running my tongue along the rim of my almost empty coffee cup, my eyes half closed, and trying to remember exactly what she'd looked like when Kuralt's line came tumbling at me. "The night is coming," I said aloud, and, suddenly, there she was in my mind, clear as an on-coming freight train at a level crossing, every detail sharp and fresh, just like a newly printed photograph. It was uncanny.

What happened next was like one of those cheery little items you find in the People section of your newspaper, and also a little like a mystery, a form of story I've been reading all my life and writing off and on for the last twenty years. I cranked out a letter to the Cedar Rapids *Gazette* editor, asking "Where is Ardis O'Keefe?" Considering over fifty years had gone by, it's surprising how many responses I got, and not just from Cedar Rapids. The clipping of my letter was sent on to friends and relatives in Illinois, Wisconsin, Penn-sylvania, some of whom were nice enough to write, all with basically the same information. She'd married a silversmith named Harris, they'd had some kids and she'd moved to Terre Haute to live with his parents during the war, which he infantreed his way through, in Africa and Italy, much like me, though I don't recollect ever meeting anyone named Harris over there. After the war, he got a job in an umbrella factory in Lancaster, Pennsylvania, rising to some kind of front office job before his retirement. Then they moved to Florida, right around the same time I was hauling my ass up this way, though none of my correspondents were sure where, or what had happened since.

That was a piece of cake for me, though. I found the um-brella factory, through long distance information (simple, isn't it?) and a pleasant woman in the personnel department there gave me the city where the pension cheques were sent, though she wouldn't go so far as to hand me the actual address on a silver platter. Confidential. Company policy. Yak yak. That's okay. I was just glad the company hadn't folded or moved to Taiwan. How many Harrises can there be in Coral Gables? A lot, in fact. Too many to contact them all, from this distance. But a brief letter to the directors of the town's three old age centres, inquiring about an Ardis O'Keefe Harris, about seventy, from Cedar Rapids via Terre Haute and Lancaster hit paydirt quick enough, and there was a letter from her, real as life in my hands, written in a graceful leftward slanting hand like they don't teach in school anymore, on fine blue paper in a greyish ink: a widow of eight years now, sixty-nine years old, only 105 pounds, and, yes, of course, she remembered me, she said – "How could I forget, the things you used to say to me, Andy, the promises you used to make?" Kind lady, with a nice touch. But if I could pin the language to the mat from time to time, why shouldn't she?

If I'm anything, it's blunt, so I write her this letter:

Ardis dear,

We made a stupid mistake back then. I've always regretted it, but it's taken me fifty years to realize just how stupid it was. That doesn't mean we shouldn't do something about it, to correct it. I'm no prize. I'm seventy-two years old and have some of the 'older man's' characteristics. I'm forgetful sometimes and occasionally cranky. But my health is still good, my mind still sharp, I have my hair, though it's thin and sort of frizzy, and most of my teeth. I've taken care of myself. I've been married twice, lived all over hell and gone, been in a war, raised a family, had a career. I guess I'm what they call experienced. And I still love you. I always have. If you'll have me, we could be married, and start redoing the fifty years. We don't

57

have that long, I know, and you can never do something now exactly the way it should have been done,
might have been done, then. But we can get started.

I would have ended it there, for the dramatic effect, but
I'm a talkative old soul once I get started, even on paper, so
I rambled on. Told her a little about my life, and about the
book I'm working on. Told her how she was sort of vaguely
in my mind that morning when I heard Charles Kuralt,
quoted her the line, told her a little about how I'd gone
about finding her. I wanted her to feel the sort of person I
am. I sent her a photo, the best of the recent ones, me with
my son Jack taken when he and his family were up this way
on a holiday two years ago, and we all went fishing up at
Diefenbaker Lake, me with my scruffy fishing vest on and a
battered hat that I've worn fishing for thirty years, filled
with flies and hooks and weights, holding up a perch that
weighed a good five pounds, if I remember right, and
grinning like hell into the camera. The world had seemed
pretty good that day, and I looked like a pretty good old boy,
like a nice man at peace with the world. I wanted Ardis to see
the sort of person I am, too.
I signed the letter "with love, Andy," and put more
stamps on the envelope than necessary.

I mentioned I was writing a book, an autobiography. Why
not?
William Saroyan, who's one of my favourite novelists,
wrote his autobiography and called it *Here Comes, There
Goes You Know Who*. I'm going to call mine *Who? Me?*
I've always had a knack for meeting interesting people,
and getting on with them. I cut Monty's hair in Africa, and
Patton's in Sicily, and I think I could honestly call them both
friends. But there's been dozens more, hundreds. And I've
always had a natural gift for gab, as the Irish say, a born
story-teller, that's me. When I was a barber back in Cedar
Rapids and Sioux City (where I went after Ardis and I had
our falling out), I used to keep my customers' ears from

drooping into my way by spinning one yarn after another, most of them more or less true. I've never been big on imagination, and fiction's just a classy way of lying, as Hemingway once told me, but detail is what makes my stories worth hearing. Nothing gets past me. People would say, "Andy, you're a born story-teller. Why don't you write a book?" And I'd chuckle and say, "Who? Me?" That's where the idea for the title comes from.

I spent the craziest war anyone could imagine. I started as a barber, in a headquarters company, and wound up in public affairs, although I never stopped cutting the top brass's hair. I didn't get beyond private first class, but I did an officer's work in public affairs, writing pieces for *Stars and Stripes*, press releases, and even a couple of speeches for George Patton, although no one was supposed to know about that. A tank commander I got chummy with, a major named Arthur Cudlup but called Lucky, was the son of a publisher of the *Arizona American*, a newspaper published in Yuma, and that led to my first full-time writing job. I'd already been doing some, selling the occasional piece to the Cedar Rapids *Gazette* and the Sioux City *Press* and even once or twice to the Des Moines *Register*, mostly profiles of people I came across I figured other folks would be interested in, or outdoor stories, hunting and fishing always having been my first real true love.

In Yuma, I did all sorts of things: a lot of outdoors stuff, some sports, obituaries (a form I came to respect), and even social notes, weddings, things like that. I wrote a column for thirteen years, even after I'd left the paper, "Andy's Way," that some people down there still remember, I'm told. I never did do much in the way of real reporting, though. I'd fall asleep at school board meetings, and I'd always want to say my piece at the city council. Once, on my way to a press conference at the chamber of commerce, I saw a broken window, stuck my head in and found a dead body. I had my camera with me, as always, and got a dandy picture of a little kitty cat leaving bloody pawprints on a newspaper lying next to the body, but my city editor gave me hell for missing the press conference. The picture won a state prize, but the city editor never let me forget how unreliable I was. I wasn't cut out for just taking notes and being invisible.

I wound up as director of public relations for the Arizona Highways Department, a job I kept for ten years, until I had a flareup with my boss, a terrible little husk of a fart who was the deputy director, what the kids these days would call a wimp. It didn't make no nevermind to me. I'd been selling stories to papers and magazines all through that period, and doing my column for some of it, and I'd even done a couple of books, outdoor adventure things for the teen-age market. Scott Meredith, the agent who got Norman Mailer a couple million bucks for a book a while back, handled them, though he didn't do as well by me. There wasn't a lot of money in it, but it was satisfying writing, knowing that kids were going to enjoy it, maybe get some inspiration.

In 1960, I moved to Montana to be a PR man with the fish and game commission, but I kept on doing my magazine writing. I was already a regular in *Outdoor Life* and *Fish and Stream* and *Boys Life.* Now I was doing things for *Ellery Queen Mystery Magazine* and *True Detectives* – one kind was fiction and the other fact, but the difference between the two has always eluded me. They're both stories, and that's what I'm good at. The telling is pretty much the same. I even wrote pieces for some church magazines, during the religion phase of my life, and I got lucky once and sold something to *Readers Digest*, one of those "most memorable character" things. I never had much use for the *Digest*, but that was my most memorable paycheque, I'll say that.

Along the way, I interviewed astronauts and mass killers, nuclear physicists and trophy hunters, biologists busting their ass to save the kind of bird most people never even heard of, and mercenaries from Africa. Congressmen, cow-boys, inventors, the last man to be executed in the state of Montana before the supreme court said no way, a little man who'd killed his wife but donated his eyes to one of those banks. I taught English and writing in penitentiaries because it seemed like a worthwhile thing to do and preached sermons in Protestant churches during my religion period, which came about the time my first marriage was breaking up.

I never graduated from any school at all, except barber college, and I never got a diploma from them because the shipment was lost in the mail, but I've interviewed college presidents, including Ike, when he was head man at Columbia. I've never been arrested, but I spent a lot of time behind bars. I'm afraid of heights and get dizzy on a kitchen ladder, but Gus Grissom is a friend of mine. I heard Patton call Montgomery a son of a bitch with my own ears, and I heard Monty say worse about Patton. The day John Kennedy was killed, I was in the governor's office in Butte, Montana, and I saw him cry. Why the hell shouldn't I write a book?

Ardis writes me this letter, getting to me about two weeks after I mailed mine to her:

Dear Andrew,

Your letter, which arrived a few days ago, has set off a torrent of memories for me, some pleasant, some not so. Truthfully, it's made me giddy. I feel like a schoolgirl, and I'm not at all sure I can trust my emotions.

I've tried to write this letter several times, and I've written it in my head dozens of times. I think I can make sense of it now.

I think you're right when you say we made a mistake in 1933. I was in love with you, just in case you had or have any doubts, but I hated you after that argument, for weeks. But you moved away and the hate diminished, finally went away entirely. After that, I didn't feel anything about you, if you can believe that, and, after I married Mr. Harris, I don't think I thought about you at all, except briefly, in passing, for over forty-five years. You said in your letter you don't even remember what that argument was about. How like a man! I remember, and I remember every hateful word you said that day. But I said hateful things, too, and I remember them, too.

I'm not sure, though, that the mistake was as stupid as you think. I can't speak for you, of course, but I've had a good life. Mr. Harris was as good a husband as a woman could want, a good provider, a good friend, a thoughtful, generous man. He died eight years ago, as I mentioned in my previous letter, and I still miss him. We had three wonderful children. One of them, our darling son James, died of polio. The other two are well, married to wonderful people, and have given me four (so far) grandchildren that are the pride and delight of my life, as is ordained. My daughter Linda and her family live in Los Angeles, and we visit, back and forth, once a year. But my son Robert and his darling wife Jan and their two children live right here in Coral Gables, not far from my house. I still live in the house Mr. Harris and I bought when we moved here, after his retirement. He, poor man, only got to enjoy it for three years before he got sick.

What I'm saying, Andy, is that I've had a life. I didn't get to be the queen of England or a movie star, but I had a life. It was mine, and still is. I've had plenty of misery, when Mr. Harris was wounded in the war and lost one leg, when our darling son died and other times, but I've been happy, too, as happy as I think any one woman is entitled to be.

You've had a life, too. You've had two marriages, three fine sons, several careers. You seem to imply, in your letter, that you've had nothing but regrets because you and I had our falling out, but I don't believe that. Life doesn't work that way, dear Andrew. I'm sure you've had regrets. All people do. But I'm sure you had happiness. You'd be cheating yourself if you tried to say you hadn't.

So we've both had lives. We can't just erase that, pretend they didn't happen. You can't turn back the hands of time, dear Andrew, as I know you know. You can't relive life, and you shouldn't want to. That's a defiance of God, and it makes your own life cheap. I don't think either of us want that.

I'm an old woman. I'm sixty-nine years old. My health isn't all that good. I haven't been with a man since Mr. Harris died. I don't want to talk about marriage, don't even want to think about it. But you're right when you say there is something be-tween us, there's still something between us. If you'd like to come down for a visit, there's plenty of room in the house. Don't, though, come with expectations that may not be possible to meet. We can see what happens.

The word love wasn't mentioned anywhere, and she signed "Affectionately yours, Ardis," a phrase that makes me frown. Affection isn't what I want. I have to smile at her use of that other hoary old saw, "can't turn back the hands of time," though. What a pair of word-manglers we'd make.

There's a photo, too. A small, fragile looking woman, with papery skin, bluish white hair that looks to be long, wrapped up in a bun like schoolmarms used to wear. I like that. Too many women cut their hair short and bob it when they get old. The colour of the photo is a little too muddy to tell what colour her eyes are, and that's something I have no recollection of, but they seem to be bright. She's wearing a sundress, with bare, freckled shoulders, and she obviously hasn't let herself go to pot. She's not fat nor unhealthily thin. There's some juice left in her, that's obvious. She's smiling, a wide open, toothy smile that means her son must have taken this shot, or someone she loves. The photo seems to be a companion to the one I sent her, or an answer. She looks good, looks like the kind of person anyone with their senses about them would like to know. But she's right. She's an old woman. And she doesn't look anything like the young woman who's been clear and sharp and dominating my memory these past few weeks. Not a thing.

Coral Gables. On the map, it looks like it's just an extension of Miami, but I'm told it's really more like a small town, with a personality of its own. I've been to Florida, of course, several times, but never to Miami, so I've never gotten down that way.

I've been taking count, and this'll be my seventeenth move, the seventeenth place I've lived since I left my father's house in Milwaukee, almost sixty years ago. He was a drunk, my old man, and there wasn't much love lost between us. When my mother died, I knew it wouldn't be long before I'd be going, because there wasn't anything to keep me. When the old man remarried, I was out the door. I didn't see him again, and I was in Sioux City when he died. I was notified in plenty of time, but I didn't go to the funeral.

"Nothin' good'll come of ya, Andy," he yelled at me when I left. I just gritted my teeth and didn't say anything back, although I could have. His prediction wasn't so hot, because, while I guess I haven't amounted to a hell of a lot, I've done okay. I'm not rich and famous, but I've always made a good living, lived the way I wanted to, made a lot of friends and no enemies I can think of, had a lot of fun and didn't hurt anybody anymore than absolutely necessary. Even in the war, I'm pretty sure I never killed anybody, although there were a few times when I fired my weapon in anger.

And I sure as hell turned out to be a better father than my old man, though my eldest son, Muggs, sided with his mother and has been cool to me ever since I left. Jack and I've always gotten along real well, especially since all the help I gave him while he was on the bottle.

I moved to Canada in 1969, the year after my youngest son, Peter, came up here to dodge the draft. When kids were first starting to do that, that and burn their draft cards, I thought it was a bunch of damn foolishness. Like any old vet, I guess, I thought a man should be proud to serve, and should go when he's called, no matter what. But by the time Peter got his notice, I'd been thinking a lot about the war and I'd changed my views quite a bit. There was a photo in *Life* of an old woman and a baby, on fire with napalm, that really turned me around. Peter was living with his mother in Phoenix and I was in Denver, where I'd gone to work for Ducks Unlimited, and he called me to ask my advice. He was only nineteen and he'd taken the divorce hardest, I think, because he was always my boy. I told him to follow his conscience, *that* was the most important thing for a man to do, to do what he felt was right, not what other people said was right.

"That's what takes the real guts," I said.

"I don't know if I have "em, Pop," Peter said, "but I want to be a man."

I followed him, partly to show him my support and partly because I'd always wanted to live up in this part of the world, ever since a fishing trip to the Kenora lakes at the height of the Depression, when even barber shops were closing down, things were so bad. We roomed together for a while in Toronto, then had places of our own, not too far away, when I went to Winnipeg to work for Ducks Unlimited again and he tagged along. But the funny thing was, when Carter came in and pushed his amnesty through, Peter went home to Phoenix and married a girl he'd been writing to. I just stayed put.

I was always comfortable in Canada, even became a citizen a few years ago, on my sixty-seventh birthday, which might make settling in Florida a bit of a problem. But I hear Florida is full of retired Canadians, so why should it matter? The social security people in Washington might smile a little, that's all.

I don't have a job to quit, but I've given my landlady notice. I told Jack about it when he called the other night and he thinks I'm crazy, of course. Maybe I am, but not doing anything would be even crazier, and I've never been one for halfway measures, god knows. Going down there like a tourist or a visitor would only be awkward, make us both feel nervous. And the expense of the extra flights – back here, then down there again – is more than my budget can stand. Since I've been working on the book, my freelancing has gone to seed, and I have to admit I miss the extra bucks it used to bring in, even though I'd slowed down a bit since I turned seventy and I had two artificial knees put in.

So I'm all packed and ready to go. It's no big deal, really. I've always been a rolling stone. And when you're my age, and live alone, you don't have much accumulation, you're always ready to pick up and go, usually to the old age home or the hospital or the boneyard, so I'm getting off scot-free, you might say.

It's important, I think, to show her my commitment, that I really mean it. "We can see what happens," she said. Okay by me. But only a fool leaves everything to chance. A fool or a younger man. Ardis is right, we've both had lives. I've had a damn good one, and I never meant to say I didn't, not for a minute. But I'd be a fool, wouldn't you say, if I let the end of it spin out without shoehorning her back in somehow. I loved Gladyse and Carol, and they were fine women. But they're in the past, and I'm here now, today, looking out for tomorrow. Night is coming, and I gotta get a move on or I'll be left in the dark.

Feathers and Blood

I N THE SPRING of 1927, on the same day that Lindbergh
was crossing the Atlantic, a young woman by the name
of Rebeccah Kristol sent my father a letter from Cleveland with the simple message: "Now."

At that time, my father was already firmly established as
a reporter on *The Day*, the Yiddish-language daily that sent
its messages of the toils and joys of Jewish life in New York
from the Lower East Side throughout the city and even into
the countryside beyond the rivers, and had begun the career
that would carry him for the next forty years and more. But
before that, there had been moments, sighs, passions, endless nights, bottles of whisky, fierce friendships and women
who, in the telling later, became blurred, indistinct as buildings viewed through fog, perhaps to spare my mother,
perhaps merely so that my father, who enjoyed telling
stories of his youth, could keep some small pieces of it
private, for his own, like good luck coins fingered and shiny
in his pocket. He never said so, but I suspect Rebeccah
Kristol was one of those coins, not just a friend from the old
days in Cleveland, as he described her when he told the
story, but one of the women who had been part of his life in
those years before my mother, before the time when my
sisters and I were given our chance to be.

Rebeccah was a strong woman, my father used to tell us,
a determined woman with ideas of her own and the courage
to put some – if not all – of them into effect. She was a

drinker and a smoker, mildly shocking behavior for a woman in those days, at least in some strata of society – even the society my father and Rebeccah inhabited – as well as a free thinker and free lover, an anarchist follower of Emma Goldman, a dabbler in vegetarianism, frequenter of cafés and theatres, friend of artists and writers, which is how my father – who was part of the Bohemian café circle, such as it was in Cleveland – came to know her. The one photograph he had of her – one of several brittle, yellow tintypes from his early days that could be found scattered in among the more abundant family portraits and snapshots of my mother's childhood and pictures of her and my father as a young couple and us children that filled a shoebox my mother kept in a dresser drawer – revealed her as clearly possessed of those qualities of character he ascribed to her, but contained not a hint of the predilections and interests. She is one of only three women in the portrait filled with men, a solemn, formal study of activity suddenly arrested in the newsroom of *The Day*, circa 1930, more than a decade before my birth. He himself is sitting at a desk in the pose I like best to remember him in, hands poised over the keys of an ancient standup typewriter, head slightly lowered, mustache bristling, cigarette dangling from a mouth pursed with concentration, his hair only just beginning to thin, still rich and black. The other men and one of the women are captured in similar freezes, at typewriters or bent over teletype machines, reading, one or two on the telephone, a few with their backs to the camera, and there is a sense of busyness and purpose to the scene that is unmarred by the other two women, who stand, stiff and vigilant at either end of the room, like prim bookends. Rebeccah is the one on the right, in a long black skirt and ruffled white blouse with a bow at the throat, her dark hair in a severe bun, her face partially shielded by thick-rimmed glasses. She was, at the time the photograph was taken, less than thirty, but there is a sort of agelessness about her face, her strong, well-defined features facing the camera with intelligent interest neither youthfully beautiful nor showing any of the decay of years. Her eyes seem to sparkle, and her mouth and chin are firm, as if they were being held into the wind. But her clothes, her hair style, even the rigid way she holds her arms by her sides, one hand seeming to be smoothing a pleat in her skirt, all point to a manner of conventionality which runs against the way my father would describe her.

"She was a changed woman when she came to New York," my father said as he showed me the picture, anticipating my thought. "Whatever happened to her in that love affair, in that marriage, in that boat ride, it turned her inside out." He carefully deposited the photograph back into its protective envelope, along with a few others from the same era, and looked at me. "She never lost her intelligence, of course, or her taste, but her curiosity about the world shrivelled up, and she became the sort of person she had always disliked, a closed sort of person. As if she was making up for something."

All of that, my father used to say when he told the story, was so much more perplexing because of the kind of woman she had been, "a woman who" – and here, if they were in the room, my mother and sisters, who were quite a bit older than me, would grimace, my sisters actually groaning – "had all the intellectual and creative abilities and instincts of a man." When she'd sent him that note, he'd kept his promise and gotten her a job, as a bookkeeper at *The Day*, the place she would remain all her working life, rising to be chief bookkeeper, the austere, darkly dressed, slightly plump woman with a wart on her nose who would greet me so cheerily on those infrequent occasions when I'd visit my father in his office, where even the air in the newsroom was redolent with the smell of printer's ink wafting in from the black-walled pressroom downstairs. He'd gotten her the job, helped her settle in, and been as much of a friend to her as he could. But they'd never been really close again, not close enough for her to go beyond telling him *what* had happened, to *why*.

It began, he knew, when she'd met the man, a salesman who had worked his way up to manager of a small haberdashery on Lake Street in downtown Cleveland, then bought out the widow of the man he'd worked for. His name, my father thought, was Greenspan, although that didn't seem to matter. Nothing about him, my father said, seemed to matter, since the problem was within Rebeccah.

The first time I can recall hearing the story, when I was six or seven, and for several retellings afterward, my father explained that she had had earlier sweethearts, and that her husband-to-be was jealous. This had "caused problems," my father said with a wink, "but nothing that feminine wiles couldn't cope with." Later, when I was twelve or thirteen, the story changed accordingly, and my father explained the "problem" was that Rebeccah was not a virgin, a condition that was sure to cause displeasure for her husband – "not all husbands," my father added quickly, "but some men care, and this one definitely." And, finally, at some point during the year I went away to college, on one of those short but intense visits home, the story came full cycle, my father relating with head-shaking wonder the facts he had come to know in detail some time later, after she'd come to New York: how, to stave off discovery, she'd planned and carried out the simple subterfuge, as brilliant and easily accomplished as the friend who had coached her had promised: the douche of a mixture of water, alum and vinegar, the feigned cries of pain, the small balloon filled with chicken blood concealed first under the pillow, then in her palm, the jab with one long, sleekly polished nail. It had gone well, my father said, but afterwards, as the husband lay sleeping, Rebeccah had walked the deck of their honeymoon cruise ship, staring into the dark impenetrable waves of Lake Erie, and come to some – to my father – inexplicable resolve. She went back to their cabin just for a few minutes, to throw a few things into a suitcase, then she'd hidden in a washroom until the ship docked in fog-shrouded Buffalo and disembarked with the first crowds, losing herself amid the noise and crowds on the dock.

It was sometime soon after that that she'd written the note to my father, the fulfilment of some late-night café pledge he'd made when they'd been close, that when she was ready to leave Cleveland, where some family obligation he was never clear about kept her bound, and escape to New York, where he was now headed, she would let him know and he would help her find a job, help her make what, in those days, and for a woman, was still a difficult passage. The note she sent – and he was sorry, my father always said, he hadn't saved it – didn't have to say more than it did, because he knew from that one word, "Now," all he needed, really: that she was ready to come, that she wanted his help, and more, that it was a cry for help, a signal for freedom.

His name, in fact, was Greenspun, Aaron Greenspun, whose family had settled in Akron, where an uncle became the first Jew to serve on a city council in Ohio. He had yellow eyes, like a cat's, and Rebeccah, dreaming of them, thought his name should more truly be *Gold*spun, so did it seem those eyes must have been fashioned. He was tall, well built, like a Greek god, Rebeccah told her best friend Belle and the other women she drank coffee with at the café, who pursed their mouths in impressed wonder as they gazed at the rumpled, round-shouldered men arguing at the next table, then giggled at the perceived possibilities, and had only the slightest curved Semitic nose in his otherwise smooth and blandly featured face to betray his origins. He was altogether beautiful, "the most beautiful thing I've ever seen," Rebeccah told her friends, conscious of her choice of words. Her attraction to him frightened her.

They had absolutely nothing in common, shouldn't have even met except there was a family connection, Rebeccah's one weakness. A Greenspun cousin had married a Williams cousin – Williams being Rebeccah's mother's family name, the Americanized version of Wilchevski that her father, Rebeccah's hard-headed, bristly bearded grandfather, had adopted in one of those Ellis Island subterfuges that had smoothed the wrinkles from so many Russian and Polish names. The old man, long dead now, had begun as a peddler but had worked his horse and wagon into a stand, then a small shop, then Williams Brothers, one of Cleveland's better furniture stores, proving his abilities as a merchant and his sagacity, he always claimed, as a name-picker. That side of the family – the store was now run by Rebeccah's uncles Meyer and Robert – seemed to have much in common with the Greenspuns of Akron and their one Cleveland offshoot, all of them prosperous, right-thinking family people who erected big brick houses near the lakefront and gave work to coloured maids who, as Uncle Meyer once explained to Rebeccah, would be jobless and go hungry otherwise, "which you, I suppose, Miss High And Mighty, would rather see?"

Rebeccah herself was considerably different. She had had the good fortune, she liked to tell her friends, of "marrying smart," referring not to herself but to her mother. Jacob Kristol was a working man and union organizer with rough hands and an intelligence striving to free itself from an inadequate education, not a trader, by any means, but a man who would smile when he saw children stealing apples from a street vendor. He had had three years of school in Russia, then another two in New York's Brownsville, enough to give him sufficient English to go to work at a factory manufacturing umbrella handles, but the bulk of what he knew of the world came from night school, correspondence courses, workshops put on by the union, and a voracious appetite for reading that had made him, in his old age, a favourite of the librarians at the stately Carnegie branch in downtown Cleveland, where he would spend most of his afternoons from the time of his retirement until his death in the reading room, crumpled over *Crime and Punishment*, which he was enjoying for the fourth time. He'd come to Cleveland as a young man, on a freight train with a trio of anarchists, to work and help organize the foundry. Then he'd stayed, marrying, as the Williamses always put it, "above his position," and fathering two children, a son who took after his mother's side of the family but died in the war, and a daughter – Rebeccah – who took after him.

Rebeccah's devotion to him was, in some respects, her undoing. Jacob Kristol had married late, so he was already an old man through most of the time his daughter knew him, retired before she was through with school and dead before she had barely reached twenty. But his impact on her was powerful, making her different from most of the girls she went to school with, leaving her bored and dissatisfied with the few boys who were willing to penetrate the veil of sarcasm and feigned intellectualism with which she clothed herself, and she would have liked to have fled from the small city provincialism of Cleveland when she graduated, but her father's failing health kept her at home. Then, when he died, a pledge to him that she would look after her mother, who was also ailing, continued to keep her bound. By this time, she had a job, an apartment and a life of her own, and had discovered the small café society of artists and poets, actors and anarchists who frequented the cluster of cafés and delicatessens along River Avenue on either side of the Rialto Theatre, where touring companies from New York would stage the latest in Yiddish productions.

"You're too good for this narrow stage," one of the actors – a handsome man with a cleft in his chin who went on to have a career in Hollywood under a new name – told her after they'd made love on the mattress of straw-filled ticking in her small, darkly lit loft. "Why don't you come with me?"

"And you'll make me a star?" Rebeccah asked, batting the long, artificially thickened lashes of her large, luminous eyes.

"Seriously," the actor said. "You're too beautiful, too intelligent to let yourself stifle in this ridiculous city where it's always either too hot or too cold."

"And in your bed, the temperature is better controlled?" Rebeccah asked.

My father tried too. "Come with me to New York," he told her when he was getting ready to leave. He had gone west with the intention of seeing the world and, hopefully, writing about it, but had gotten no farther than Chicago before his money ran out and he'd circled back to Cleveland, where he'd heard, from a poet fleeing the place, of a job on a Yiddish newspaper. He spent three years there, learning the craft that would carry him for the rest of his life, before he felt he was ready to go home, and he would have liked to take her with him, this beautiful creature with wild, tangled hair and nicotine and paint stains on her long, delicate fingers, like some sort of souvenir of the great hinterlands across the Hudson River, proof of his passage.

Rebeccah kissed him, gently, like an echo. "You know I can't, Morgenstern," she said. "But I will someday."

"Will you let me know?" my father asked fervently.

"I'll let you know when I'm ready," Rebeccah said.

Before that happened, she met Aaron Greenspun.

Perhaps she'd meant it, always meant to leave, to find a broader world to the east, in New York, where so much of the nightly café talk centred, perhaps even in Paris, where she longed to study art at the Sorbonne, but time passed, her mother lingered, then died, freeing her from her final bond, but still, somehow, she stayed, and before she could muster her energies for that flight, he appeared, changing everything.

It was at a family gathering, the first one of any real consequence since the marriage of the cousins, and he was there, being led through the gauntlet of Williamses by Aunt Ruth, who took Rebeccah fondly by the hand when she came to her.

"And this is Rebeccah, our darling black sheep."

The black sheep was a tag Rebeccah had smilingly endured for years, even before her father's death, but tonight, with her hair in a woolly, swirling halo around her head and dressed all in black, even to her stockings, the tag seemed exceptionally appropriate, and she was radiantly bewitching, a fact which was hardly lost on the tall, handsome man in Aunt Ruth's tow. Nor was her effect on him lost on Rebeccah. They smiled at each other and a current of sexual tension crackled between them like an electric spark running along a twist of broken copper wire.

"The black sheep? More like a black diamond," Aaron said, in Yiddish that was almost cultured in its precision.

"Coal, you mean," Rebeccah said. She gave him her most luminous smile, showing all her teeth, and made a noise that was somewhat like a hiss.

"No, no, a sheep, a poor little lamb," Aunt Ruth said, putting her arm around Rebeccah and rocking her gently against her shoulder. "This child just lost her mother, my darling sister, so treat her gently."

"Aunt Ruth, that was almost two years ago."

"And still unmarried. Just a lamb, a poor lost lamb, but a *black* lost lamb, so what's to do with her?"

Aunt Ruth gave both their hands a squeeze and looked from face to face, then seemed to make a decision. "Be nice to each other, children. Rebeccah is a lost black lamb, Aaron is a stranger, a Jew among Jews, of course, but a stranger nonetheless." She moved on, making no indication that he should follow.

Aaron shifted his weight from one lean hip to the other and cleared his throat. If Rebeccah truly was a black sheep, he was a white shepherd, dressed in dove-grey trousers with a sharp crease – just the kind, her father used to say, the bosses use to cut the throat of the working man – and a white linen jacket with an ironed handkerchief in the breast pocket. And his yellow eyes, gazing shyly at her. "A white knight," Rebeccah said.

"Pardon?"

"That's you. I'm the black sheep, you're the white knight."

"A white night," he said, gesturing with his chin toward the window to underline his pun, "that's once a year if you're lucky, don't you agree? A full moon, starry sky, not a cloud."

Rebeccah smiled at him. There was an attraction, of course, and no sense in denying it, but she already knew enough about him, from family gossip, to know better. She took the edge of her lower lip gently between her teeth and made a decision.

"That's too dizzying an abstraction for this poor lamb," she said, and began to move away.

His hand on her arm brought her up short. "Wait." He looked embarrassed by his abrupt gesture. "I'd like to see you again."

"Again? I'm just going across the room to have a canapé. My stomach is growling. Look over there in a moment and you'll see me."

"I mean," Aaron said, twisting his resolve, "again, after this. Some place else. Perhaps we could have a meal."

"I don't like to cook," Rebeccah said with suspicion.

"I mean in a restaurant," he said in sudden English, as if it were a secret he wanted no one overhearing to understand.

She took a step back and looked him over, from the top of his sandy brown hair, neatly parted in the centre of his well-shaped head, down along the smooth contour of brow, nose, cleanly chiseled mouth and chin, the starched white collar, down the perfectly tied necktie, the immaculate linen jacket, pausing for a moment at his crotch, where, despite the loose drape of his trousers, she believed she saw a barely perceptible movement, then down the crease of those trousers to the glimmering black wings of his oxfords, then up again, letting her eyes take their time while he stood motionless, waiting their verdict. "I want you to know," she said finally, "that you represent just about everything that I detest and abhor about this society, capitalism at its most rapacious, mercantilism at its basest, petty bourgeoisie mentality at its narrowest, dandyism, masculine superiority, class and sexual arrogance...." Her hand darted out from her side in a palm-up gesture of dismay, as if she were overwhelmed by the enormity of the list she was prepared to recite, but her voice trailed off.

Aaron observed her with the same aloof detachment she had spent on him, a small smile seeping into his lips, and he shrugged, a shrug coloured with a boldness that made her think she had, perhaps, been wrong. "I may represent those things," he said. "I think you're wrong, but I won't argue with you now, here. I may *represent* them, but that wouldn't necessarily mean I *am* them. You *are* wrong there."

Four days later, he showed up at the department store where she worked as a window dresser, resplendent in a blue and white striped gabardine suit and a straw hat, a bouquet of flowers in his freshly manicured hand. "We're in the same business," he said as he greeted her with the flow of employees through the staff entrance at six o'clock.

"Not exactly. You sell, I decorate, though I'll concede there's a connection. More importantly, you own, I toil." But she was pleased to see him, flattered by the flowers he now proffered, making a gallant sort of dip with his head and shoulders, his free hand behind his back.

"The same business just the same. Mercantilism at its basest. And the fact that you're a Williams had nothing to do, I suppose, with your getting a job at Loew's."

"I'm not a Williams," Rebeccah said fiercely. "I'm a Kristol."

"Excuse me, no disrespect meant to the memory of your father, who I'm told was a fine man, I regret I never had the pleasure of meeting him. Working here rather than in the family store eases the conscience, don't you agree?"

Rebeccah let a smile slowly form. "That's a contradiction I'm still grappling with, yes." She observed him coolly, conscious of the slight pressure at the back of her neck caused by having to tilt her head upward to meet his eyes. "I don't know that meeting my father would have been a pleasure for you, though. He was a man who said what he thought."

"Like his daughter?"

"Like his daughter, yes."

"There's no accounting for taste," Aaron said, with a light laugh. "Don't you agree?"

He took her to as good a restaurant as was possible, considering the way she was dressed, and afterwards to a place on the lake where they drank wine and danced. He took her home in his automobile, a Packard with shimmering chrome, and, on the street, gazed thoughtfully up at the dark windows of her loft, which was on the upper floor of a building that had once been a warehouse and was now honeycombed with small apartments. "You must be lonely there," he said with warmth.

"Not really," Rebeccah answered dryly, considering the options that faced her now. "There are ghosts."

But he didn't ask to come up, didn't make a move to kiss her good night. Instead, he offered his hand and shook hers vigorously.

After that, they saw each other often, dining out, dancing, attending the theatre and concerts, going to the museum and galleries. He had little interest in art, he admitted, and a tin ear, but he seemed happy to accompany her wherever she wished to go, and expressed an interest in learning about the things for which she had passions, which were many. He even, on the two or three occasions she took him, after the theatre, to the Royal Café for coffee, endured the thinly veiled insults of her friends. Rebeccah made no attempt to defend him and watched thoughtfully as he gingerly fended off Belle's parries, like a man wearing white gloves suddenly handed something slick and foul smelling.

After two months, she was summoned to her Aunt Ruth's for Friday dinner. "And Aaron?" Aunt Ruth inquired after the dishes had been washed and Uncle Avrom had taken the dog and his pipe for a stroll in the late summer evening. The two women sat in the kitchen, drinking cool tea in the flickering candlelight.

"Aaron? That name sounds familiar. Wasn't he a fellow in the Bible?"

"The Bible! You've heard of that, Miss Fancypants, what a surprise."

"My father mentioned it once or twice, said it was suitable for use as kindling, if dead leaves were not close at hand."

"Your father! God rest his soul. He probably did say that. You like him?"

"My father? Of course I liked him." Aunt Ruth had been her mother's closest sister, and Rebeccah had a special affection for her, visiting often since her mother's death. But this was the first time she'd know her to intrude.

"Aaron! Oh, you *know* who I mean. Aaron Greenspun. The man is crazy about you and you don't know who he is."

"Oh, Mr. Goldspun."

"It's Greenspun, dear."

"I know, Aunt Ruth. That's just a little joke."

"A joke! The man wants to marry you and you make jokes about his name that should be your name soon."

Rebeccah stared at her aunt for a moment, then laughed. "Marry me? Aunt Ruth, the man has only kissed me once, and that so softly it felt like a butterfly batting its wings against my lips. And *that* only because it was my birthday.

When he escorts me home after an evening together he shakes my hand like it was the handle of a pump and he was dying of thirst."

"The man is a gentleman," Aunt Ruth said sternly. "You don't appreciate that, but you'll learn to."

"The man is beautiful but hollow," Rebeccah retorted. "He's like that candle, flickering, precious, hypnotic if you let yourself look too long, but of no substance." She leaned over and, as if to demonstrate her point, brushed her hand through the small flame, extinguishing it.

"Candles!" Aunt Ruth snorted through her nose. "You're burning yours at both ends, Miss Fancypants. Are you twenty-six now, or is it twenty-seven?"

Rebeccah wrinkled her nose to show her displeasure, but kept her voice soft. "Twenty-five, thank you, just as of three weeks ago, as you well know, since you sent me that lovely satin robe." She paused, tilting her chin up slightly. "You *witch*. I thought that was an odd gift to be coming from you. You're preparing my trousseau, aren't you?"

"Your mother, God rest her soul, isn't here to look after you. You're incapable of doing it yourself, so someone has to. It's a burden, but I take it happily, Bubela."

The two women stared at each other through the growing darkness that had pounced on the room when the candle went out. Finally, Rebeccah blinked. "What do you mean, he wants to marry me?"

"Just that. Would it be plainer if I spoke in English?"

"You're crazy, Aunt Ruth, forgive me for saying so. How do you dream of such things?"

"There's no dreaming, Miss Fancypants. The man said so himself."

"Said so. To who? You?"

"Not to me, of course, silly," Aunt Ruth said. "To Uncle Meyer. He was a bit flummoxed, the poor man, his nose always in the store's books, he hardly knows there's a real world spinning around him, he asked me to have a word with you, and your Uncle Avrom to look after things. Oh, for goodness sake, Rebeccah, sit back down."

Rebeccah was on her feet, her hands closing into small,

tight fists at her side. "He told Uncle Meyer he wanted to marry me? Aaron Greenspun did that?"

"Of course he did, Bubela. Now sit down."

She was speechless, words spinning around in her mind but failing to properly lodge on her tongue like gears in a machine that won't engage. Worse, she felt, inexplicably, a profound sense of shame, as if she had been caught out in some disgusting betrayal, and blood rushed to her cheeks, making her feel faint. "Who... who...," she stammered.

"Who does he think he is? A gentleman, that's who." Aunt Ruth put her hand on Rebeccah's wrist and tugged at it until she sat down. "Let me ask you this, Miss Modern Woman, Miss Artist and Literary Type. If your father, God rest his soul, were alive, and if Aaron Greenspun or any other man, I mean any other man of breeding and manners, this isn't your friends like Morgenstern or that actor I'm talking about, but men who still have the Old Country in their minds and hearts, if such a man wanted to marry you and your father was alive, wouldn't you expect such a man to have the courtesy of talking to your father. *Not*" – she held up a silencing hand – "to ask permission, just to inform. Wouldn't you expect that? Wouldn't you even, maybe, be hurt, just a little, if such a man didn't do that, Miss Head-in-the-Clouds?"

Rebeccah allowed that maybe she would, "if it was that type of man, yes, maybe. Not if Morgenstern didn't do it." And she laughed at that thought, of my father paying a courtesy call.

"Well, what an admission! But Mr. Greenspun *is* that sort of man. He's a gentleman and an Old Country man. And wait, wait just a second, darling, let me ask you one more thing. Since your father, God rest his soul, *isn't* here, wouldn't it be proper then for Mr. Greenspun to talk to some other member of the Kristol family, if there was one nearby? Your father's brother, Mort, maybe, except that he lives a thousand miles away?"

Rebeccah nodded slowly.

"So, all right. Your father, God rest his soul, isn't alive, nor, God rest her soul, is your mother, my darling Rachel, and your father's brother and other relatives are a thousand miles away. So who should Mr. Greenspun talk to about his intentions but your Uncle Meyer, woolly headed though he is, he *is* the head of the Williams family, your mother's people."

"He could have talked to me, damn it," Rebeccah said in English.

Aunt Ruth smiled and patted Rebeccah's hand, which had grown cold. "He will, Bubela, he will. As soon as I tell him you'd like him to. Oh, come on, come on. He's a gentleman, I keep telling you. And maybe just a little bit shy, too."

Rebeccah went home and, over the next three days, as she brushed her teeth and combed her hair, as she steamed her vegetables for dinner, as she painted, standing nude under the skylights of her loft, she contemplated her life. She was, in fact, twenty-five years old, and, as her father had died at sixty-eight, her mother at sixty-three, she was well into what was likely the second third of her life. There had been no money left after her mother's illness, so her father's wispy promises that maybe, someday, she would go to art school, had entirely evaporated. She had delayed her departure to New York and points further on so long that, now, the thought of leaving Cleveland terrified her. And, worse yet, the paintings she had done, piled up like neatly stacked picket signs waiting the next strike in her father's old office at the union hall, even the painting she was working on now, were shit, no other word for it, in Yiddish, English or any other language. She sighed, lit another cigarette and went to stand in front of her one concession to vanity, a full-length mirror she had justified when she bought as essential to her study of anatomy. She stood there, in the bright, white northern light streaming down from the ceiling window, for a long time, observing the beginning sag of her breasts, the little puckering of skin along her belly.

On the third day, Monday, when Aaron came to call for her at the store, she found herself looking at him more closely than usual, *examining* him, with her painter's eye, as if looking for defects to match the ones she had found in herself. He had shaven within the hour and there were tiny pinpricks of dried blood clustered along the firm line of his jaw, but his cheeks and neck, when she reached across the table suddenly to stroke them, taking him aback and bringing a pleased, bashful smile to his strong mouth, were smooth as a baby's. His yellow eyes glistened like those of a cat watching the progress of a mouse across the room, and she had to admit he was simply beautiful, as flawless as a baby that had not yet begun to puncture its possibilities. But, at the same time, he was hollow, as she had told her aunt, filled with vapid observations about the weather, the people who worked for him in his shop, the politics of the city. Two weeks before, she remembered, after the theatre, an Ibsen play, his only comment had been a vague "What a way to live."

"You don't have an idea in your head, do you?" she asked suddenly, surprising herself that the thought had translated itself into words, slipping out of her mouth before she could stop them. Aaron blinked, looked surprised but not particularly displeased, as if her comment had referred to his new jacket, a grey seersucker he had taken off the rack that afternoon.

"I have an idea that I'd like to get to know you better. How's that?"

Rebeccah smiled despite herself. So it was out, the overture that, from almost any other man of her acquaintance, likely would have come on the first night, certainly on the second, but from Aaron Greenspun had taken two months. She wondered if he had spoken with her aunt over the weekend, whether something she had said had emboldened him. Well, it didn't matter. The next step was up to her.

"That would be very nice," she said. "Yes, I'd like that."

That was all there was to it. So simple, that small exchange, but now there was an understanding between them, and that night, for the first time, when he had escorted her home, he kissed her good night, and she knew the inexorable journey to their marriage had begun.

The engagement was announced within weeks, but the marriage itself didn't take place until the following spring, after a suitable period of adjustment to the idea and an opportunity for Aaron to purchase and, with Rebeccah's guidance, furnish a house, in the growing suburb of Shaker Heights, where streets lay like quiet ribbons beneath tall canopies of leaves. The honeymoon was to include an overnight trip on a paddlewheel schooner that plied Lake Erie, taking them from Cleveland to Buffalo, from where they would go by train to Niagara Falls, there spending several days admiring the scenery. It would be aboard the ship, on its first night out, in their stateroom, that their marriage was to be consummated. It was not a fit topic for conversation between betrothed, but Aaron, always a gentleman, did have this observation to make, three weeks before the wedding, when Rebeccah was still assembling the items for her trousseau: "And as to the rest ... what will come afterwards... well, I just want you to have no concern. I'm not entirely without experience" – here he offered her his shyest smile, while his eyes blazed with boldness – "and I can promise you that I'll be gentle. It will be something wonderful, the two of us, don't you agree?"

Rebeccah awaited that something wonderful with a great deal of concern, in fact, since she was not without some *considerable* experience herself. The subject of virginity was not discussed, but it became clear to her, both from Aaron's manner and occasional small things he said, that he assumed he would be the first man to share sex with her – although he knew she had many male friends, most of whom he disapproved of – and that it was important to him. Honesty seemed out of the question, and the strategy of deception appeared to be inevitable.

"That will be no trouble at all, don't worry your head about it," her friend Belle told her. She was a woman of indeterminable age but at least beyond forty to judge from the wealth of experience she had crammed into her life, a Romanian who had traveled for several years in France and England on her way to America, a friend, so she said, of Virginia Woolf and Emma Goldman, a painter of note who had benefited Rebeccah with encouragement and gentle criticism, a lesbian, though that was not a term then in vogue, who had buried three husbands already, one in each of the previous countries where she'd lived. "Men are such children, it's easy to deceive them. Flatter them and they're only too happy to believe anything, no matter how unlikely." She puffed on one of the slim black cigars she had developed a taste for in Paris and raised her magnificent eyebrows. "When it comes to sex, it's all the easier since, in bed, they are so helpless. So *strong*, they think they are, just because blood rushes to one pathetic portion of their anatomy and makes it stiff. At the same time, the rest of them turns to jelly." She shrugged her shoulders and gestured with a slim, black-gloved hand, as if uncovering some vast expanse. "Men are such children, take it from me, darling Rebeccah. They preen and swagger, they bellow and fight, they spend money like it was water and let compliments flow from their tongues like honey from the rock, they even *marry* you, so desperate are some of them, all to get you in bed, then, a little kiss, a little pat, a jiggle, a thrust, another jiggle, and it's all over. They roll over and lie there like exhausted warriors who have single-handedly defeated great armies, a beatific smile playing about their lips like a butterfly among flowers. No, don't worry your head darling, it will be easy to deceive your Mr. Spun-From-Gold. We'll devise a plan."

The deception was remarkably simple, consisting of an easily mixed douche of water, vinegar and alum, guaranteed, Belle promised, to give Rebeccah the rasping friction of a thirteen-year-old girl, and a small quantity of chicken blood, concealed in a pink balloon, the sort that children blow up at birthday parties. The rest, Belle explained, was merely a sleight of hand, a bit of acting and, she said, "that famous guile we women are supposed to have in such abundance. Let's see if it's true." And, on the couch in Belle's studio, not far from Rebeccah's own loft, they practiced the weary motions, with Belle taking Aaron's part.

"Ah, my darling, my sweet cheri, don't be frightened, I weeell be gentle," she sing-songed in English rich with French resonance, and the two of them burst into schoolgirl giggles, rolling together on the sofa like young athletes, though it went no further than that. "Ah, my darling," Belle gasped, breathless with laughter, "you are so, how they say? Wonderfully... tight."

Rebeccah herself went to the pharmacist for the alum, and prepared the mixture as to Belle's instructions, starting its use two days before the wedding, to be sure. "I feel like the inside of a pickled egg," she reported. "Ah, how wonderfully tasty," Belle retorted, arching her brows.

But Belle, on the day of the wedding itself, so it would be fresh, attended to the blood, visiting at the slaughterhouse a *kosher* rabbi she was acquainted with, who provided what she needed, no questions asked.

The wedding was small, by the standards of the community, with only family, from Akron as well as Cleveland, and a few of Rebeccah's and Aaron's closest friends attending. Rebeccah had doubted most of her café friends would be interested, or would approve; besides, she had found herself, in recent months, drifting away from them, with the exception of Belle and a couple other women. Uncle Meyer, as head of the family, and the wealthiest, hosted the party at his home in the Heights, though Uncle Avrom, as the favourite uncle, played the part of the surrogate father, standing up to give the bride away. Aaron broke the muffled glass with one determined stomp, there was dizzying music, crowded tables of food that all seemed to be flavoured with honey, and glasses of sweet wine that couldn't be emptied. Then, as her head spun, Rebeccah was led by the hand to a waiting motorcar by Aaron, her husband – *her husband* – and they were off to the docks.

Her head was still filled with spinning wafts of wool when they were shown to their cabin, and as soon as the porter was gone Aaron had her in his arms, covering her mouth, nose, ears and neck with moist, indistinct kisses. She extricated herself, took her overnight bag and locked herself in the small bathroom where she made one final application of the douche before putting on her nightgown. Then, with the balloon cupped in her palm, she made her entrance.

"You look wonderful, darling," Aaron said in English, his yellow eyes seeming to dance in the soft glow of the kerosene lamp. "You get into bed, I'll just be a minute."

She did as he said and, as soon as the door softly shut behind him, slipped the balloon under her pillow. Then, with her eyes gradually slipping into a sharp focus on what was either a stain or a shadow on the ceiling, she waited, her breath ragged, her heart pounding, just as if she really were a virgin.

Afterwards, as Aaron slept, Rebeccah put her satin robe over her gown, slid her feet into slippers, and crept from the cabin to walk along the deserted deck. The night was thick and dark, like an old woollen cloak, and cold. She stood against the rail, shivering and clutching her arms, staring down at where, from the choppy roll of the deck beneath her feet, she could tell the foaming waves of the lake were splattering against the ship's hull. But she could see nothing, and even the sound of the waves was absent, drowned out by the whining of the engines, which must have been close by to where she stood. She could have just as easily been aboard one of Jules Verne's fantastic ships, sailing through the darkness of space, as on the paddlewheeler *Albany*, somewhere in the middle of Lake Erie, suspended between two countries and two worlds. The deception had been so simple, so absurdly successful, just as Belle had promised. Aaron had been still a little drunk, his shining eyes excited but only half open as he slipped into bed and turned to her, and he'd been hasty, clumsy, needing, despite her pretense of innocence, her discreet hand to guide him. The alum had done its job almost too well, and there'd been pain, for him as well as her, and then it was over, almost before it had begun, leaving her barely enough time to reach back beneath the pillow for the balloon, sliding it down along her sweaty side, before he rolled away. She clenched it tightly in her palm, pricking it with the nail of her index finger, and smeared the tepid blood along her thighs and into the dripping wet hair covering her aching vulva. She had lain there for a moment, feeling like the victim of some bizarre religious ritual, waiting for him to lift the sheet, seeking the evidence for himself, but as it happened he was already drifting off to sleep, one hand tossed lightly across her breast like a statement of trust and possession, and he never did look.

Just before he screwed his face closer into the pillow and fell asleep, as quickly and firmly as a stone being dropped into water, he half opened his eyes and murmured: "That was wonderful, darling, don't you agree?"

She hadn't said anything, just watched, in the flickering light of the lamp, as he fell asleep. She'd insisted he leave the lamp burning, so she could see him, those brilliant cat's eyes, so he could see her, because he was so beautiful and she wanted to feel beautiful. But after they started, he had closed his eyes, and it had seemed to her he could have been anyone. Just the same, there had been a moment, as he slid into her, a moment above the pain as her nerve endings and skin responded on their own, when they had moved together as one, when her passion had risen with the alacrity all those months of courtship seemed to have been foreshadowing and their breaths had merged into one fierce, staccato rhythm. She thought about that moment as she stood along the railing, her teeth chattering with cold, her eyes streaming with tears as they stared blankly into the darkness below. There had been that moment, that was all. There had even been one moment when, allowing her imagination to run wild, she had believed she might love him. But it had just been that one moment, and then it was gone.

Something of Value

THE THING I remember most about her was her smile. That was what killed me. Her mouth was wide but the lips thin, or gave that impression because she wore no lipstick or any other makeup, and the combination gave her smile a shadow of irony that pierced me, knocked me into the boards. She was a big girl, slender but tall, tall as I am and seemed taller, a girl who filled a doorway when she passed through it, big-boned, with large, high breasts and long straight hair falling past her shoulders, wide eyes moist and round as a fawn's. "A handsome woman, indeed," Pedro said, mocking me. To me, of course, she was much more than that.

We were freshmen together at Turnfield, an ivy-covered college in New England, the year John Kennedy was elected president of the United States and all seemed right with the world. This year, watching Dole and Clinton on cable TV, that time seems a lifetime away, that place somewhere on a different planet. My class had a reunion a couple of years ago, but I didn't go, much as I was tempted to see the place again, a few of my old classmates. Too much has happened to me, the war and everything else, though it's no fault of theirs.

Few of the students were particularly religious, certainly not Pedro or I or the others we palled with, but the college had been built by a church and, though it was now independent, was sustained by tradition. Every morning at ten, we filed into the chapel for morning services, one class at a time because the college population had outgrown the building, a steeple-topped square of stone and gleaming marble that stood solidly on the top of the larger of the campus's two hills, overlooking its valley. First the freshmen, five minutes for a hymn and a prayer; then the sophomores, and so on. On Sundays, though attendance wasn't compulsory, we were encouraged to attend the lengthier services conducted through the morning by Rev. Dobbs, the round-headed chaplain whose dramatic facial scar, running from above one eye, along the crescent of his cheek, down to the corner of his mouth, was always a lively topic of conversation.

On the very first day of school, there was a special service for the freshmen. Dobbsey gave a prayer and there was a lovely little Bach fugue played on the magnificent pipe organ that made Pedro, who had a passion for Baroque, sit up and pay attention, his fingers drumming on his tweed thighs. The president of the college, an Italian-looking, moustached man improbably named Willis, who seemed out of place amid the Episcopalian trappings, gave a welcoming talk in which, as a dramatic opening, he told us to look to our left, then to our right, at the student sitting in front of us, then to twist our heads around and smile at whoever was just behind. "Take a good look at those faces," he intoned gravely, "and try to remember them. In a year's time, one of them will likely be gone. And in four years, for those of you lucky enough, intelligent enough, *determined* enough to make it, only two of those faces you see beside you or in front or behind you today will still be here."

We all looked again, craning our necks and grinning, laughing self-consciously and saying things like "so long, pal," or "been nice to know ya." Pedro was on my right; we were roommates, newly met. "Isn't *he* original, though," he whispered, rolling his eyes to the vaulted ceiling. I don't recall who was on my left or in front of me because, as it turned out, *I* was the one in our little cluster to be gone by the end of the first year. She was behind me. When I'd twisted my neck and turned the first time, she was doing the same, so I hadn't really seen her, not her face. The second time, there she was, and our eyes locked, just for a moment. I had never seen anyone as beautiful, not a girl my age, not someone real. I guess I must have smiled, a small, closed-mouth smile I still have, but she didn't respond – it would be some time before I would finally see that smile of hers, and she'd be giving it to someone else – and if she was thinking anything, I don't know what it was.

Her name was Muna, which I've since learned is an Arabic word meaning "wish," but at the time it was merely a delicious, meaningless sound for my lips and ears to revel in, and seemed just right because everything about her struck me as unusual. She was the daughter of a diplomat and had lived in a string of exotic, romantic places, reputedly spoke seven languages, and was beautiful in a way far removed from the blond, healthy good looks of the other girls on campus. A few weeks after that first glimpse in the chapel, I told Pedro, with that open honesty boys of that age sometimes have, that I was in love with her.

"Not that I have much hope. A girl like her isn't likely to want to have anything to do with someone like me," I said, hoping he would contradict me, say something reassuring like "Don't be a schmuck, you're her type exactly." But Pedro wasn't like that.

"Quite right, you are a bit of a sod, old chap," he said. "Can't even speak a decent French. The magnificent Muna. Don't expect her to be *munificent*, not to you."

Pedro was a pudgy, tousle-haired boy who looked middle-aged in his expensive but worn tweed jackets and waistcoats, which he pronounced "weskits." I'd given him his nickname because he was studying languages, Spanish especially, but he was British as could be, was even addicted to strong tea, brewed from morning to late into the night with a forbidden electric kettle stored in a hatbox and a ceramic teapot that we kept dried flowers in to fool the maids. His father was a down-on-his-luck writer, a novelist who'd come to the States to tilt at Hollywood but hadn't clicked, "desperately poor, or poorly desperate, depending on how one looks at it," Pedro said.

Most of the Turnfield students were well off and had gone to private schools, places with names like Choate and Groton and Miss Pembroke's. Several of the boys in our class had gone to Kennedy's old school and boasted of meeting him when he'd come down for a football game the previous year. One girl was the daughter of the governor, another was a member of the family that controlled RCA, and there was the son of a movie star, a sad-eyed, slack-haired boy who killed himself in the spring by riding his motorcycle off a bridge. They all quickly pledged to fraternities and sororities, but a few of us, like Pedro and me, were what were called "independents," meaning we had chosen to stay aloof, or hadn't been chosen.

Some of us "indies" banded together that winter in our own informal club, with secret passwords and the beginning of a language of nicknames and puns Pedro and I – mostly he – created, designed to insult the fraternity boys without their realizing it. We had no building, of course, and no parties. We met every morning, just after chapel, at the student union and drank coffee and ate donuts which we bought for a nickel each and dunked in the coffee, and smoked cigarettes and talked, politics and poetry and gossip, endlessly till our eleven o'clocks.

I was one of the few Canadians at the college, and I was only there because of hockey. If I'd been playing that fall, I probably would have joined a frat, because, as Pedro said, "Lord knows, you're ordinary enough, you should be doing fratpalls," but, as it happened, I tore the ligaments in my knee during the first week of practice. I was still on the team, technically, and I didn't lose my scholarship, but I wasn't chosen by the fraternity I wanted when upper classmen came around with solemn eyes and invited freshmen over for tea. Joining the one that did express an interest, which was made up almost entirely of jocks, would have opened me up to more of Pedro's scorn than I thought I could bear.

The others in our private group were a skinny boy with a lisp and a cackle who later became a composer of popular songs and who everyone called Pissface, Pedro's name for him; two Jews – Manny and Moe, Pedro called them – who had been politely shunned by the fraternities; our class's sole black student, the son of a government lawyer from Washington, who had been chosen but politely declined; a very tall boy from Boston who was too uncoordinated to play the basketball he looked to have been born for; and an immensely fat, horrifically acned boy from New York, who said little to anyone. There were two girls as well, both poets and both named Margaret, though one was called Peggy: Margaret Varley had a nice body but buck teeth; her friend, Peggy Verdeen, had perfectly normal teeth she hid within an unsmiling, pleasantly plain face, but a lumpy body. They were lesbians, I suppose, but we knew little of such things then. As I recall us, we were nice people, intelligent, decent, but a little different. We took comfort in each other, the way friends do, and sustained ourselves with the belief that, somehow, we were superior.

I don't think Muna even knew we existed. She had her own group of friends, girls from the sororities and clubs she belonged to, junior and senior boys. If she walked through the cafeteria while we were gathered at our table by the big window, she would look straight ahead, just as she did when she passed me in a hallway or on one of the meandering brick pathways linking the campus's elegant stone buildings, some of them bearded with ivy. We shared no classes, but it was a small school so we were bound to pass from time to time, and I set a challenge to myself to get her to speak to me. When we did pass, I'd say hello, in my deepest voice, somewhat earnestly, and try to make our eyes connect, the way they had for that brief moment in the chapel. It cost me a lot to do that, but it didn't achieve anything, even the first time, when I was still on crutches and must have been an empathetic sight. She never said a word, never met my gaze, just walked past, her shoulders back, head high, hair flying. I would want to turn my head to watch her receding hips, but I didn't dare. If someone had seen me, I would have been ashamed.

"You're making progress, Puckhead," Pedro said one time when we'd passed her as we strolled back to the dorm from the library, wearing the ridiculous beanies the freshman boys were forced to endure for part of the fall. "She didn't barf this time."

"She wanted to, though, just didn't want to blow her cool."

In fact, she had glanced at us with icy disinterest, the way a cat might observe a spider, but she had never looked lovelier, her honey-coloured hair pressed tightly to her face like a helmet by the red-striped muffler around her neck, and my throat ached with longing in the chilly air.

That winter, with my knee improving, I spent most of my time on the ice, practicing, or battling with my French. It was ironic that I should have been doing so poorly in French, since I came from a country where it's widely spoken, though not much in the part where I was from. I had done poorly at it in high school, but always managed to get through, more because of my skills with the puck than with verbs and pronouns. That's the way it is in a small town. At college, it was different. The instructor, Madame Lavalee, a thin, dark woman with a pinched face and glasses that seemed to press in on her nose, had an elegant Parisian accent and an exaggerated air of self-importance, as if mastering French grammar was the most noble goal a human being could aspire to. She hated my accent and had little tolerance for the long hesitations that were part of my oral translations. I flunked the mid-term, which sent me into a cycle of defeat: study, give up in exasperation, do poorly in the next class, more exasperation, and so on. Pedro, for whom languages came as easily as gliding across the ice did for me, tried to help, tutoring and cajoling me, but nothing worked, I seemed to have a block. As it turned out, I would flunk the final as well and have to take the course over in the spring.

The other burden I had to bear that winter was Shawn Rattigan.

"You're the fuckin' Canuck, *eh?*" Those were his first words to me, first week of the term, standing naked and ferocious in the common shower room shared by the dozen boys in our corridor of the freshman dorm, snapping a towel menacingly. He was a muscular, clean-featured boy with fox eyes and a sandy crewcut, and I took the same sort of instant dislike to him that he took to me, really for no good reason.

"Yeah, I'm from a civilized country," I told him back and we glared at each other, the way athletes will do after they've roughed each other up during a game, the way male animals will when they meet at the borders of their territories. Then we both grinned, there was banter, good-natured now, splashing, the inevitable *crack* of towels and the cacophony of the locker room, but a tone had been set between us, something had begun.

Shawn and a boy named Tick shared a room three doors down from ours, and they were the nucleus around which a constellation of dormitory life revolved. They were both on the junior varsity football team and had pledged to the fraternity which took most of the better jocks. Through their influence, a couple other boys from our corridor had been pledged to the same fraternity; the others had either gone to rival frats or, like Pedro and Pissface and I, were indies.

That didn't mean we were outcasts, though. College life doesn't work that way. I had a number of friends in the dorm who joined fraternities, including Roger Platt, a moody boy from Boston who tried to hang himself in the spring and wound up in a mental institution; a handsome, muscular ski jumper from New Hampshire called Wild Bill James; a tall, skinny boy from Newark, Lou, and his roommate, Tony, a squat Italian from Brooklyn, who played rock and roll all day long in their room, where many of us would congregate to listen, drink Cokes, smoke and talk. All of these boys were in frats, but they didn't let that change or sour them, it didn't make them hate those of us who weren't.

But Rattigan and Tick were different and, for some reason, took it as a personal affront that I had spurned the frat they joined. Their dislike spilled over to Pedro – whom they called Penguin. Shawn was from somewhere in Connecticut and had that polished, country club kind of manner that seems to come from riding horses with English saddles and playing tennis. Tick was from Michigan, Grosse Pointe, maybe, where his father was a lawyer for General Motors. The two of them had roomed together at Groton, been the stars of the football and swim and track teams there, and now they were set to blaze something new for themselves. They were far from being the smartest boys at Turnfield, and they weren't the best athletes or the richest. But they had an arrogance that set them apart, made them special.

I've thought, sometimes, that my time at Turnfield might have been happier if I hadn't hurt my knee so quickly, before the season even began. I was good, and had a good record, but I was from far away and no one there but the coach had even seen me play, so they didn't know. And life is so much smoother for athletes; they always seem to have a lustrous patina of corruption about them that makes women want to touch them, teachers like them, boys and men respect them, for no good reason. It makes them be accepted. Not by everybody, but by the people who seem to count. I didn't have that, and, as a result, I met some other people, people I probably wouldn't have met otherwise, good, interesting people whose company I enjoyed. But I always felt I was on the outside.

Always, Rattigan ate away at me, all my discontents with the college and that year made into flesh.

In early December, as the term was dragging its agonizingly slow way toward Christmas, Pedro and I were up late one night, along with most of the dorm, cramming for a Western Civ exam, and at about two a.m. Brenda Lee started to pour her heart out of Shawn and Tick's room, loud enough for the whole corridor to hear, even with our doors closed.

"The Rat and Tickle Show is on again," Pedro grumbled, looking up sourly from his book. We could hear shouts of "turn it down" and "can it, willya?" in the hallway and the music wavered for a moment, the volume lowered, almost to a bearable level, then erupted even louder than before.

"Don't go 'way," I told Pedro and walked stiffly down the hall to their open doorway, squinting into the hazy light filtering its way through sour smoke.

"That chick can really sing. Mind turning her down, though?"

Rattigan looked up from his bed, where he was sprawled with one arm draped over his head, cigar in mouth.

"Well, well, the hockey hero. He walks, he talks. Glad you like the sounds."

"That's only half of what I said."

"I heard it all, Canuck. I'm not deaf. No need to shout."

I took a step into the room. "C'mon, man, some of us are trying to study."

"So study. We're studying, too, *man*, for a *music* test. Fart off and leave us to it, *man*. G'wan back to your penguin."

I took another step toward him, but I could see Tick stiffening in his chair, knuckles tightening around a beer can. His dark hair, longer than Shawn's, was rumpled, a lock of it in his eyes.

"C'mon, Canuck, get out of here," Shawn sneered, cocking his head to show his smooth profile. "G'wan, Gimpy, scat."

"Don't call me that, man," I said very slowly.

"Oh, sorry, Gimpy, maybe we should call you Organ Grinder instead. Whaddya think, Tick, should we...."

I went for him, pulling him off the bed by his shirt front, raising my elbows to ward off the bearhug Tick swung around me. I don't know how it would have ended, with bruises and blood on all of us, maybe, but it was cut short quickly as it had begun.

"Hey, cool it, you guys," someone was yelling, and hands were pulling us apart. "C'mon, cut it out, shit, we have a fucking *test* tomorrow." It was Tony and Lou, the rock and rollers, who always turned their sound down at midnight at the latest, and Wild Bill and a couple of others.

They pulled us apart, the hi fi was turned off, we were needled till we all said we were sorry and shook hands all around, Shawn grinning malevolently. And that was that.

Except that the damage done between us remained there like a scar on a tree where a branch has been broken off, irreparable. He was always around, the Rat, with a snide remark, a wisecrack, a taunt.

I don't mean to suggest that year at college was one long

agony, though, far from it. I enjoyed most of my classes, my new friends, and particularly the freedom of being away from home, something I'd felt cheated out of when I was younger because my parents wouldn't let me go off to play junior hockey. I'd been good enough, but I had to be content with our high school league.

Pedro and I would go for long walks in the countryside and he would jabber in the dozen languages he knew bits and pieces of. Often I would accompany him to the chapel, where he had taken to playing Bach on the organ, and I'd work my way through French verbs as the rich, intricate music poured over me. I drank more beer than all the rest of my life combined, and hitch-hiked everywhere, with Wild Bill, to Boston and New York, seeing the sights, listening to jazz. Like everyone else, I watched on the flickering TV as Robert Frost, his shaggy white head bowed, repeated the last line of his poem, "… and miles to go before I sleep," and JFK challenged us to ask what we could do for our country. It wasn't my country, but the words stirred me. What could I do that would be of value, I wondered.

And always, that whole winter, there was Muna, moving around the campus in the periphery of my vision like a dream or a cloud, tall and cool and aloof, ignoring my greetings, refusing to meet my eye when we sat at tables within sight of each other in the union or one time in the library, when I came around the end of a stack and almost walked into her, drifting through my dreams like some phantom doomed to walk the earth for eternity for a crime no greater than having a face that could kill with its beauty.

I was preoccupied with her, writing her letters I didn't dare mail, and the other girls on campus had little interest for me. I went on a few dates with one, a slim, sloe-eyed girl with coal black hair to her shoulders named Wendy, but we never got past the goodnight kiss stage, not because she wasn't interested, I don't think. It was me.

And I burned with agony whenever I saw her with another boy, felt sick the day I saw her emerge laughing in a light snow from behind a marble pillar of the chapel with Shawn Rattigan, that sneerlike smile of his pulsing.

Dave Margoshes

At Christmas, I went home and let school seep out of me, skating afternoons with old pals, sleeping late, eating good and trying to make some decisions. I talked things over with my father and we agreed I'd give French one more real shot, my best shot, and see what happened. If I couldn't make it, then we'd decide in the summer whether I'd be better off in the community college at home or shucking it all and going to work, maybe even trying out for a semi-pro team. That suited me and I went back feeling better about a lot of things. I'd determined to forget about Muna and give Wendy another try.

But as soon as the rhythm began again, things went sour. My knee seemed strong and the coach thought maybe I was ready. But I hurt it again in the first game I played, badly enough to ensure I'd be out for the rest of the season. And I flunked a French quiz that was a warmup to the final.

When I called Wendy, she was busy, leaving me to hobble alone through the snowy campus Saturday night, watching my breath rise against the light from the lampposts near the girls' dorms, listening to laughter spin off the hills. Wandering past the row of fraternity houses across the campus, jabbing at myself the way you worry a sore tooth with your tongue, I heard a door open, laughter, footsteps crunching in the snow toward a car, and I thought I saw Muna, smile luminous beneath her swirling hair, the arm of her escort sheltering her. I felt useless, rotten.

One afternoon, crossing the campus in a snowstorm, I surprised myself by labouring up the marble steps of the chapel and ducking through the heavy oak door into the dim silence. I shook the snow off my head and leaned against the back of the last polished pew, taking the weight off my throbbing knee. I gazed at the ornate stained glass windows which flanked the organ and pulpit and tried to capture a strain of the music Pedro would set free when we were here together, but the melodies were too elusive. After a few minutes, Dobbsey came in from a rear office, the livid scar on his forehead and cheek bright above the purple collar of his robe. He knew me – he saw Pedro and I often enough and once or twice had come and sat beside me as I listened to

Pedro play – and bustled down the central aisle toward me now, smiling and bobbing his oddly shaped head.

"Is there something you'd like to talk about, son?"

I would have liked to unburden myself – would have liked to reach out and touch his face, ask him the question every student at the college wondered about – but could bring myself to do do none of those things. "No, thanks, Padre," I said, grinning, "just taking shelter from the storm." I turned away before he could say anything else.

The semester spun down to its end and the spring inside me tightened more every day. I studied, but couldn't concentrate for more than a few minutes at a time. I'd raise my eyes from the page, French verb endings swimming before me, and the smiling image of Muna would glide past, an apparition on ice, cool and crystal clear – yet seemingly wrapped in gauze, so that light radiated from her skin, something I can't explain. I must have said something aloud, called out, because Pedro looked up from the translating he was doing at his desk and clucked his tongue.

"Hey, shit-for-brains. Why don't you take a cold shower?"

"Fuck off, pukeface."

I got up and paced across the room, banged my fist against the wall. Somehow, the verbs and the girl had become entwined, as if Muna had come to believe, as Madame Lavalee did, that the study of French was the most important calling one could imagine, that a man who couldn't master its intricate patterns could not possibly be worthy of her. In my dreams, she came to me, hair falling over her eyes, wavering smile offering a glimpse of heaven, one hand on the top button of her blouse, whispering words in French I couldn't understand.

Late in February, a few weeks into the second term, I was on my way out of the dorm and I stopped to kid with a bunch of guys in the lobby. Tony and Lou were there, singing doo-wop as always; Manny and Moe, who lived on another floor but gravitated toward the guys on ours; Roger Platt, just weeks away from his suicide attempt; Pissface and a couple of others. They were talking about the dance the next Saturday, a winter carnival that was a college tradition, the last fling for winter, with spring just a month away. All of the guys gathered there in the lobby had a date or were sure of one, except for Pissface, who never went anywhere with girls except Margaret or Peggy. And me. I had phoned Wendy, but her roommate said she wasn't in, and she hadn't called back, had avoided me in the hallways. I had even, for a moment, given thought to asking Muna, just calling out of the blue and asking her. What could I have lost?

So I was startled when Moe said *he'd* asked her.

"You're kiddin', man," Tony said. "That classy chick?"

"Hey, I didn't say she said yes," Moe said quickly. He was from Boston and he had that pinched, nasal tone.

"What *did* she say?"

"Well, she said... no...." His cheeks reddened as he was interrupted with laughter. "She already had a date, that's all, that's what she said, anyway."

"Why'd you even ask?" Lou said, rolling his eyes.

"I don't know." Moe shrugged, his heavy shoulders moving slowly under a bulky sweater. "She's in my history class and we're in a discussion group together. She's nice." He pronounced those last words solemnly, as if they would explain everything.

There was a silence while we considered that appraisal, and Lou nodded his head gravely, looking at me.

"A nice piece of ass, yeah."

We all looked up and there was the Rat, standing in the corridor doorway, his wool jacket open but the muffler already tied around his neck for the cold slap waiting for him outside the big glass doors.

"Hey, man, nice way to talk," Platt said quickly.

"About that piece of meat?" Rattigan approached us, grinning. "Muna Snyder you talking about? That one? Big tits, empty head? That the one you mean?"

"Hey," Moe said. I glanced at him sideways and saw his face reddening again.

"She's just a cunt with a body wrapped around it, that's

all," Rattigan said. My temples were pounding and a veil seemed to fall over my eyes, so I'm not sure, but I think he had turned to me. The one thing I did notice was that Tick wasn't with him.

"Hey," Moe repeated, but I didn't hear anything after that. I sent my fist straight for Rat's face, but his balance was better than mine, and I realized later he must have been expecting it. He stepped backwards and I only got a piece of him, and I lurched forward. He was ready, and he banged the heel of his fist down on the top of my head, forcing it down. He got me with an uppercut that just grazed my chin, but then his booted foot went heavily into my bad knee and I went down, my head exploding with stars.

There were voices shouting around us, and hands groping, but Shawn was on top of me, his elbows battering my face. The pain in my knee was excruciating, and my mouth must have been open, either in a scream or gasping for air, I don't know, because my tongue was bleeding, and later, it was sore, swollen. My fist connected against something, I don't know what, and I could hear someone saying "Don't say that, don't say that," over and over, and a hysterical cackling sound that was Pissface, laughing.

They pulled him off me finally and Roger Platt knelt beside me, rubbing the blood off my face with his shirt. Someone was asking "Who started it? Okay, who started it?" as if that would settle anything.

And Rattigan was standing hunched over, his jacket off but the muffler still wound around his neck, panting, blood on his face, his tongue flashing against his teeth. "What's a matter, Canuck, somebody insult your girl?" he spat.

"She's not my girl," I said, tears seeping out of my eyes.

"All right, man," Tony commanded, taking Shawn by the arm. "You said enough, okay? Knock it off."

"She's not my girl," I said again. I think it was the truth of that that hurt the most.

. . .

I had an appointment with the dean of men three days later, and I was still showing signs of the fight when I arrived at his office in my dark sports jacket and a black knit tie. My mouth and one eye were puffy, there was a welt on my forehead, and I was limping badly. My face was reddish and I felt hot.

The dean was a grandfatherly man with a large head, thick grey hair, and smooth baby-like skin. His tweed jacket had leather patches on the elbows, as if that had been ordained. He had been a professor of classics for thirty years, and boys I knew who had dealt with him said he was gentle but firm. I'd already been to the chaplain, and Dobbsey told me the dean was my only hope.

He looked me over for a moment before telling me to sit down, puffing smoke out of the rounded bowl of his pipe like a toy engine on a Christmas table. "You seem not to have fared too well, have you? What's that they say, though? You should see the other fellow?" He smiled, his broad pink face boyish.

"He's not as bad as me."

"What's that?"

"He's not as bad as me. I'm sorry, I can't talk any louder."

"Of course, sorry. I don't suppose you want to talk about it at all, do you? That's not why you're here." He put his hand on a folder lying before him on his desk.

"No, sir."

"No, of course not." He edged his chair an inch closer to the desk and put his elbows on it, forming a cradle for his chin with the backs of his hands. "Now, what's this about French?"

I had signed up for the introductory course again, hoping I'd have a more sympathetic teacher and that things would go better. And the teacher *was* better, a man this time, also French but less picky, but it didn't seem to matter. I'd failed the first quiz badly and was all but paralyzed during class.

The professor, M. Gratin, had taken me aside. "There doesn't seem to be any point to this," he'd said.

"Professor Gratin says I seem to have some sort of block against it," I told the dean. "I've always known that, but I couldn't get Madame Lavalee to understand."

"Or I, I'm afraid," he interjected. "I don't *believe* in blocks. Anyone can learn anything if they put their minds to it. I'm awfully old-fashioned about that, I'm afraid."

"Well, I don't mean to get into an argument about psychology," I said, enunciating the words carefully.

"Oh, sorry, dear boy, I didn't mean to sound argumentative. It's just that I don't believe in *blocks*. I thought you should know that. Go on."

We were silent for a moment while I considered. It wasn't easy for me to say things I wanted to. I had hoped Professor Gratin's recommendation would be enough.

"Well, I honestly have to say I've put my mind to French. I've tried. It's been important to me, really. But I can't."

"So you want permission to waive the language requirement." The dean opened the folder on his desk and selected a sheet of paper, blowing smoke thoughtfully. "Gratin thinks that's what should be done. I've had a note from Rev. Dobbs, too. Hmmmmm."

I sat silently, waiting.

"You know, of course, why we *have* the requirement, don't you?" he asked finally.

I started to nod my head, then shook it no. "I guess not."

The dean leaned back in his swivel chair and glanced briefly out his window, which looked across the campus to the chapel, and then gazed about his office, as if the answer to his question was there on the walls, along with the framed diplomas and the signed portrait of Kennedy, the stuffed pheasant on the bookcase.

"It has to do with the well-rounded intellect, of course. You know about that, don't you?"

"Of course, sir, but...."

The dean raised his hand. "You're going to tell me you can be well rounded without French, isn't that it?"

"Something like that."

He shook his head sadly, like a grandfather explaining to a child why the match had burnt his fingers. "Then I'm afraid you *don't* understand. You see...."

Suddenly, I was angry, the way I'd been when Rattigan was saying those things. They didn't make sense, they weren't true, and I couldn't see why anyone should be allowed to say them.

"No, I'm sorry, sir, *you* don't understand. Forgive me for interrupting, but, please, let me say something. I'm here, I mean at the college, because I want to be, because I believe in the well-rounded intellect, as you put it, and I want that in my life. I'm a hockey player and I could be a pro now, or, well, a semi-pro, but I *wanted* to come here. I *want* to learn French, believe me, not just because it's a good thing to know and all that, but because in my country it's a *useful* thing to know. I *want* to learn it, and I've tried. But I can't. I hate to say that. I don't mean I don't want to, or it's too hard, or I can't be bothered, I mean I *can't*, and it really hurts to say that, to admit I can't do something."

I stopped and glared at him, my temples pounding, my mouth sore. He bobbed slightly in his swivel chair, blowing smoke idly at the ceiling, gazing at me as if I were a new fish for his aquarium. I wanted to reach across the desk and rip that pipe out of his mouth and smash it, to tear the patches off his jacket.

"I can't, and all I'm doing is wasting my time keeping on with it. I'll flunk again, and that will be as far as I'll be able to go. I'll have to drop out of school or transfer somewhere else, if I can even find another place that will take me with two Fs on my record, and that will be that. Is that what the well-rounded intellect is all about?"

My clenched hands were wet, and I realized I was standing, pressed against the edge of the dean's desk. He observed me mildly, puffing on his pipe, and I sat down, opening my hands. "I'm sorry."

"That's all right, my boy, no need to feel sorry. It's good, sometimes, to get things like that out, clears the air and makes you feel better. And I'm sure you will. Now" – he leaned forward, stabbing at me with the stem of his pipe –

"consider this, though. I give weight to all you've said, no doubt you mean it sincerely, really feel that way. But giving in is the worst thing you can do, don't you see that? Then you'll have to say to yourself, admit to yourself all your life, that you couldn't do something. Now wouldn't *that* be awful?"

"But I *can't!*" I shouted. I managed to stay in my chair, but when I left his office, I found my palms were torn where my nails had dug into them as I pounded them against my thighs.

"There is no such word," the dean said gravely. "*Can't* and *impossible*, those are two words I've banished from my vocabulary. *Won't* and *difficult*, those are words I understand." He leaned back, pushing the chair away from the desk and crossing his legs. "And as to wasting your time, well..." – he waved the pipe like an orchestra leader's baton – "there's no such thing as wasting one's time in the academic world, no, no, not where there's something to be learned, no matter how small, how seemingly trivial. Everything is of some value, no matter how small it might seem."

I walked back to the dorm in a daze. The dean's words kept spinning around in my head, but they seemed to be coming out of the grinning mouth of Shawn Rattigan. I'd have to drop out of school, I knew that. I could try with Spanish or Italian, but it would be futile. My head was spinning and I tore loose my tie and collar to let what must have been steam rise from my neck. The smoke from the dean's pipe clung in my nostrils like the sickly sweet pollen of wolf willow, which grew thick as grass in the meadow behind the house back home. As it turned out, my face was red with fever, and when I got back to the room Pedro would take one look at me, then bundle me up and help me to the infirmary where I'd spend five days, unconscious for much of the first three, with mononucleosis and tonsillitis that had my throat as red, the doctor said, as any he'd ever seen.

But for the moment, I was stranded somewhere between the dean's office and the dormitory, on the brick path that led past the chapel, where old Dobbsey was standing on the steps in his satiny robes, awaiting the trickle of students for noon prayer, the scar on his face pulsing like a beacon. He waved to me, but I didn't return the gesture, turning away. I was wavering there, trembling with fever or rage, I don't know which, when I saw Muna approaching. The bell had just rung and people were streaming out of buildings, the path was suddenly clotted with them, passing by without seeming to notice me. I stood there, watching her come closer, and there are moments, now, when I feel I could be there still, my whole world frozen. Then Pissface came past, scuttling by sideways like a crab from behind, slowing down, then receding, backwards, his face squinting, the nervous cackle breaking out of his moist lips. "Man, you look *weird*."

I just stood there, my eyes on her, until she came up almost abreast of me, her long legs in a smooth stride, her hair sort of bobbing with the motion like a figure on a running horse seen from a distance. I could see her breasts rise and fall with the motion of her stride, except I know I can't have seen that, it was February, cold, we were wearing coats. She slowed, leaning down, just a little, better to see my face. I don't know if she knew about Shawn and me, whether she'd heard about the fight, but the campus was a small place, people knew each other, people talked, news traveled fast. I don't know what she knew, or what she felt, whether she even knew I was alive, but I swear, just before she passed by, I'm sure she smiled.

Pennies on the Track

ALFWAY UP THE hill, the engine sputters and dies. For two, three, maybe four beats, the car continues its forward motion, upward, but slower, slowing, not quite in slow motion but edging toward it, like Wile E. Coyote or Elmer Fudd in one of those cartoons where they've run off the edge of a cliff and they're suspended in space, legs still churning, what's happened to them taking its time sinking in. Then the car comes to a hesitant stop, like the earth shuddering on its axis or the heart gathering itself in rather than beating in one of those arrhythmias, and everything – I mean what is happening but also the blue air itself, strained thin as if from altitude – is very clear, and I can see not only the expression on my father's face, which is a grin, a *foolish* grin, but what his hands are doing, pulling at the whining hand brake, snapping the key back and forth in the ignition, and the fear flashing across my mother's eyes just beneath the flowered brim of her hat, the warm brown interior of the car, the scratches and scrapes on the leather, and even outside, the avocado-green canopy of leaves above us that tells me it is spring, the honeysuckle bushes growing like scrap heaps alongside the road, the gravel on the shoulder, each chip separate, like snowflakes, and, of course, spinning my head quickly to take it in, the long, tunnel-like sweep of hill behind us, its jaws spreading into a grin wider than my father's – all of this I can see as the car, for that one moment trapped by the laws of physics between its desire to continue forward and gravity's insistence in pulling it down, trembles, awaiting instructions that cannot come.

Then there is motion: a bursting of movement sharp as the innocent explosion that sends birds hurtling out of treetops. The car – it's a Ford, I know because that's what my father always bought – begins its inevitable roll backwards, slowly at first, the quickening pace that will lead us to destruction implicit in its force. My father's grin widens as he looks over his shoulder, then deepens into something like a grimace, his teeth showing. "Oh shit," he says, or "damn," or "thunder" – I don't remember the word itself, just its force, but he *does* say, "Hold on, everybody," that I do remember. My mother says: "I *told* you to have that looked at," because the car has stalled before, though not on a hill (this is not part of the memory itself, not *my* memory, but part of the intelligence which has gathered around the story, part of the legend, as is my father's decision to use the gears rather than the brakes. "We want to go, not stop," he is remembered as saying). My father too is moving, his head smoothly swinging backward and forward as if packed in ball bearings, his shoulders rolling under the seersucker cloth of his jacket like fish thrashing in water, his hands darting like birds. He jams the stick up and out, his foot treading the clutch pedal like an organist caught up in rhythm, the gears grind malevolently but the stick pops into place and the constipated engine coughs, clears its throat, coughs again and roars into life. The car jerks, picking up speed. My father swings the wheel suddenly and the car, as if it is on one of those platforms they use to turn locomotives around with in railroad marshaling yards, takes an abrupt right turn, its rear end smothering into bushes that scrape and claw at the fenders and trunk and running boards and rear window, embracing us, and again the car shudders to a halt, trembling like a girl who's just been kissed. Then my father is pulling on the gearshift, his feet tap-dancing between the clutch and brake pedals, and we're moving forward again, jerking out of the bushes' embrace, swinging down, straightening, moving faster. My father's head swivels one last time to the rear, taking me in, my eyes wide not so much with fright as with wonder. "You okay, Buster?" he asks.

His head moves forward to the rushing road, then to my mother. "No harm done," he says. But he doesn't try the hill again. Wherever it is we're heading to, we take the long way around.

My sister claims she was there, that she covered her eyes with her hands and didn't look out again until it was all over, but I have no memory of her. She was certainly not in the front seat with them, all those swinging elbows, and, in my memory, there is no room in the cramped back for anything but me, small as I was, and my fear.

This is not my earliest memory of childhood, but it may be the first which is specific to my father. It is certainly my first memory of him as brave, as something I might have called or thought of as a hero.

When I was six, I set fire to my bed.

There were always candles in the house, and kerosene lanterns, because the hydro would frequently go out in bad weather and my mother, though she was a city woman, had acquired a taste during the war for evenings with all the lights off, the family sitting around the fireplace, the lantern by the chair where my father read glowing like the sun glimpsed through haze. I had a fascination for flame, like many children, and I don't think it was an unhealthy one, though my father, if he were alive, would look at his outstretched hands, palms turned up, and laugh at that thought.

On this night, the war had been over for two years and the lights were on in the house. I was in my room, under the bed, which, because the bed was high and the fringed edges of the bedspread hung down almost to the floor on all sides, was like a neat, well-lit cave or a clearing within a dense woods. I had toy soldiers, a candle – a small white stub of wax encrusted onto a chipped white saucer – and a book of matches, and, when the candle had been lit, the cave was

109

even brighter. I knew I was not allowed to play with matches, which may have been why I was under the bed, out of sight. I played with my soldiers and time passed. I was not conscious of it, but I moved the saucer with the candle to the edge of the battlefield to give the soldiers more room. The flame fluttered beneath the fringes of the blue chenille spread, then one of them caught and suddenly one entire strip of fringe, running the length of my bed, was aflame. "Mummy!" I shrieked, not thinking of her specifically, not thinking of my father, only reacting. I shrunk into a ball, clutching my shoulders with my crossed hands, raising my knees and lowering my head. "MUMMY!"

They were there immediately, both of them, she a few steps ahead, and, as she came through the door, I responded to the sight of her ankles and feet the way a dog trained to attack a stranger might have, scrabbling out from under the bed, on elbows and knees, the way a crab moves, my shoulders hunched, until I was clear of the bedspread, which ignited the back of my polo shirt as I went by, then leaping up, although my feet buckled beneath me and I folded in like a flaming accordion. I was howling with fright and the first intimation of pain but I was conscious of two things: my mother stopping, her face white and frozen into a horrible, twisted parody of itself, and my father *not* stopping, moving past her with some kind of stubborn, overweight grace, bending down and swooping me up, aflame, smothering the flames with his chest and arms. Then he handed me, still screaming but extinguished, to my mother and grabbed up the flaming bedspread, bunching it in his bare hands and pressing it to his chest, smothering it the way he had done with me, pressing the heat into his own flesh, absorbing it, then throwing it to the floor, stamping out the remaining licks of flame and sparks with his slippered feet.

I had stopped screaming, transfixed. My mother was rocking me against her body, my head pressed to her collar bone, and her head tilted down so that her mouth was just above my ear, into which she was crooning, "my baby, my baby," over and over, and my father turned to us, his shirt burned and his chest and face black, his eyebrows and the shock of shoe-leather brown hair that usually trickled down over his forehead gone. There were no flames, but the smell of them, of the burning chenille and hair and skin, was strong in the room, and my father, his back to the light hanging from the ceiling, seemed to glow, as if he were still aflame, as if, rather than extinguish the fire, he had absorbed it, become one with it.

The blacktop road from Clinton runs alongside the river, loose and lanky but relatively straight, until it reaches the abandoned mill at Potter's Mill, with its loosely spread community of half a dozen houses, then it becomes a vee, with the main branch angling north, toward Potter Lake, the smaller road bending sharply and lumbering across the river in the form of a two-span metal bridge. From there, it dwindles to a narrow gravel road that struggles up a steep hill to a short wooden bridge spanning the CN tracks before it meanders on through meadows and woods, ultimately, in some logic of its own, curving back to link with a blacktop road leading to Clinton.

I was on the railroad bridge when my father passed by on his way to the village in early afternoon and, by coincidence, I was there again when he returned several hours later. It was late afternoon now, almost suppertime, and the heat of the day had gathered into a pocket of dust and intensity that made it difficult to breath. My father had the jacket of his gabardine suit folded neatly over his arm, his tie and collar button were undone, and his face was flushed red as a slab of meat from Gabreaux's butcher shop as he rose to the tip of the hill. Rivulets of sweat poured down his face from his scalp as if an underground spring existed in the dense foliage of his hair. I had been watching him for some time as he made his slow way up the hill, and it wasn't fear I felt but some vague unease I could neither identify nor explain.

He stopped, chest and shoulders heaving, and puffed his cheeks, blew out slowly. He was, I suppose, in his late forties, an average-sized man slightly overweight but in good health, the cancer that would kill him a dozen years

111

later not yet a tic in the rhythm of his blood. The acidic smell
of rye whisky stood on his breath like poorly camouflaged
sentries betraying their position and I knew he had been
sitting in the pub at the Clinton hotel, where it was always
cool and you could see through a window to the corner
where buses to Toronto and other places stopped. He
looked at me but he didn't smile.

"Missed the stupid bus," he said, gesturing down the hill
with the arm that held his jacket. I didn't say anything.

"Been here all day?"

"Just came to see the afternoon freight."

"How many cars?"

"Never the same but they all been long this summer.
Yesterday, there was 117, plus the caboose and two engines."

My father pursed his mouth, the smooth skin on his chin
wrinkling with the effort, and nodded his head slightly.
"The commerce of the nation is healthy. Not bad a tall."
My father had no head for or interest in business, but he
considered himself knowledgeable about politics. He had
cut himself shaving and there was still a tiny square of
tissue paper stuck to his jawridge just below his ear. I
reached out to flick it away and he jerked his head back
involuntarily and swatted at his jaw as if he had felt the
delicate footwork of a mosquito. He smiled now, almost his
full grin, and some of my unease lifted, as if a sudden breath
of wind had sliced through a smell hanging over me, carrying part of it away.

"Better get on home," he said, shrugging his shoulders.
The straps of his suspenders, striped blue and dark red,
almost maroon, stretched with the motion. He took out the
neatly folded white handkerchief he always carried in his
back pocket and mopped his forehead, brushing back his
hair, which had grey mixed in with the dark brown like light
flakes of snow. He folded the handkerchief without looking
at it, using his thigh for support. He gazed down the tracks
toward the east.

"Train'll be here any minute," I said. I had a picture in
my mind of us both standing on the bridge watching it
thunder past, counting the cars, pointing at the funny ones.

"Not this time, Sport. Not too fussy about watching trains, anyway. Have to get home while your mother still remembers who I am." He put the handkerchief away, and, this time, *he* touched *my* head, brushing at my hair with a palm still shiny and hard with scars from fire, but I didn't flinch. "See you later, Sport. Don't be late for dinner."

I liked the bridge because it's the highest point for miles and gives up a view in all directions. Without changing my position, but by turning my head to the right, I was able to watch him walk down the dirt road that traversed a barbwired field where dairy cows grazed, then curved into a woods behind the Clements farm that hid the cottages and led, if you followed it far enough, in a wide arc, to the blacktop road leading to Clinton, where, if you turn south, it continues on to the highway leading to Peterborough. I watched him, his body growing smaller and smaller, until he passed the point where the road bends, still a quarter of a mile before our driveway, and he disappeared from view. By that time, the whistle had already blown and I turned my attention to the tracks, getting off my bicycle and standing at the railing with my hand on a crossbeam, gazing east at the approaching train.

There is a slight curve to the tracks just before they plunge beneath the bridge so it was possible to see a partial profile of the engineer, his elbow hooked on the open window of his door, the grey-striped peaked cap pulled firmly down around his ears, just above the eyes. I waved and he waved back, our arms lifting in ritual that required no thought. The locomotive was so enveloped in dust and grime it was virtually colourless. The bridge shook as the freight roared beneath it like an animal taking to its burrow, and I could feel wind rushing up at my face from between the rough boards. I moved quickly to the other side, but, as always, the train had been faster and the locomotive was already emerging. I shook my head, lifting my chin until my line of vision bisected the line created by the outflung branch of a thorn tree on the north slope of the hill. I waited until the second engine had passed and then, using the branch as a reference point, began counting the cars. There were boxcars, many of them with the CN logo but others saying CPR and Grand Trunk and Great Northern, and flatcars, some of them empty, others carrying farm machines, big tractors and combines, and tank cars with strings of numbers on their sides. The train moved with a lurching smoothness, and waves of heat rising from the tops of the cars made many of them seem to blur into each other, so I had to concentrate hard. There were only ninety-seven cars, and I felt let down that there hadn't been as many as the day before. "Record still stands," I said as the caboose rattled past. I waved again, but there was no brakeman visible, no reply.

I watched as the train got smaller and smaller, the way my father had, and waited until it disappeared. I walked to the end of the bridge and onto the grassy bluff, then down a path that led to the brow of the hill. Shallow steps had been carved into the sloping dirt wall below and I had to pick my way carefully down the steep incline to avoid falling. Toward the end of the slope, the steps gave way to slippery gravel for the last yard or so, and I jumped from the last step to the bottom, my sneakers making the gravel crunch. I walked east, placing my feet carefully on each tie, starting at the one across from a lightbox, and counting to a hundred. I crouched down between the tracks facing east and peered down at the dust lying lightly on the shining steel rail. The only trace of the penny I'd put there earlier was the faint impression of the young queen frowning up at me, her profile etched in a rime of copper dust thin as winter breath. I grinned back at her. "We are not amused," I said aloud. After a moment, I ran my finger lightly across the track, wiping her away. "We are *not* amused."

All this time, through the watching of the train's approach, the counting of cars, the scramble down to the tracks and along them, and the ironic communion with the coin's spirit, I was not thinking of my father. But as I arose, he came into my mind, as if he had been waiting his turn and it had now come, and he didn't leave my mind until, fifteen minutes later, I saw him, his face not yet bloodied. All I had seen of him in the morning was his crumpled form under a blanket on the chesterfield in the cottage's main room – he had been up late the night before, my mother said, and we should leave him be, and I was gone, off with my friends, before he got up. But I'd been on the bridge, with Randy and Travis Sloan, twins who lived in the next cottage, when he came by on his way to the village, startling me with his cleanly shaven cheeks and the suit.

"What're you boys up to this beautiful Saturday?" he said, giving me a hug. "Not planning on running away, are you?"

"Just playing. Why would you think that?"

"Oh, maybe you're unhappy." He shrugged and flashed his famous grin, the one my mother used to say – though she hadn't for years – could have made him prime minister if he'd had any sense for politics, could have made him anything he put his mind to if he had any ambition, and it seemed to me that he looked at me closely, looking *for* something, and then, because he winked, was relieved not to have found it. "Tracks always make me think of that, because that's the route I took when I ran away when I was a boy, younger than you fellas."

"You ran away, Mr. Ossarian?" Randy asked.

"Sure. Lots of times." My father pursed his mouth. "Not that I recommend it. I had plenty to run away from, or thought I did. I don't suppose you fellas do, eh?"

He told me he'd forgotten an appointment he had in town today and was on his way to the village to catch the bus. He was stupid for forgetting and shouldn't have come out last night. He'd try to be back tomorrow, maybe in time for church. He didn't say why he wasn't taking the car, and I didn't think to ask. He brushed my hair away from my eyes, the same gesture my mother was fond of, as if that lock of hair offended them, though neither of them ever suggested I get a crewcut like the twins', and he moved off, looking back once, when he was halfway down the hill, just where the Halliwells' fence began, and waving.

"Your dad's weird," Travis said, when my father was safely out of hearing, and I wanted to hit him.

I didn't, but my irritation festered like a splinter, and later, when we were swimming in the river and Travis splashed me, I told him he was stupid, and there was some pushing then, bewildered Randy coming between us before anything happened, and that's how I came to be on the bridge alone later. I was sitting on my bike, leaning against the railing, my left foot on the bottom rail for support, facing south, looking down the hill at the abandoned Halliwell house where, shortly after the war ended, they had found the body of a baby in the well. I was thinking that if I had a pair of field glasses or a collapsing telescope like I'd seen in pirate movies I'd be able to see everything people were doing within the scope of that field of vision, including the sad, quick closing down of the lives of babies, the disposal of their bodies in full sight of anybody who might be watching when it would be assumed no one would be, and I was staring intently across the river at the vague outline of Helen Mackie's house on the small bluff above the road just before it turned onto the bridge, wondering if, with a telescope, I'd be able to see her bedroom window, could watch at night as she readied herself for bed, could see the blinding whiteness of her panties and bra, when I noticed the figure of someone walking along the road just below her house. I made field glasses of my hands, propped my elbows on the railing and watched. The figure came down off the road and onto the bridge, across the first span, and it was a man, dressed in white, then onto the abutment, then the second span, stopping once to peer downward into the river, then on, back onto the road, growing bigger with each step. The whiteness was a suit and a straw hat, and, just a moment before I would actually have been able to recognize him, I realized it was my father. I tightened the focus of my glasses and watched him as he drew closer, along the road and past the Halliwells and up the hill, until he was close enough for me to see the frown.

He had been drinking the night before too, the fresh smell of it on his breath cutting through the stale, sour sweat clinging to his body after two hours in the sweltering Ford as we gave him our hugs, but that was not unusual; what was, was the way my mother, who never liked it, was harping at him, scraping at him the way the razor had this morning, nicking the blue-veined skin of his cheeks and jaw, drawing tiny pools of blood.

"Leave it alone, Allie," my father asked her. He was seated at the kitchen table with a cold beer, in his undershirt and suit trousers, the suspender straps loose at his waist, his socked feet in slippers. From Victoria's birthday to Labour Day, he fended for himself at home during the week, then joined us at the cottage Friday evening, letting the relaxation of standards that tempered the rhythm of his summers overtake him even in the presence of my mother, who, at home, would never tolerate an undershirt anywhere but in the privacy of the bedroom.

"How can I when you remind me all the time?" she said, her voice so bitter it surprised me. She gave me a sharp glance and I averted my eyes quickly so she wouldn't know I'd been watching them. I got up, made a business of stretching, got my ball and glove, and went outside. I stood under the apple tree tossing the ball up at the almost ripe apples and catching it, seemingly absorbed in what I was doing, but my ears cocked to their voices seining through the screen door.

They were arguing, I knew even without hearing all the words, not about his drinking, which was never really a problem, but about money, our lack of it, my father's inability to make as much of it as he should, and his even more maddening inability or disinclination to care, a feeling – or lack of it – she took to mean an inability to care about her, my sister, and I. I knew even these subtleties of the argument because they had had it so often, I'd heard it so many times. I don't mean to suggest that my parents fought all the time, or that they fought with fervour and irreducible bitterness, they didn't, and I believe my mother still loved her husband as much when he died, and he his wife, as they had when we children were small. The only reason this particular argument sticks in my memory was its ferocity.

My father had been a promising young man when they met, but he was forced to drop out of school short of his architecture degree, after she became pregnant with the child that would have been my older brother if it had lived,

117

and settle for a draftsman's job. He was with the 12th Calgary Light Engineers during the war, serving in Italy and Africa, but never firing a shot, helping to design billets for troops and modifying villas for temporary headquarters, a service he accepted willingly. After the war, with two young children to feed, it had seemed easier to go back to the drafting table, which he loved, than to school, which he hadn't. He worked in a large firm on Yonge Street doing blueprints for buildings designed by younger men who had avoided war service. This didn't bother my father but rankled my mother, and that *did* bother him. The arguments were always worse, the indignity that caused them harder for my mother to live with, in the summer, when we were at the cottage, which had belonged to her parents. Being here was a constant reminder that we couldn't have afforded it on our own, just the way we couldn't afford a bigger house, a newer car, one of those television sets everyone was getting, and so many other things.

The light faded, and I put my ball and glove on the porch and sat on the step listening to the sound of my parents' voices, their long silences. Tinny radio music drifted across the thin line of trees from the cottage where Randy and Travis lived, Perry Como complaining about the moon in his face. "Goddamn it, Tom, why don't you be a man?" I heard my mother shout, her voice suddenly rising above the hushed tone like a bird flinging itself out of the orbit of its flock, soaring high against the blinking sky. In response there was a bang that I knew was my father bringing his fist down on the table, then the sound of breaking glass. Then a door slamming. Then silence.

It grew dark. Frankie Laine on the radio. Then the Ames Brothers. Then "ShaBoom." A door opened. Behind me, my mother's steps on the kitchen linoleum. "Robby, you should be in bed, dear."

"In a minute, Mum."

"Not in a minute, Mum. Now. Right now." She had a cold and had been sneezing through the day. Now her voice was thick and faint, as if she were speaking through gauze. Her footsteps retreated, the door closed again. I sat on, listening to the music, lifting the ball and dropping it into the glove's smooth leather pocket. A car, my sister's boyfriend's old blue De Soto, came down the long, looping driveway from the road, passed the turnoff and slowed down as it approached. It stopped a dozen yards from the cottage, the engine humming. After a few minutes, the passenger door opened and I could smell my sister's familiar perfume as she stepped out. "Good night, Henry," "Good night, Amy."

She stood in the moonlight watching him drive away, then came and sat down beside me on the step.

"What'dya see?"

"*Hell and High Water*. Lousy, but Richard Widmark is great. I love his eyes. What're you doing up anyway, Buster?" She looked over her shoulder through the screen door at the light from the kitchen softening the dark porch. She leaned her head against mine. "They been at it all night?"

I shrugged. "It don't mean nothin'."

"I know, Buster, but I wish they wouldn't."

We sat on for a few minutes, not saying anything, listening to the faint music from the Sloan cottage and breathing in the smell of her perfume, safe in the comfort of each other's bodies. Then we went inside, where my father was sitting at the kitchen table with a bottle and a glass, reading the *Star*. He looked up at us, blinking for a moment as if waiting for recognition to register, then grinning, the light of that smile washing over us in a gesture of permanence that sent me to bed willingly.

I was remembering all this as I rode my bicycle toward home now, not because I had lost my faith in that, but because of the look in my father's eye when he'd pulled his head back with a jerk as I swatted at his chin, the sound of his voice as he gazed down the track from the bridge that afternoon, "I had plenty to run away from, or thought I did. I don't suppose you fellas do, eh?", and I was filled with a longing thick as hunger rising up from my gut all the way to the back of my tongue, longing with neither direction nor purpose that I could tell, driving me not toward him necessarily, but keeping him in my mind as I pedalled home.

Chips of gravel small as my thumbnail sprayed in both directions as the wheels of my bicycle rolled off the bridge and onto the hard-packed dirt in the centre of the road. I pedalled with my head up, shoulders back and arms straight out to the handlebars, in imitation of a horseback rider in a show ring, my legs moving like pistons independent of the small, wiry body above them. Half a mile down the road, the Clements' driveway branches off to the left, leading to their house and barns, behind which lie the cottages. I took this shortcut, the bike bouncing up and down in the ruts, and went across the barnyard, the Clements' sheltie, Joby, barking at me without menace or interest. I had to walk the bike across a narrow stretch of cultivated field, the corn as high as my shoulder, and lift it over a barbed wire fence I crawled under. Then I rolled down a grassy incline to a hard dirt trail that came out just behind the Sloan's cottage. "Hey," Randy said. He and Travis were sitting on the grass in front of their porch in their swimsuits, eating ice cream from chipped blue bowls. I waved, but didn't say anything, my legs pumping hard.

I wheeled around the corner of our cottage just as the baseball bat was coming down against his shoulder. He had put his suit jacket back on, and the bat left a smudged grass stain on the white upper sleeve as it slid down. "Bastard," my mother yelled, "Why'd you come back, bastard? Bastard, bastard, bastard. I'll kill you." Her face was bright with what might have been fever.

I braked and slid forward off the seat, straddling the bike's bar with both my feet on the ground. My breath was coming fast, and my polo shirt stuck to my back like parchment, sweat rolling off my face the way it had off my father's as he laboured up the hill. My mother and father were standing in front of the porch door, she barring his way in, the baseball bat – my bat, which had been on the porch, in a corner with the ball and glove – rising again for another blow. My father stepped back, one small step, as if to give her more room to swing, but he didn't lift his hands. He said her name, "Allie," softly, repeating it again and again like a child.

"Bastard," she said, and the bat came down, on his head this time, and he reeled back from the force of the blow, a blossom of blood springing up on his forehead, but, again, he didn't raise his hands, and this is the moment I take with me, the mind's photograph I snapped then that has lost no clarity or lustre over the years since: the bat rising yet again and falling, with less force, this time on his shoulder, just at the fleshy point above where the ball of the arm connects, the tears springing from her eyes, the soft round circle formed by her mouth as she said the word so low I could barely hear her, "God," the bat falling from her hand and clattering to the soft ground beneath their feet, end first, then tilting over, sparking against her shins in its fall, him standing there, blood pouring down onto his collar, eyes closed as if, by shutting out the sight of it he could protect himself from her anger, mouth looped open into some lopsided combination of pain and grin, his hands at his sides, the fingers jerking with concentration the way they had when they took the flames from me for themselves, waiting for the next blow.

Goodbye to All That

THE RAIN BEGINS to fall just as I get my last ride, and, by luck, it's one of the counselors at the camp, he's going right there. I've been lucky all day, making it from the city into Vermont in a little under five hours, with three rides.

I say lucky because I must look like something out of an acid trip: my hair's longer than ever, down around my shoulders, Veronica Lake style but scraggly. My beard's a couple of months old now, bushy enough that it covers my collar. My jeans are pretty worn, my tennis shoes beat-up, but up top I'm glowing like a Broadway marquee with this absolutely wild shirt I picked up this morning as a possible final gesture at one of those trashy men's shops on 42nd Street: a weird floating red and black design on top of a deep purple background.

Doesn't scare away the rides, though. The afternoon has been one of those sweet-smelling, sticky, New England scorchers and I got picked up twice by kids in convertibles, one a vintage Impala, mint, the other a worn-out T-Bird, the Beach Boys and Creedence blaring out of their boxes, and it's been easy riding. The third ride, from Pittsfield almost to Bennington, was with a monk in a Jeep pick-up crammed with groceries – I shit you not. A slobbering St. Bernard perched on the boxes, licking salt off the back of my neck. As darkness crept up, we were just crossing the state line, deep in a debate about Thomas Aquinas, and clouds were beginning to gather. The temperature dropped quickly, and a little wind caught up with us. I asked him what I should do, but he just shook his head: "I'm glad *I* don't have to decide, glad it's not *me*." Render unto Caesar ... he *didn't* say that.

I wasn't sure exactly where the camp was, but the monk gave me directions, even offered to take me all the way, but I didn't want to trouble him. He dropped me at the turn-off to the monastery. I only had to wait about five minutes, standing in the nice breeze, the air heavy with that incredibly fresh smell of earth breathing that comes with summer rain, until the counselor barrels along, in a battered Plymouth, all chrome and fins and rust, just as the first drops come sputtering down onto the dusty shoulder of Route 7. As I climb in, I see the name of the camp, Indian mumbo-jumbo I recognize right off, scrawled on the front of his sweatshirt, and I laugh.

"Come on," he says. "This buggy ain't that bad off."

His name's Barry, he's a dental student from the Queens who's been at the camp, as camper and counsellor, every summer since he was six. Turns out he and Dick are buddies, in charge of adjacent cabins, and we trade Dumb Dick stories as the rain pours over the windshield, its wipers straining to catch up, with the ferocity of a car wash. I'll find Dick in Lodge One, he tells me, checking his watch again and frowning; they're having some sort of a peace council this evening, he tries to explain, but I can't make too much of it, really. Barry's been to New York to see his girl and is late getting back. This powwow is one of the highlights of the season, he says, and he knows he'll catch hell from the chief.

"That's the head counsellor. Everything's Indian with us. Some days we even eat buffalo stew. Horsemeat or some shit."

The camp is something like an Indian village in a B movie, with Joel McCrea as the army scout who wins the peace. There are totem poles all over the place, and the cabins, each one named after a tribe, Mohawk and Algonquin and so on, are decked out with phony tops made of poles and canvas above the rafters to make them look like teepees. They're arranged in a big circle around two low-slung quonset huts unevenly sided with logs housing the recreation hall and dining room. The biggest of these buildings is fronted by the largest totem pole, tall enough for a flag and carved with bad copies of noble savage profiles, and a low rickety porch from which hangs a sign, a rough-cut slab of wood into which the words "Lodge One" have been burnt. Barry pulls the Plymouth up in front of the porch, and the three steps it takes me to get from the car hardly gets me wet. He roars off, tires spinning gravel and mud.

Standing under the shelter of the eaves, I drop my backpack and guitar case behind a pillar and smooth out my hair, run my fingers through my beard. I try to figure whether I'm better off tucking in my neon shirt or leaving the long tails hanging out, covering up frayed spots on the thighs and ass of my jeans. In this setting, I guess I could pass, except for the shirt, for a prospector or a renegade, one of those colourful characters Joel McCrea always has along as a sidekick.

I leave the tails out, which is maybe the wrong move, because when I walk through the door about three hundred little Indian boys and a dozen or so big bucks turn their heads and stare at me like I'm General Custer come back from the dead for a second round. Dick's at a table on the far side of the room, his face glistening with war paint, a feather in his hair. There's one of those terrible moments that seem to hang on forever while all sound and motion cease and everybody gawks at me. Then Dick lets out a war whoop and comes striding up to me in that funny way he has of moving, like he's about to topple over and if you don't want him to fall on you, brother, get the fuck out of the way.

"You silly bastard," he whispers. "What're you doing here?"

"I come to smoke peace pipe, white eyes," I say.

"Get out of here, we'll be through in a few minutes."

Then he wheels around in his moccasins and strides away, like the lord of a manor who's just dispensed with a beggar or a grumbling tenant, and whispers something to a big old guy with a paunch and steamy glasses who's been glaring at me. I haven't gotten much further into the lodge than the doorway, so I just back out, letting the screen door slam shut, and settle myself on the porch railing, which groans but seems willing to hold up under me. Inside, there's all sorts of buzzing and giggling, and the big chief calls for order, slapping his fist on a tom-tom.

Barry comes running through the rain and dashes up the stairs, his hair plastered. He's stripped off his shirt and daubed his chest and face with streaks of bright red lipstick that raindrops cling to. "Find him?"

"Oh yeah."

"I'm gonna get skinned."

"Looks like it."

He goes on inside, and I light a cigarette, wondering if they have the same brands in Canada, will I be able to stick with Luckies or have to switch if I go, and listen to the rain beating down on the lodge's tin roof. I'm just a little tired.

Through the window, closed against the rain, I've got a pretty good view of what's going on inside. Some of the kids are as little as five or six, others as old as thirteen or fourteen. Three or four twelve-year-olds in warpaint are trying to scalp a couple kids wearing red bandannas and floppy cowboy hats. Dick's in it too. He must be an enlightened Indian, friend of the white man, because he keeps stopping the rubber tomahawks from falling. The skit seems funny enough – I can't hear the lines, but laughter rumbles through the window and over the sound of rain ricocheting off the porch roof. The kids nearest the window are squirming around on the floor, looking over their shoulders at me, giggling and pointing. They're all eating cookies and drinking milk.

When it breaks up, the kids pour out, whooping and leaping off the porch like paratroopers, and scatter in all directions. Dick comes out wiping the paint from his face with a bandanna. I can see the outline of his ribs pressed against the skin of his scrawny torso, like poles defining the shape of a teepee.

"You heap powerful medicine," I say.

"You schmuck. You'd walk into the UN Security Council

while they're in session. What're you doing here, anyway?"

We shake hands, a habit that prep school beat into Dick.

"Happened to be in the neighbourhood, so I thought I'd drop by. Thinking of going to Canada. Want to come along?"

"Canada? What for?"

"Got a letter from my uncle. Some cat named Sam, maybe you heard of him? He wants me to join him in some venture he's got cooked up in the mysterious Orient. I don't much go for Oriental women. You know how it is, an hour after you lay them you're horny again."

Dick's lips purse in an unconscious impressed expression. He looks me over like I'm a car he's thinking of buying.

"That's the shits. You're running?"

"Don't be so crude. First of all, I haven't decided what I'm doing. I'm thinking about it, hard. But if I do go, I'll walk, not run. *Migrate*. Not like a lemming, hopefully. I've always wanted to be an expatriate. Hemingway, Fitzgerald, like that. This just might be my chance."

The rain's letting up and Dick's itching to wash the gunk off. He shows me where to stow my gear in the lodge, and we head down a muddy path through the light spitting to his cabin, which is called Seneca. Very cute. The kids are already there, sprawled out on their bunks reading comic books in the candlelight. They look to be about eleven or twelve.

"Who's your hairy friend?" one of the kids asks, and giggles ripple through the cabin from bunk to bunk. There are four double-deckers and one single, which Dick gestures me toward. "My sister," he says, the giggles erupting into howls.

Dick busies himself at the cabin's one cold-water sink, its enamel badly chipped, while I parry wisecracks with the kids.

"How come you didn't bring your gee-tar?"

"It's electric, not candle-power."

Dick opens a footlocker at the side of the bed and takes out a clean sweatshirt with our school's name on it. I wish I had one of those. "Ten minutes till lights out."

There's a unanimous moan from the kids, but no real protest.

"I run this ship of fools with an iron rudder," Dick says. "When did you hear?" He's brushing his fine sandy hair, short and neat as ever, in front of a stained mirror over the sink.

"Three days ago. They gave me a week to put my affairs in order, as they say, but three days was all I needed. Since Marilyn Monroe and I split up, I don't have a whole hell of a lot of affairs. Sold my stocks, divorced my wife, murdered my kids." I wink at the closest bunk, which erupts into giggles again. "That's all there was."

"Schmuck," Dick says.

"Then I burnt my boats behind me – ever see a thirty-foot yacht go up in flames? Quite a sight – and packed my trusty knapsack. And hit the road, Jack. And some people say moving is a drag."

Dick's mouth makes its sour purse. I can hear the gears grind behind his clear grey eyes, breaking this thought down into bite-size chunks. I'm not so sure that, now that the brief sweet moment of recognition has passed, he's all that glad to see me.

"Well, maybe not all my boats. Anyway, I figured, why not stop off an' see youse and maybe ol' crazy Tom. Take soundings. Canada's up north, ain't it?"

Dick puts his brush away on the shelf above his bed, stacked neatly with shaving cream, aftershave, cologne, the works. He looks very respectable, even for an Indian war-chief. His wash pants have a crease and his tennis shoes are still white. The little curl of hair that clings to his wide forehead looks clean enough to squeak if you pull it. His long loose jowls glow red from the scrubbing they've just gotten. His ears are sunburned.

"Where'd you get that crazy shirt?" he asks.

"Quite becoming, don't you think?"

Dick puts his kids to bed, tucking them in like a mother hen, and blows out the candles. "And no reading comics by flashlight," he warns.

"How'll you know if you're gone?" one of them asks.

"I'll see it with the eye in the back of my head, and I'll come back and slice of your noses. Or your peckers. Those of you who still have them."

"Mr. Angstrom has an eye in the back of his head," a kid tells me, very matter-of-factly. "But it's usually bloodshot."

"And no beating off, either," Dick says. "It'll make you blind."

"Or bloodshot."

"Let's *us* get blind," I say. "Let's go collect crazy Tom and get stinking."

The rain has stopped completely, and we walk back to the lodge slowly, feeling the wetness of the grass seep into our sneakers. I never went to camp, and I'm thinking back to how we used to play in the streets when we were kids. "I wonder if I'd have wound up any different if I'd come to a place like this," I say aloud.

"Yeah, some mean counsellor would have cut off your pecker."

Dick steers me to the pay phone and I call North Adams information, then have the operator connect me. "If we're in luck, he'll be out of town," I say, grinning. Dick's probably thinking just that.

But Tom answers on the second ring. "Beirut police headquarters, Inspector Ahmel here."

"I want to report the rape of my camel. The bastard ran off after doing it only once."

"Carl, you sweet bastard. How are you? *Where* are you, you son of a bitch?"

"I'm at camp whatchamacallit. Dick's place. Not too far."

"I thought you were playing in a band in Pennsylvania, the Pinocchio Mountains."

"The Poconos, yeah, I was there, I'm retired now. I'm on a royal tour of the northern states, thinking about slipping over the line to join the Mounties. Need a powwow. What'ya say we meet you over in New York and get stinko?"

"You mean for old times' sake?"

"Something like that."

"That's the best offer I've had all evening, but fuck old times. Let's get stinko for the sake of the here and now, the sweet moment at hand. How far are you from Bennington?"

I tell him where we are, and he gives me directions to a bar right over the state line near Hoosick.

"I give up, who *is* sick?"

"I'll see you there in half an hour, shit-for-brains. I'll have a rose in my teeth so you'll recognize me."

"Have Rose bring a couple of friends," I say.

Dick has fetched my pack and guitar, and we throw them in the back of his heap, a Volks bug of uncertain age. Everything I own's in the pack, which is to say, everything I've taken with me. I spell out the situation for him in more detail on the drive over. He doesn't say much, just frowns a lot.

The bar's about two hundred yards into New York, a nondescript, greasy looking place, sprawling, crusted with neon almost as bright as my shirt. The parking lot's jammed with Vermont and Massachusetts plates, and, inside, every booth's filled with college kids wearing Indian-name sweatshirts. Everybody stares at us when we roll in, ogling my beard just like those little Indians did, and the noise level dips a few decibels, but just for a couple of seconds. Then the heads swivel around and the eyes lower, the din rises again, like a radio being cranked up after the landlady leaves. We sit at the bar and order a pair of Schlitzes. Dick's still being pretty quiet, telling me about this new novel that's really turning him on, *Catch 22*.

Tom comes in after we've done in our first beers, wobbling on his battered cowboy boots and wagging his huge shaggy head. "Carl, baby." He gives me a bear hug and blabbers on, what a great shirt, what a cocksucker I am for not writing him, like that. He jabs Dick in the ribs and kids him about working in a camp. They don't really like each other very much.

"So wha's happenin', man? Goin' to Canada? Ain't Expo over? Oh, I get it. Feeling a bit of a draft?"

Tom looks even more disreputable than me. No shaggy beard, but several days' thick, dark stubble, and his hair, like always, is a bird's nest, growing straight out of his head like a Brillo pad. His T-shirt and black jeans are grease-stained beyond cleaning. His big, raw face is swollen with sunburn blisters, and underneath his John L. Lewis brows his eyes do war dances Dick's kids can only dream about.

"I am, as we say in the trade, thinking of splitting the scene," I say. "Khaki is just not my colour. Want to come along for the ride?"

"Wouldn't that be great," Tom says. "No, wait. I can't. I got a date tomorrow night. Too bad. But you should see her."

"I'm thinking of getting me one of those French-Canadian broads. Maybe she'll have a sister for you. Their waists are so little, those Frenchie girls, you can put one hand around them."

"Clever, very clever," Tom says. "That leaves the other hand free. Very clever. You sly fox." He winks at me and jabs Dick in the ribs with his big elbow. "Ain't he a sly fox, though?"

We order beers. A booth under a revolving Budweiser clock is emptying out and we swoop on it.

"So you're going, or what?" Tom demands.

"I dunno. Give me three good reasons why I shouldn't. Give me *one* good reason."

"What would you do up there?" Dick asks, always practical.

"I've been wondering about that myself. I'm kind of lacking in the profession department. My skills are practically nil, and I'm a functional illiterate, you know. I guess I'll do the same thing up there as I've done down here."

"Hey, that's great," Tom says. "I was just reading, Canada's got a shortage of assholes that're good at scratching themselves. It's critical. They'd be tickled to see you."

"I could bring music to the north woods. Music to soothe the savage beasties who live there. I could write songs for Nelson Eddie and Jeanette MacDonald."

"Who the fuck're *they*?"

"I could write a musical for them, based on my life. 'The Loneliness of the Long-Distance Draft Dodger.'"

"Yeah! Jeez, what a flick that'd make. Fuck Jeanette MacDonald. *Doris Day* starring as The French-Canadian Little Waist. Sandy Kaufax as the Dodger."

Even Dick laughs, the lines around his mouth softening. Then we talk about all kinds of shit for a long while, school, girls, books, music, Tom's job on a highway road crew, even politics, the war, though Dick keeps changing the subject. We lay to waste a lot of little brown soldiers, even Dick, he and Tom taking turns buying. I'm not any closer to making a decision.

The swirling clock above us is saying about midnight, and the place is pretty well cleared out. Dick is starting to get yawny and fidgety. He's been quiet all evening, and he got kind of cool over something Tom said, about some girl we all know. I guess he's thinking, too, about those screaming Indians along about six or seven in the ay-em.

"I believe I'm feeling pretty good," Tom says.

"Oh, yeah, but we're still a long way from being stinking," I remind him. "When do these New York state bars close?"

"Don't you go gettin' yourself all worried about that little ol' thing. Ol' Tom's got a few tricks up his sleeve yet. Speaking of which...."

He nudges me and Dick, and I look in the direction he's leering at. These three chicks have just come in, one with unbelievable tits. The other two aren't bad either. They're wearing sweaters, not sweatshirts, and they don't look the camp type, healthy but not wholesome. They take their time looking the place over, which is what we're doing to them, then choose a table within voiceshot of our booth. The big one sits across the table farthest from us, facing us.

"That's puttin' your best foot forward," Tom says. He and I are pretty giggly, and Dick's frowning at us the way he did at his little charges.

"Think they're Bennington girls?"

"I hear Bennington girls do it."

"No shit."

"Oh, yeah. I read it in a book. *The College Man's Field Guide to Twat*. But *she* ain't no Bennington girl anyway. They don't allow tits there."

"Those aren't Bennington girls," Dick says flatly. "Green Mountain." That's a junior college for girls not far away over on the Vermont side. It has a reputation as a great place to go for a party, especially during the summer.

"What'ya say we double the guest list at this table?" Tom says. "After all, we don't want Carl to forget what good ol' American big-waisted girls are like, right Tricky Dick?"

Dick fends off Tom's elbow. "Let's not. I've got to be getting back pretty soon."

I don't really care one way or another. I've had a good summer. But Tom won't let up. He calls over to them, "Hey, ladies, can we buy you all a drink? We're having a little party." He's pretending to be drunker than he is.

The chicks giggle, confer, then pick themselves up and come over. Tom leaps up, almost stumbling, and pulls extra chairs around our booth. In the shuffle, Tom winds up on one side, inside, with the big girl next to him, I'm on the other side with another girl, and Dick and the third girl are on the chairs.

The big chick is really something, icebergs under her tight white sweater. She's pretty in a sort of blank, Debbie Reynolds way, blonde all over, gum-chewing, constantly in motion, and she's big all over, almost fat under the waist, with tight blue jeans bunching around her thighs. But you just can't help staring at her chest. It's like she has a sign hanging around her neck saying "Look at me, look at me." Her friends are nice looking too, coedy, cute. Turned up noses and puckered little mouths, and firm little chins that make you think about the hard, perfect teeth behind their cheeks.

We trade names all around, but I'm not paying attention. The big girl, naturally, is the talker. The one sitting next to me, a nice shiny Italian, has a few things to say too. The third one, another blonde, doesn't make a peep after the names.

"You boys look like you've been partying for quite a while," the big blonde says, something like that. I'm not really listening.

"We're giving a bon voyage party for Carl Marx here," Tom says. "We're his brothers. I'm Chico and that's Harpo. Carl's going off to Siberia to join the foreign legion."

The waitress takes our orders, beer all around except for the Italian, who has a gin and tonic.

"Come on, *really*," the big girl whines. "You guys work in the camps?"

"The chain gangs," Tom says.

He and the big chick keep it going for a while, whipping quips and sly little insults back and forth like a shuttlecock that's losing its feathers. It turns out they *are* from the junior college. They loosen up some after their drinks come, and Tom keeps nudging me with his knee under the table, sometimes flashing me a rolling-eyed grin. Dick's yawning, looking bored, a little pissed.

Eventually, the talk comes back to me and Siberia. Big Tits is having as tough a time keeping her eyes off my beard as I am keeping mine off her chest. It comes out I may be going to Canada, "which might as well be Siberia," Tom says, "to join the RAF."

"What's that?" the shiny Italian asks. She's kind of nice, with smooth olive skin and eyes dark as olive pits, and, by this time, I have my hand on her knee and she has a hand on my hand.

"The Regal Air Force, naturally," Tom says.

"What's the matter with the U.S. air force?" Big Tits asks, looking at me. Her eyes are narrowing, as if it's just starting to dawn on her she's being conned.

"Oh, the RAF is much more glamorous," Tom says. "And more musical. Our friend here is the famous composer of martial music, Franklin S. Souza. American forces already have their marching tunes so he's *got* to go to Canada. All they've got is 'God Save the Queen,' which tells you a lot about Christianity, when you think about it. They *need* him. Besides, all the great American artists go to Canada and join the RAF. That's what Faulkner and Hemingway and all those guys did."

"Hemingway was in the ambulance corps in Italy," Dick says, yawning.

"Exactly. He hadda get out, that's the point. Go where you're needed. Italy had lots of wounded, so ambulance drivers were in short supply. Canadians march a lot, so they need marching music. Anyway, they have cleaner wars up there."

"Oh, come *on*," Big Tits says. She looks right at me. Her breasts graze my elbow as she leans across the table. "Why, really?" she asks seriously. She looks like she really wants to know.

I'm tired. I'm almost stinking, too. "I haven't made up my mind yet," I say. "I'm thinking about it, about going to avoid being drafted. What's known in the trade as draft dodging."

There's one of those awful silences. Dick looks like he would very much like to be someplace else. Jefferson Airplane's on the jukebox across the room, and you can hear every word of the lyrics, "One pill makes you larger, and one pill makes you small, and the ones that mother gives you don't do anything at all, go ask Alice when she's ten feet tall."

"Canadian wars *are* cleaner," Tom confides to us all. "American wars are dirty. Canadian wars have proven to be 76 per cent cleaner than all the other leading brands of war combined. That comes from a scientific survey to be found in the current issue of the Christian Dentist Journal." His voice has the clean-sounding innocence of a child who has wandered into the middle of adults' conversation.

"What do you have against the army?" Big Tits say finally. "You one of those peace creeps? A communist? You want the Viet Cong to win the war?"

"I don't like to talk politics," I say. "I'm not a politician. Politics don't have anything to do with it. I just don't like...."

"Then you're a coward?"

"No," I say slowly. "I don't do that either."

"What *do* you do?"

"Well," I start, and I really can't help but laugh. I can almost hear, word for word, and see, movement for movement, what's going to happen next. "I scratch a lot." It seems like the easiest thing. Tom guffaws.

"I can believe that," Big Tits says coldly. "I doubt if the Canadians will want you for their clean wars."

"Hey, babe, be fair," I say. "I may be scraggly but I'm clean. I happen to have bathed just this morning. My own mother bathed me herself. In mother's milk. My mom's tits aren't as big as yours, but they're more sincere."

She gets up; the others do too. The little Italian has long since brushed my hand away. Very deliberately and slowly, almost telegraphing what she's going to do, the big chick picks up her glass and throws its contents at my face. I see it coming, the frothy white head and the yellow liquid shapeless in its flight, like a pattern in a Rorschach test, but I don't duck. The splash of beer breaks up across my nose and swishes down through my beard, warm and sticky.

"Thank you," I say. "Beer is considered quite good for that, I understand. But you needn't have bothered. I shampooed my beard this morning too."

Then they just go. That's all there is to it, except for Tom roaring with laughter and Dick clearing his throat. The waitress comes over and begins to wipe the table, giving me a disgusted look to show all her worst expectations have come true. I go to the men's room and wash my face, staring hard into the mirror. "Why do you bother?" I say to myself, but the pompous son of a bitch doesn't bother answering.

We all go out into the mist. The stars are dimly visible above us, and the moon, what there is of it, is making a good try. I get the guitar and my pack out of the Volks. Dick and I shake hands, and he slides in and starts up the engine, its hoarse hiccuping roar pathetic against the even drone of the crickets in the pasture on the other side of the road. I feel sad, without knowing exactly why.

"I guess I won't be seeing you again," he says.

"Hard to say."

"I hope you know what you're doing. I hope you're doing the right thing."

"Whatever that is."

He smiles, says something I don't quite catch, and is gone.

Tom's car, an old Ford that looks like a refugee from a demolition derby, is parked under the neon sign announcing the bar. The car began its life blue, but someone started to paint it purple, making it look like my shirt. As we climb in, the light goes out with a staticky hiss, and Tom fumbles with the key. There hasn't been anything said about me spending the night with him, it's just worked out that way. There wouldn't have been room for me in the teepee, anyway.

"We never did get really stinking," I say.

"Oh, Ol' Tom's still got a few tricks up his sleeve. Don' you worry none."

We drive back into Vermont, through Bennington, and then down Route 7 into Massachusetts. Tom drives slowly, with exaggerated care, keeping his eye out for cars with bubblegum machines on top, and we don't talk much. We listen to rock and roll on the radio, WBZ in Boston.

We turn onto a dirt road, go for about a mile, then pull over to the side where the road deadends. We get out, and Tom leads me through the dark along a little grassy trail that soaks my feet again. He stops when we came to a fence, iron spike and railing. Beyond it, in the faint moonlight, I can see grave markers and tombstones. He shrugs, twists his mouth into a quick smile. "Ol' Tom's got some fuckin' aces up his sleeve yet," he whispers thickly.

We climb the fence, and Tom leads the way through a thicket of birch to a large crumbling mausoleum. "Like you to meet my family," he says. I can just make out his grin. "Not all of it, a course, you're not 'xactly the kind of guy I'd bring home to mother, but here's the grandfolks and great-grandfolks. Both sides. We're a close, old family. And here" – he reaches down and lifts a loose stone in the floor of the mausoleum's patio and retrieves first a six-pack of beer and then a fifth of bourbon, half full – "here's some old friends, the Schlitz boys and my good pal Jim Beam. Sit yerself down, podnuh."

It's cool in the graveyard, and a little spooky. We sit on the cobblestones, our backs hard up against the stone wall, and finish getting stinking.

"I always leave some liquid refreshments here," Tom says. "It stays cool in the stones. I come here a lot, to meditate on my past, and my future." There's a pause, filled by a chorus of crickets. "No one thinks to look for me here."

We toast Tom's past and his future, then mine, then the world's. As an afterthought, we even toast Dick's future.

After a while, we're quiet. Tom's asleep, his head slumped forward, chin poking into the hollow of his throat, hair glistening with dampness, and I sit on, watching the night dissolve like hard rain on the windshield of a moving car, smoking a bitter cigarette and humming quietly into the lip of my beercan. I'm thinking about the girls at the bar, the look in the big girl's eye, the cold splash of beer in my face. Everything seems so clear now, straight as the line down the centre of a highway. "Why do you bother?" I say aloud, but again, there's no answer.

Tom and I wake almost simultaneously, with a start. A bird's singing somewhere, and the sun's directly above us, booming down like a cannon on my pulsing temples.

"Gawd, I feel awful," Tom says. Sweat's running in great rivulets down his brow. "Handy being here, it'll save them delivering the body."

"That's funny, I feel like a million."

"Yeah? A million what?"

We collect the beer cans and struggle through the grass and over the fence to the Ford, which is steaming in the sunshine, its purple streaks looking like psychedelic rust stains. In the daylight, the cemetery seems cheerful, almost friendly, like a park, its headstones exotic statues and drinking fountains. We drive slowly to Tom's house, Tom moaning a little, shielding our eyes from the sun with our hands. The Ford doesn't have visors, or much of anything else, far as I can tell. Nobody's around, his folks already left for work, and I take a shower while Tom makes coffee and an omelet. He makes it with Irish whiskey in place of milk. It sets me up.

Tom drives me into North Adams, where I buy some cigarettes, and then up onto Route 7. We're just driving for a while, not saying much, until I tell him we're far enough. It's about ten miles north of Bennington. I think about the monk in the Jeep, the wet-tongued dog. The sanctuary of the monastery.

"I really covered a lot of territory," I say.

"Yeah, but you lived, man. I guess I shouldn't ask you why, huh?" Tom asks softly.

I don't have to ask him what he means. "Why the fuck not? Can't give you much of an answer, though. I've known this was coming since I quit school. I don't know. Ask Big Tits." We both grin and I raise my hands. "Just seems like the thing to do."

Then there isn't much else to say. Tom gets out of the Ford and gives me a bearhug. "Sure you don't want to come along?" I say. "Plenty of room in my pack." It would be nice.

"Naw, I don't think I'd better, podnuh." He grins and kicks a pebble into the road. "Not now, leastways. Maybe if I get that letter too." After a moment, he adds: "And if it seems to me like the thing to do."

"Right." I pick up the guitar case. The handle feels good in my hand. "Well, don't do anything I wouldn't do."

"Right. Prob'ly will, though. You got such finicky fuckin' taste."

There doesn't seem to be anything else to say, so he gets back into the Ford, wheels it around, and roars off. We wave, and I stand watching after him, until there isn't anything more to see.

It's another scorcher. I just sit in the grass for a while, on the side of the road. Then I walk. I'm pretty lucky. A guy in an air-conditioned Caddy picks me up after a few minutes. There's no breeze about at all, so it's nice.

He's a middle-aged guy, nicely dressed and all – I figure him for a fag. We get to talking. Turns out he's a third cousin by marriage or something to Norman Thomas, the big-deal socialist. He says he has a nephew in Canada, a dodger, thinks it's a pretty good idea. We stop after a while, and he buys me lunch, insists on paying. I'm sure he'll make a pass later, but no, he's just nice.

This Moment, With All Its Promise

THE IDEA OF finding her family – her real mother – came to Kathy the day her daughter graduated from high school. She'd always thought she might, since that day, almost forty years earlier, when her mother and father, stiff with formality and apprehension, had told her she was adopted.

"Whose little girl are you?" her father had asked.

"Yours, Daddy," she squealed, hugging his warm neck. "Yours and Mummy's."

"Yes, that's right, Darling, you're Mummy and Daddy's little girl." That part had been rehearsed, hundreds of times. She was seven and had begun to ask the innocent questions that hurt them: why didn't she have any sisters or brothers like Louisa and Hildy and some of her other friends had, where had she *come* from, questions she later used to wonder why she had had to ask, as if, not asked, they might have gone unanswered, leaving so much beneath the surface. What came next was new.

"But you're someone else's little girl, too," Daddy said, taking her on his knee. "How about that?"

"Someone else's?" She hadn't known – for just a moment – whether to be frightened, that she might be taken away, or exultant, that she was different, special. Both of those feelings swept through her, then passed as quickly as they came, and left her confused, and *that* had never really left.

Someone else's? How could she be? How could someone have given her away?

After that first introduction of the idea and her parents' awkward explanation – the man and the woman who love each other, the tube and the cave, the seed in the soil, pregnancy and birth, then the Mummy who was alone and didn't feel strong enough to do all the things that had to be done to take care of a brand new baby girl all by herself – she had talked about it from time to time with them, together until she was ten, and then, after her father's death, with her mother, but always, she realized later, looking back, with more of a sense of idle curiosity than of urgent need.

"I wonder what my Mum's doing right now?" she would suddenly say, and her mother would look up at her from the needlework in her lap or across the table and smile but say nothing, there being no suitable answer, or "I wonder if my Mum's ever been here?" as she gazed out the tightly rolled-up window of the car.

"I don't think so, dear," her mother would say. "Toronto's so far from Kelowna. I imagine she married a man from there and has a family of her own now."

"You and Daddy moved."

"Your father was transferred or we never would have. To leave the coast on our own? Never! Why would anyone do that?"

When she was at university, her room-mate the second year, a tall Jewish girl with hair coarse and tangled as a bramble bush, asked her if she'd ever tried to find her birth mother, and that was the first time she'd heard the phrase or given serious thought to doing more than merely wondering about her.

"I never thought about it," Kathy said, feeling slightly guilty, as if she had, out of innocence or ignorance, she didn't know which, somehow betrayed a trust too secret to have ever been put into words.

"Never?" Ruth asked. "Weren't you curious?"

"Sure I was. Just… not enough, I guess."

"You *goy* are so funny. You claim the family is so important but you ignore each other, disown each other.

You're studying history and you haven't even looked into your own."

Kathy was stung, and would have been angry if she and Ruth hadn't already become such close friends. "I guess I didn't want to be disloyal to my … my *mother*," she said, stumbling over the word. "If one is my *birth* mother, what does that make the other one? And which one's the *real* mother?"

"Disloyalty doesn't have anything to do with it," Ruth said. "Are you disloyal to your father, all right, your father's memory, when you go out with a boy, when you kiss? One is one, the other is the other. *They* know the distinction; you need to, too."

They had this conversation and variations of it dozens of times after that, both through the long days of school and the shorter, more frenetic ones of the years that followed, career years, marriage years, years of her own children. Kathy knew Ruth was right, but, in her heart, she remained unconvinced. Looking for some place on a map of Canada, her eyes would stray, with a volition of their own, to the west coast, to Vancouver, where she had been born, and to Kelowna, where, her adoptive mother had told her, her birth mother had been born and raised and likely had returned, her lessons of independence bitterly learned. She began to think of the woman who had raised her, who she knew loved her, as her "Toronto mother," the other as her "B.C. mother," as if the only divisions between them were geographical, and when she and Herbert went to Victoria for their honeymoon she found herself thinking of that B.C. mother almost every day as they strolled along the wharf in front of the Empress Hotel or along the beach littered with kelp and shells at Botany Bay.

"My real mother lives here," she told him, "in B.C., I mean. Did I tell you that?"

"You want to visit her? I survived one of your mothers, I ought to be able to last through a second one."

"I don't know where she is, silly. I don't even know her name."

"Does your mother know? I mean, your…."

"Just her first name, Alice." She pronounced the word with loving solemnity, as if it were a slice of pear in the mouth of a hungry child. "And that she had light brown hair and green eyes, like mine. She only saw her once, so it was hard for her to remember, but she always said she *thought* I probably looked like her."

"We could look for her," Herbert said, and Kathy squeezed his hand, grateful, thinking how lucky she was. He had been very sweet in those days, giving no clue to the way he would change after the children came, closing in on himself like a tortoise caught in the beam of a flashlight. "There must be some way."

"There isn't," Kathy said, though she didn't really know that, and she clung to that belief like a child's blanket.

But for some reason, when she saw Terri in her robes on the stage at Point Grey Collegiate, her eyes fierce with something that might have been pride or independence under the flat board of her hat, the idea came into Kathy's head that perhaps there was. More than twenty years had passed, the gulf between Herbert and her was wide as the Pacific, her mother was in a nursing home in Toronto and would likely be dead within the year, she was living in Vancouver with Keith, who was clever and friendly and gave her whatever room she needed to maneuver in whatever undertaking she was in at the moment, the boys were grown and gone and now Terri was all but gone, and why shouldn't she do something for herself for a change? She smiled at *that* thought, because she had been doing things for herself – what *seemed* like herself, though it wasn't always – for six or seven years now, since she'd finally left Herbert, but she never tired of mouthing that incantation, saying it to her friends and seeing them nod their heads wisely, as if she had spoken in a code only she and her expanding sisterhood could understand. She smiled at Keith when he pointed at something on the stage and let her eyes follow the long reach of his hand. Well, why shouldn't she?

"As you go out into the world, you will think back to today, fondly, one would hope, and recall the brightness of this moment," the guest speaker, a judge, was saying. She was a stout woman, whose smartly cut white hair seemed crisp and regal enough to have been a wig, a woman from somewhere in that mysterious generation between Kathy's, in which women were only just beginning to learn about and assert themselves, and her mother's, in which women were defined solely by their relationship to their husbands and fathers. "This moment, with all its promise, can be a memory or a blueprint, the first step in the sequence of steps which merge to become the rest of your life," the woman said smugly, as if it were that easy, and Kathy grimaced, nudging Keith, who was fond of positive thinking and self-talk. "That's up to you, young ladies."

Kathy lost interest in the rhetoric, and her mind wandered. "A memory or a blueprint," she repeated under her breath, and she began thinking about how it could be accomplished, finding her mother, her *real* mother, after all these years. But why not? She'd been a journalist, after all, and she had research skills. In her mind, she could see the pages of a Henderson directory turning, could smell the fragile pages of old telephone books, the musty odour of dead history rising from yellowed clippings in the morgues of newspaper offices where she'd sometimes gone to find information on a client. She began making notes to herself.

To Ruth, with whom she still was close, she wrote this letter:

Baby Ruth,

Guess what?

After all these years, I've decided to try to find my real mother. Will you help me? I've asked Keith, but now that he's a vice president he's so busy he barely has time to acknowledge *me*, let alone some shadowy past I may have. He's been kind to my mother – you know what I mean – so I guess I shouldn't be ungrateful.

This was all your idea to begin with, don't forget, but I imagine you'll say my actually doing it is just the latest step in my dance into the arms of the bourgeoisie, just the way marrying Keith was, and I'm not saying you may not be right.

Help me anyway. I don't really need you to *do things*, I think I can handle that end, just believe in me and what I'm doing, just put your mind to giving me persistence and guile.

Hope all's well with you. Talk soon.

Love,

K.

To the child welfare branch of the Human Resources Ministry she wrote this letter:

My name is Kathleen Hindemith Logan. Hindemith is my maiden name, the name of my adoptive parents, Robert and Lois Hindemith, who lived at 2751 Point Grey Road in 1953, when I was adopted, under the aegis of the B.C. Children's Aid Society, which I understand the ministry has absorbed.

I would like to learn more about my "birth mother." I know only that her first name was Alice, that she was in her twenties and had been living in the Vancouver area but was originally from Kelowna. I know nothing about my biological father. I've always been told that my birth date was Nov. 23, 1952.

I understand that provincial legislation makes it impossible for you to put me in direct contact with my birth mother or to identify her for me, but I understand further that there is certain information I am entitled to. I would appreciate receiving as much information as your files and the law allows.

For what it is worth, I've discussed my interest with my adoptive mother, who is still alive but ailing, and she supports me.

Best wishes,

Kathleen Hindemith Logan

Two weeks later, she received this reply:

Dear Ms. Logan,

Thank you for your letter about the circumstances of your birth, which has been passed on to me for action and response.

Your understanding of the legislation is correct, although you should be aware that legislation is constantly under review and could be changed.

I have prepared a summary of our files on your case, which is attached. I hope you find it helpful. Please feel free to contact me should you desire any interpretation of the material or any other assistance. Good luck in your search.

Sincerely,

Donna McAdam, MSW

Kathleen Hindemith

You were born Nov. 23, 1952, in Grace Hospital, Vancouver. Your birth was a difficult one following a 59-hour labour and medium forceps delivery. You weighed seven pounds, four ounces, and required resuscitation. Because of a series of boils, you remained in hospital for five weeks. Following this, you came into the care of the Children's Aid Society, which was asked by your birth mother to find a permanent home for you.

You are described as a very pretty baby, with beautiful big green eyes with brown flecks and hair that was fair and a little curly.

You were bright, alert, well-adjusted and content. Your development was a little behind the average, no doubt due to the difficulties of your birth, and your adoption placement was delayed until you had achieved an average rate, which was around the end of the third month. You went to live with your adoptive family Feb. 26, 1953, and your adoption was completed Aug. 23 of that year.

The only other information on your progress we have is that you sat alone at 8 1/4 months and said a few words by 13 months.

Your birth mother was in her early twenties when you were born and had herself been born in British Columbia. She is described as tall and basically slenderly built, with light brown hair that had been curled but was actually straight, and light green eyes. She had a small scar on the left side of her nose, but this was not disfiguring and she was attractive. She was a quiet person, fond of reading, sewing and knitted many things for you. She loved you and felt your security would be best achieved in an adoption home. She took a long time to reach this decision, but felt she had made the right one.

She was educated in Kelowna, but left school before the end of Grade 11. She later attended business college and was employed as a clerk at a department store in Vancouver at the time of your birth.

Her health was generally good, but she was in labour for three days and it took her several months to recover her strength after your birth.

She was the second oldest in a family of seven children. Her parents had been born in Canada, but were of Irish descent. Her father owned a small business. Your birth mother described him as a clever, kindly man, but completely dominated by his wife. He would have liked to help your birth, but your grandmother refused to have you or her daughter in their home. She and your birth mother had never been on good terms.

Your birth mother gave us the following information about your birth father, who had no contact with the society.

He was in his early twenties – younger than your birth mother – and was unmarried and in good health. He was born in Prince George, B.C., of Italian immigrant parents and had gone to Vancouver in search of work. He had planned to marry, but his family persuaded him against this because he was unemployed, his age and the great value placed in the family on education. His family consisted of six brothers and three sisters. One brother was a lawyer, another a doctor, and one sister was a teacher.

Like your birth mother, he was tall and slender, but, unlike her, he was dark, with black hair and eyes and a swarthy complexion. She described him as a serious man, passionate and sincere, but with a quick wit. She was not bitter toward him, but was toward his family; she spoke of him with remorse.

He did contribute financially toward your care.

She was lucky immediately. In the Pacific Northwest History Room at the Vancouver Public Library, she found a 1952 telephone book for Prince George and, in its yellow pages, she compared the listings for doctors and lawyers and found only one Italian name that was the same, Dr. Stephen DeNiro and A.F. DeNiro Jr. She read the names with a chill, thinking of the actor Robert. "God," she thought – "that sexy hunk." In the current Prince George phone book, there was no listing for Dr. DeNiro in the yellow pages, but there was a residence listing. Under lawyers, there was an F.G. DeNiro, but not an A.F.

She wrote this letter, sending copies to both DeNiros:

Please forgive this intrusion, which, I realize, may be upsetting.

I'm seeking information about a man named DeNiro – I don't know his first name – from Prince George who I believe was my father. I know he had both a lawyer and a doctor for brothers.

He was involved with a young woman from Kelowna, in Vancouver in 1952, and apparently intended to marry her, but was persuaded otherwise. I was born in Vancouver in November, 1952, and was given up for adoption. My adoptive parents, whose name was Hindemith, moved to Toronto when I was young and I was raised there, and have lived most of my life in Ontario. I've always known I was adopted and have been curious about my natural parents but, while living so far away, was able to keep that curiosity in check. I recently moved to Vancouver, and my desire to know more about my origins has grown tremendously.

Here she paused and considered carefully before ending.

Any information you might feel comfortable providing me with would be most gratefully appreciated.

Yours most sincerely,

Kathleen Hindemith Logan

In the three weeks that passed before an answer came, she continued her evening research at the library, but with less luck. Even in the fifties, Kelowna had been a good sized town, big enough to have a Polk directory, but too big to make finding people in it easy. Painstakingly, investing hours to the search, she went through the commercial section looking for businesses of any kind owned by people with Irish names. These she checked against the residential section, seeking references to children, a daughter named Alice would have been wonderful, large families, anything she could capitalize on. Nothing came of this, nor was there any immediate response to the letters she sent to the one business college in Kelowna and the several in Vancouver and the Vancouver department stores, seeking information about an Irish-surnamed young woman named Alice whose path may have crossed theirs in the early 1950s.

Then this letter, from F.G. DeNiro, solicitor and barrister, of Prince George:

Dear Mrs. Logan,

I am writing on behalf of my father, A.F. DeNiro, and my uncle, Dr. Stephen DeNiro. I apologize for the delay in responding to your letter of July 25. I had no personal knowledge of the information you requested and was unable to immediately contact my uncle, who was on holidays, or my father, who no longer resides in Prince George. Both are retired.

It appears your inquiries concern my uncle, Robert, who I never knew, and that your information may be substantially correct. Both my father and my uncle Stephen recall that Robert was involved with a young woman – a rather "messy involvement," in the words of my father. Their recollection is that there was a threat of pregnancy and an attempt to coerce their brother – who was barely out of his teens at the time – into marriage, and, when that failed, an attempt at extortion. Neither my father or my uncle Stephen can recall having had any knowledge at the time of there actually being a birth, or having any knowledge of the woman in question following the rupture in her relationship with my uncle Robert.

The fact that you have obtained our family's name – and I would be most interested to know how you obtained it – would appear to indicate there may be some basis to your claim, however.

My uncle Robert, I'm sorry to say, was killed in the Korean War. He enlisted – against the desires of his family, I should add – soon after the entanglement with the woman and was killed very soon after arriving in Korea with the Princess Pats.

Neither my father nor my uncle Stephen have any interest in having direct contact with you, but I would be willing to provide you with more information – limited though it may be – if you can satisfy me that your claim is valid. Perhaps you could forward to me a copy of your birth certificate and any other information you may have at your disposal that would serve as evidence to support your claim.

I must caution you to carefully consider, however, exactly what it is you want from the DeNiro family.

Sincerely yours,

Frank G. DeNiro

She wrote back immediately.

Dear cousin Frank,

I take the liberty of addressing you that way because it seems obvious to me that we *are* cousins. I'm enclosing a copy of a document provided to me by the Human Resources Ministry. I believe it speaks for itself as to the validity of my "claim," as you put it. I fully understand your surprise and discomfort, so forgive my pique for the tone of your letter.

As to what I "want" from the DeNiro family, rest assured it is not a share in the estate or a place at the table. As I write, there are tears in my eyes, not tears of grief to learn my birth father is dead – my adoptive father, who was a kind, thoughtful man who, by his presence in the absence of the other, became my "real" father, died many years ago and I don't intend, emotionally or intellectually, to mourn a father again – but tears of confusion. I don't *know* what I want, damn it, from the DeNiro family, the city of Prince George, the province of British Columbia, the universe, fates and so on *ad infinitum*.

I started out wanting to find – *know* – my birth mother. I must confess my natural father never entered into my thinking until, in my pursuit of her, I came across his trail. His involvement with me, despite good intentions, appears to have been little more than insemination and perhaps a bit of financial support – and the circumstances surrounding that are far from clear. If I am "flesh of his flesh," as the Bible puts it, it is tissue connection of the flimsiest in nature, genes and nothing more. To my mother, despite what *may* have been poor intentions, I am joined by flesh, blood, bone and sinew. Emotional webbing. Sisterhood. History.

I apologize for this outburst. A photograph of your uncle Robert – my father – would be very much appreciated. The surname of my mother – and any other information about her your father and uncle

Stephen can recall – is what I really want; that would be the end of my involvement with you.

Fondly,

(Cousin) Kathleen

But she didn't mail that letter and the one she replaced it with was considerably more circumspect.

Even Keith, who had faith in the symmetry of the universe, its ability to unfold itself not only inexorably but in patterns that are discernible, said it was too easy, what happened next, laughing not only at the tone of the second letter from the young lawyer DeNiro but at its implications.

"It's like Sherlock Holmes getting a clue in the mail," he said, handing the letter back to her. "'Check out redheads,' something like that. Where's the fun to that? Sherlock would toss that out, try to forget it."

"Right, and back to the Polk without a clue. Sherlock never turned his back on a clue, Le Strade."

And it *was* easy, almost as if someone was leading her by the hand. "The woman my uncle Robert was involved with was named Alice Malloy," her cousin's letter said. "My father remembers that much, and that she came from Kelowna. As my father and uncle are adamant in their refusal to have any direct contact with you, I'm really afraid there's little more in which I can be of service to you. I'm enclosing a photograph of my uncle Robert, taken shortly before he left for Korea, which I hope will be of some comfort to you. Should your search bring you to P.G., feel free to give me a call."

The photograph was blurry and faded, and the face of the young man in uniform it depicted was vague as a smudged thumbprint. He stood at a sort of parody of attention, the trousers and sleeves of his uniform too short for his long limbs. Beneath his service cap, a shock of unruly black hair was clearly visible, and, below that, a strong, longish nose and many, many teeth. Kathy wondered if her kin in Prince George had selected the best photo available or deliberately sent the worst. She shook her head over the blurred grin and held it against her breasts, as if her heart were a special decoding machine.

She went back to the library. In the 1952 Kelowna Polk she found a hardware store owned by Peter Malloy. In the residential listings, she found his address at 427 Ridge, and his wife, Margaret. Kathy wrote that name in her notebook and gazed at it intently: Margaret Malloy – this was the grandmother, she was certain, the woman who had refused to allow her daughter and her child into their house.

She found them in the 1952 telephone book and up through 1977, then they disappeared. There were other Malloys, over a dozen. She wrote vague letters to them, expressing a desire to contact Alice, the daughter of Peter and Margaret Malloy. Was she kin to them? Could they help?

While she waited replies, she turned to the microfilm of *The Kelowna Record*, starting with August, 1953. The weddings and the engagements were reported on Saturdays, not many that summer, but a growing number in the fall and winter, many more the following spring. And that May, this item:

Malloy-Lally

Peter and Margaret Malloy are pleased to announce the engagement of their daughter Mildred to Daniel Lally Jr., son of Daniel and Mary Lally Sr. The wedding is to take place July 6, 1954, at St. Mary's Catholic Church.

She found Daniel Lally in the 1954 phone book. The following year, there were two Daniels. The Polk listed the new one as a roofer, his wife Mildred. She traced them through the phone books, addresses changing, the older Daniel disappearing in 1982, the younger remaining, the listing still there. She telephoned.

"Oh, God," the woman said. "Is this some kind of a lousy joke?"

"It isn't. Would you rather I wrote? I shouldn't have called, but I've been looking so long and I found your name and number today and I just couldn't resist."

"Alice is – was – my older sister, but I don't know anything about a baby. What did you say your name was, honey?"

"Kathleen Logan. My adoptive name was Hindemith but that wouldn't mean anything to you. I was born in Vancouver. I know your mother and father knew, but maybe the other children didn't."

"I certainly never knew anything about something like that. Listen, honey, you should talk to my sister Lou. She's the oldest. But honey, listen, didn't you know Alice was dead?"

Kathy blinked. She'd known from the beginning that was possible, but she hadn't believed it would be that way. "No, Mildred, I had no way of knowing."

"Oh, sure. If she *was* your mother, I'm sorry to be the one to tell you, honey. You shoulda started looking sooner. She just died a coupla months ago."

"God," Kathy said.

"She had a good life. Listen, you call Lou. She lives in Winnipeg. I'll give you her number."

"And your mother? Is she still alive?"

"The Gorgon? Are you kidding? She'll never die. But don't you go anywhere near her, honey, not if you want to keep your head."

Kathy called Lou. There was a long silence after she explained. "Kathy, is it? What d'ya look like?"

"I'm short. A little overweight right now, but usually I'm okay. I have small bones. My hair's light brown and wispy. Green eyes."

"She died, you know."

"Mildred told me. My timing was lousy."

"She never forgot you, honey. She didn't talk about you – her husband and kids never knew. But she didn't forget. *I* know that. What's that?"

"Nothing," Kathy said. "I'm just crying."

Somewhere in the night, a car door slammed, and Kathy awoke with a start, the memory of the evening before spilling out before her like a spool of thread in the paws of a kitten. For a few seconds, she couldn't get a deep enough breath, a hand on her chest, an old feeling of panic pulling at her groin like minnows nibbling at her toes in the lake when she was a child. She felt as if she were drowning, her whole life flashing before her eyes as they said it would, not in a steady stream but jerkily, one frozen image after another, photographic cards quickly dealt on a playing table, but the scenes they depicted were not of her, her own life, but another one, totally foreign, a life that could have been hers, a life unlived.

Beside her, Keith lay heavily beneath the blankets like a log submerged in water, both harmless and lethal, his breath light as the flutter of air brushed into motion by the first raindrops, and Kathy let her hand slide across the sheet and touch his hip, feeling the solidity of bone beneath the soft layers of flannel, skin, and flesh. It remained to be seen if he would stay as sweet as he was or go the way of Herbert, or the man she'd known briefly between them. Nonetheless, that anchor allowed her mind to stop spinning, and the farthest reaches of her lungs opened, letting in the insistent air with a rush satisfying as orgasm. She lay still, gathering resolve, hearing again Byrna's high laugh, seeing the wonder in Terri's eyes as they'd scrolled back and forth from face to face. "Mom, it's *you*," the girl had said the moment they came to the table. She hadn't seen it herself – there was a resemblance, yes, a similarity of features that was interesting but not conclusive, but as she lay in darkness seeing the wideness of Terri's green eyes again, eyes so much like her own, eyes so much like those of the stranger across the table, her daughter's certainty translated itself into her own. "I really am that woman's sister," she thought.

The glowing phosphorus hands of the bedside clock read 3:47 a.m., obscenely early, but sleep seemed unlikely to return. She slid her legs to the side of the bed and got up with as little disturbance to the covers as she could. She made her way down the dark hallway to the bathroom and groped for her robe, big shapeless terrycloth, then to the study, turning on the lamp above her desk, where she did her work. Even through her child-rearing years, she'd kept her hand in, freelancing, and when she'd left Herbert she'd fallen easily into the other side, writing newsletters and speeches for a number of organizations and companies before landing a permanent job with the bank, which, of course, had led to Keith. Here in Vancouver, she'd mustered up the courage to label herself a "consultant," freelancing PR again from home, which suited her just fine. After a year, she had enough business to occupy half her day, which again suited her.

She turned on the computer and went through the familiar ritual, calling up program and directory. There were over two dozen items in the directory called *Mum-hunt*, mostly letters. She gazed at the familiar list for a moment before getting up and walking to the window, opening the curtain, and staring out into the dark, empty street. Sometimes when she couldn't sleep, Keith long since gone to the world, she'd stood by this window and imagined she could feel the presence of kindred spirits, other night people like her standing by similar windows in similar houses staring at similar streets elsewhere in the city, throughout the coastline and mountains and valleys of British Columbia, throughout Canada, the world, thousands of people staring out into darkness, their eyes reflecting the same empty street, bound by a commonality tough as cat gut – imagined that she was part of some community of loneliness. Tonight, perhaps because it was so much later, or because she'd slept, or had wine with dinner, the street was darker, its emptiness more a presence than an absence, and, though she pressed her ear to the cool glass, she could hear no sound of traffic on Marine Drive, just half a block away, and the world seemed truly devoid of life, as if she was not part of some common herd separated by walls, streets, rivers and oceans, but the only person alive on the face of the Earth.

She slipped back into the bedroom to collect her cords and a T-shirt and took them with her to the bathroom, where she brushed her teeth and showered, letting the stinging spray wash away the last vestige of breathlessness. In the kitchen, moving easily in the combination of natural light of dawn seeping in through the east window and the small fluorescent light on the stove hood, she put up coffee, drank orange juice, made two slices of lightly buttered toast, nibbling on one piece as she waited for the coffee, then sat down in the eating nook, which, in another hour, would be bright and cheerful but now was diffused with thin grey light giving the air around her the soft quality of gauze. Finally, after her second cup of coffee, the pulsing numbers on the clock radio said 5 a.m., and she pulled the telephone from the shelf.

Ruth answered on the fourth ring, sounding not sleepy but distracted. "Yes."

"Aren't you awake *yet*? It's eight in the morning, for Chrissake."

"You know I am. What are *you* doing up, Kath? God, it must be the middle of the night in Lotus Land. Conscience bothering you?"

"You know I don't have a conscience."

"Living in a rain forest, who knows, you might have grown one."

"Soil's not fertile enough."

"Miracles can happen."

"You know it. I had dinner with my sister last night."

"Your sis… you found your mother!"

"Yes and no."

"Yes?"

"I found her."

"And the no?"

"She died two months ago."

"Oh, Kath, no. I'm so sorry."

"Do you believe in vibrations? Not spirits, necessarily, but vibrations? Maybe it's just electricity?"

"You know I do. Hold on a second, I was just making coffee."

Kathy's gaze fell on the calendar on the wall, from Van City, each month a child's drawing of peace. August's was a chunky pink unicorn rearing up beneath a four-coloured rainbow in a field of scribble flowers. The unicorn's horn was short and shaped like a football, or maybe it was supposed to be a bomb? She thought of Ruth, her swirl of black hair greyish now and cut close to her scalp, like a slightly rounded Brillo pad. She'd like that picture – unicorns were her specialty.

"I'm back."

"Ruth, she died June 17, just a week before Terri's graduation. That was the night she came into my mind, while I was watching and being a proud mother."

"I remember, you said."

"Is that crazy?"

"No. Maybe it's wonderful. Not that she's dead, but...."

"It wasn't anything horrendous. Not cancer, I mean, or a stroke. She had rheumatic fever when she was a child and her heart was always weak. She got a cold, and that turned to pneumonia, and one morning she just didn't wake up. She was sixty-eight, and Byrna said she'd been fine up until then, healthy and happy. It's better to go that way than the way *my* mother is, almost ten years older than that and shrivelled up and sick and hurting all the time, or without even the comfort of memory, if you can call that a comfort. Damn." She turned her head, as if to hide the sight of the sudden tears from the telephone, and there was silence for a moment. Then: "Byrna said they never expected her to live that long. There were three kids, and Byrna said she could never keep up with housework and things the way other mothers did."

"Byrna?"

"That's the sister. Half-sister. I don't see much resemblance but, God, Ruth, you should have seen Terri. She looked like she'd seen a ghost. All through dinner she kept staring at her and whispering to me: 'Mom, it's you, it's *you.*'"

"You had dinner together?"

"Last night. I've hardly been able to sleep a wink. She only lives in the valley, down in Pitt Meadows."

"Is she nice?"

"God!"

"Oh."

"I shouldn't be such a snob."

"You shouldn't be. But how do you stop a lifetime of habit?"

157

"Her husband's a car salesman. Really. Not *used*, but it might as well be. Al."

"Oh. Al and Verna."

"Byrna. With a B and a Y. Al and Byrna. Al said it was too bad they didn't live in Calgary so they could be Al and Byrna from Alberta."

"Oh, God."

"'That's what I always say.' Great fellow, Al. He and Keith got along famously. You know Keith when he gets into his good-old-boy mode. Thank God for that. They amused each other talking machinery. Terri just gawked."

"And Byrna from Alberta dispensed family secrets?"

"Such as they are. It's all exactly as I imagined. Everything very ordinary. Christ, Ruth, this is not exactly the search for Anastasia or Bridey Murphy. Speaking of which, can you believe my mother's name was Malloy? Ordinary, very ordinary."

"So what kind of an Irish name is Byrna, with a B and a Y?"

"Mumsie married a Svedish fella, Lars Svenson, dontcha know? Honest to God. A carpenter. They had a little white house with a picket fence in Chilliwack and three little white children with picket smiles. All disgustingly ordinary. With me there would have been four little Svensons."

"But you would have been DeNiro, right? Kathleen DeNiro? Son of Robert DeNiro. If they'd married, I mean. And to think, I *know* you."

"But they didn't. I would have been Kathy Malloy if she'd kept me, hard as nails, and a brogue thick as porridge, thank ye. God, all that WASP upbringing, and now it turns out I'm a regular ethnic hotpot."

"I think I'd have liked Kathy Malloy."

"You'd better have. She'da kicked the bloody bejesus outta you if you hadn't. With all that Irish and Italian in me, I don't know how I ever got on with a kike like you. God, I might have grown up to be like Byrna, instead of the wonderful, talented, fascinating creature I am. Kathleen Malloy DeNiro Svenson Hindemith Alcorn Logan, that's me."

"Just like an onion, Kathy darling."

"I make you cry, Ruthie baby?"

"*Layers*, dear. Lots of layers."

"Yeah, that's happened to me, too."

They laughed, and, for the first time since about five in the afternoon the day before, as she was dressing for dinner, choosing the blue-and-white patterned dress and the white silk scarf with the same practiced eye she used when dressing for a meeting with a client, she felt the rigid bar wedged in her crotch and extending upward through belly and diaphragm to her throat soften, like a fist beginning to open. That fist, she was sure, had been closing for weeks, wrapping itself around possibilities and squeezing them shut.

"So what now?" Ruth said. "Granma?"

"The Gorgon? I dunno. Everybody keeps steering me away from her like she was Attila the Hun. She's eighty-six and still lives in her own house, with the youngest daughter, who everyone describes as 'a spinster and so lucky to have Momma to be of use to.' Congratulate me – I finally have a spinster aunt. It's enough to make you puke."

"Nice family you're worming your way into."

"I thought the *Hindemiths* were respectable and dull."

"It's only your friends you get to pick, darling. Can you hear my eyelids batting?"

"No, I can pick this family or not pick them. Or pick *on* them. I can worm my way into their bosom, as you so subtly put it, or I can turn my somewhat lumpy back on them. Some nights I smile myself to sleep daydreaming about flying up to Prince George and parachuting into my uncle the good doctor DeNiro's front yard, my skirts blowing up in the wind and no pants on. Scandalize the life out of the old fart. 'Just making a house call, uncle. My mother's daughter, after all. Tart runs in the family.'"

"I thought you didn't care about the DeNiros."

"I don't, but that's the point, isn't it, Ruthie? Can *you* say, 'Oh, I don't care a fig for my father's family'? Can anybody, without covering their heads first to ward off the pile of bird guilt that will be dumped upon them? But I can. They're not connected to me, except by some stupid accident of biology. Hey, it's the latest fad: no-guilt family, and I've got the patent."

"And the … what is it? Malloys?"

"That's another story, Ruthie baby."

"And the end of the story? Come on, I'm breathless."

"I don't know what the end is. Grannie *is* eighty-six years old, after all. Byrna's pretty sure nobody's told her about me yet, although the rest of the family is buzzing. If I call her, she might have a heart attack. *That* would make me guilty."

"And what does she have that you want anyway?"

"Ah, Dr. Ruth, with her uncanny ability to penetrate the fog and put her finger four inches from the heart of the matter, on the spleen."

"And?"

"I don't *know*, damn it. What do you expect from me, responsible adulthood?"

"The child is the mother of the woman, my dear."

They laughed again. "Thanks for this," Kathy said. She put the receiver back in its cradle and poured herself another cup of coffee. It was full daylight now, traffic was moving in jerks and starts on the street, and around her the house seemed to be stirring like a child whose brittle-edged dreams were drawing it smoothly and fishlike toward the surface. Keith would be up soon, yawning and scratching and shuffling like some aloof bear in a circus act, going through his toilet with his back to the audience. Then Terri, her eyes so damn green and sharp the ferns always seemed to wilt in shame and envy beside her. She'd be gone in another few weeks, off to university, and the nest Kathy had fouled herself would be empty again. Somewhere out *there*, to the vague and distant east, her boys were probably up already, leading their separate lives, clumsily fitting their limbs into garments they'd skilfully bought to fit, or found girlfriends clever enough to do for them.

That had been their biggest complaint, both of them, thirteen and fifteen, when she'd walked out on Herbert. *Needing space of her own, it's her turn now, mommy and daddy don't love each other any more, that was all well and good and* their *affair, after all, but who's going to buy our clothes, mom,* dad *can't do it.* When they'd moved in with her two years later, after all those stupid negotiations, it was her hands they'd seemed most relieved to be reunited with, dishwater hands, mending fingers, and whatever hurt there may have been between them, betrayals, seemed to be able to be squeezed out with the pressure of their hands on hers. Terri had been different, of course, younger and a girl, already starting to rub up against Kathy at the time of the breakup, she'd been even more fiercely loyal to their father than the boys, the last one to see through him. Then, rejoining with Kathy, six months after the boys, had been a reflowering, not just a coming-back-together but a going-beyond, a miracle.

She stood by the kitchen window gazing out at a delivery truck that had pulled up across the street, wondering if the material for the same kind of miracle between herself and her grandmother was in one of those boxes, ready to be delivered, and feeling connected again, a part of *something* out there, even if she didn't know what it was.

Last night, Byrna had been cagey, willing to believe, but not certain she wanted to, and that was okay, Kathy hadn't expected open arms, tears, and one of those newspaper feature-page reunions soggy as stale bread with hugs and kisses. Byrna hadn't brought a photograph, denying Kathy the one tangible thing she *did* want – "We never were big on picture-taking in our family, but I know I've got one or two *somewhere.* I'll find them, I promise." They'd get together again – "There's so much to talk about," Byrna kept saying, though very little was actually said – and there was even talk of a sort of family gathering, at Thanksgiving, perhaps, or Christmas, Byrna's brother and sister, *all dying to meet you,* Aunt Mildred and maybe Aunt Lou, maybe some of the other aunts and uncles and cousins, though it wasn't clear how far the story had spread, how many of them were willing to listen.

She found herself thinking of the grandmother again – *her* grandmother, Margaret Malloy, distant and aloof, her arms folded across her breast like some kind of Celtic warrior, eyes narrow and hard as the Blarney stone, whatever

161

the hell *that* was. "You were the one," Kathy said, surprised to actually hear the words, loud and harsh in the kitchen as a rap on the door. "You were the one who said no, damn you, just like you were a goddamn condom and you could shut off life, just like that, just like it didn't matter."

She turned away from the window, blinking fiercely. "Memory or blueprint," the smug lady at Terri's graduation had said, and that was fine enough, but how the hell do you *read* blueprints if you haven't been to architectural school, tell me that, smug lady? Well, it didn't matter. She knew – with suddenness and clarity sharp as an alarm clock knifing through sleep – that she *would* read the thing, make up her blueprint as she went along, just the way she always had. She picked up her coffee mug and headed for the den, starting to compose the letter to her grandmother in her mind. The letter itself wasn't the important thing, knowing what to ask was, of her or anyone else, knowing what she wanted – as cousin Frank had so bluntly put it, clever fellows those lawyers – and that, she knew, lay outside the walls of the house, not within it, out *there*, where she was going, not where she'd already been.

A Distant Relation

THE SAME YEAR, late in the last century, that my grandfather left his wife and children to cross the ocean to New York, where it was thought he might make a better life, his brother, whose name was Isaac, left his family as well and went, with a similar purpose, to Montreal.

The two brothers had never been close. As children, only two among many brothers and sisters on a farm, they had been rivals for their often-absent father's attention, and as adults they had little in common – Joseph, my grandfather, a writer and an intellectual of sorts, Isaac a brawler and a fixer, good with his hands. This, apparently, was the extent of what my grandfather had to say about this brother. They did not have any direct contact, but, through other relatives, they heard news of each other, and, consequently, my father was dimly, disinterestedly, aware that he had an uncle and aunt, a brood of cousins, in Canada. Why one brother had come to one North American country while the other went to the other, my father didn't know – perhaps their destinations had merely been an accident. All he did know, in fact, was that he had relatives in Montreal, a city that, while it was considerably closer, seemed as distant and exotic as the cities of Poland and Russia that figured in *his* father's recollections. In his own travels, north into upstate New York and New Hampshire, and west into Ohio and, eventually, to Chicago, my father never gave these relatives a thought.

So when, early in 1930, he met his cousin Reuben one

evening in the crowded Automat on East Broadway, he was flabbergasted. They were first cousins, sons of brothers, with a noticeable similarity in the shape of their face and features, but the distance between them was more than one merely to be measured in miles or the texture of blood.

My father, who was a reporter at *The Day*, was with his friend Vogel, his counterpart at *The Forward*, the Socialist paper. Together, the two men, rivals but friends, kept their eyes on the city's teeming garment district and their boisterous, muscular unions. On this night, they were eating together because, within the hour, they were due at a meeting of Local 37, the cutters, who were agitating for a strike within the industry – the merits of which my father, who was opposed, and Vogel, who was enthusiastically in support, were arguing. My father was eating hotdogs and beans, for which he had deposited three nickels into the slots beside the glass window, one of dozens of such windows in the wall separating the dining area from the kitchen. On his tray was a cup of almost white coffee, from which he sipped as he ate, and a bowl of red Jello with a crown of whipped cream; both of these had cost a nickel extra. He had squeezed bright yellow mustard over his plate and was eating with gusto, aiding his fork with a crust of bread.

Vogel, who rarely ate, was slurping from a cup of black coffee and chain-smoking cigarettes. He was a small man, little larger than a child, with a narrow skull, and already had the same nervous mannerisms which, years later, when I would come to know him, were always so noticeable: a twitch in his eyelid, an irritation in his ear that made him continuously tap at the base of his jaw with his fingertips. Both men were in their thirties, my father a year or two older than his friend, unmarried, dressed in dark suits and ties, in good health, their hair still thick and dark, though my father's was beginning to both fade and thin.

To their table now stepped a man who, my father would later say, when he recounted this story, he looked up at with a shock of recognition. He had never seen the man before, but knew with certainty that there was a link between them.

"So, you're Morgenstern?" the man said, in Yiddish, a

vaguely accusing tone in his odd voice that suggested he would not accept a denial.

"Sure," my father said. "And you? I know you, maybe?"

"You know me, no," the man replied, allowing a small lifting at the edge of his lips, lips that were remarkably like my father's own. "I'm your cousin, Rueben, from Montreal." The man was about my father's age, perhaps a few years younger, and, like my father, was of medium height, medium build. He was wearing a dirty wool overcoat, dark blue but with a jaunty red stripe running along the bottom and rubber galoshes, the buckles undone. He extended his hand. "I asked for you at *The Day*. A very nice young woman said I might find you here. I worried how I would know you but she said I shouldn't, that I would know you immediately. She was right."

"There is a slight resemblance," my father allowed, reluctant, for reasons he couldn't then fathom, to admit how great it was. "But tell me, Reuben, how did you even know of me? I knew I had relatives in Montreal, but not their names or anything about them. Yet you knew of me, knew where to find me."

My father's cousin emitted what struck the other two men as a peculiarly mirthless laugh. "Come now, Morgenstern, don't be so modest. People in all directions of the compass read the works of your illustrious father and brother in the pages of *The Day* and *The Morning Journal*. Even in Canada, even in Montreal."

"That I can believe," my father said. "And me?"

Reuben shook his head in protest. "Again, false modesty, cousin. Even you, though you've changed your name, are well known."

Reuben excused himself and went to get a cup of coffee for himself and second cups for my father and Vogel. The two friends exchanged glances. "A flatterer," Vogel said, with obvious distaste. "This one, I don't like the looks of, Morgenstern."

My father laughed. "He looks just like *me*."

"Looks like is one thing," Vogel said, tapping his jaw. "It's the look in his eye I don't like."

Reuben returned with the coffees on a tray and sat down. The two cousins exchanged news of their families, and, while my father finished his meal, he learned that his uncle had died but his aunt by marriage still enjoyed her health and that he had half a dozen cousins in addition to Reuben, all grown, most of them still in Montreal. The family business, a furrier shop, had fallen on hard times, however, and had recently closed its doors. When my father pushed aside his tray and lit a cigarette, the cousin leaned forward and lowered his voice. "I could have a private word with you, maybe? It's a matter of... what would you say? Delicacy?"

"Don't mind me," Vogel said, implying that he might merely turn away and not listen, but he rose and joined two other men at a nearby table, Singer, the novelist, and Javelit, a compositor at *The Forward*.

"Delicacy means one of two things," my father said, not unkindly. "Women or money. Or both."

His cousin smiled ruefully. Like my father, his hair was starting to recede from his high forehead, and he passed his palm over his skull now in a nervous gesture, patting the hair into place – a gesture my father recognized with a shock as identical to one of his own father's. "Right on both counts. It's taken all my savings to bring us to New York. Things are not so good in Montreal. The shop, as I told you, closed, and I haven't been able to find anything. I hoped things would be better here."

"I might be able to help you find something," my father interrupted. "I know some people."

"That would be wonderful," Reuben said, looking grateful. "In the meantime, there's a place to live to worry about. Food on the table. For myself, I wouldn't ask. I have a wife, a child."

My father allowed himself a moment to think of his own father and the uncle he'd never met, men who had left their families behind while they sought their fortune in another country. Why would this man take his wife and child with him, he wondered, exposing them to whatever risk there might be? He also thought about Reuben's other options. My father was far from the man's only relative in New York, of course. He thought of his own father, who was famous for his parsimoniousness. He thought of his older brother, but approaching Sam for a loan would be akin to slamming a door on one's own foot. He thought of his younger brothers, but Izzy had a young wife and two small children of his own and Henry was in law school, and was himself the recipient of occasional assistance from my father. "Certainly I can lend you some money," he said.

"Loan, of course," Reuben said quickly. "I'm not asking for a gift. I'm not asking for charity. It's a loan, and I ask only because of the woman and child. That should be understood."

"Of course," my father said. "Understood. How much do you need?"

Reuben didn't hesitate. "Fifty dollars is the sum I had in mind. Is it too much? We could manage on forty. Fifty would give me more time to find something. It sounds like a lot, maybe...."

My father held up his hand. "That's all right. I can manage fifty. Better that, than you should have to borrow somewhere else later, or have to come back to me. I don't have that much with me, of course."

It should be understood that fifty dollars was a fairly large sum of money at the time, what five hundred would be today, or a thousand. But, as it happened, my father was doing well, even though it was only a few months since men in expensive suits had plummeted through the air from tall buildings a short walk from where they now sat. It was an anomaly he would eventually pay for, but, at the height of the Depression, a few years later, he would be making close to one hundred dollars a week and he earned not far from that now. He lived modestly, in a boarding house, not out of meanness but because of the convenience, and often ate in restaurants, but his tastes were far from expensive. He had no automobile and few women friends, though he had recently made the acquaintance of the woman who would be my mother. What money he did spend was in the cafés and bars of the Lower East Side and along Broadway, at the theatre, which he often frequented, and at the used bookshops along

East Broadway and Orchard Street where he would often spend more than he should on a rare edition.

He gave his newly found cousin ten dollars from his wallet and made a date to meet him the next afternoon, after he could make a withdrawal from his bank. Reuben pocketed the money, thanked my father profusely and excused himself. "My wife will be so happy," he said in parting. "It will make her happy to know she's married to a man with generous relatives. Family is worth more than wealth, the Bible got that right."

My father lit another cigarette and drank the last of his coffee, now cold. He looked at his watch. Vogel sat down beside him. "Money?" he asked, his eyelid twitching.

"What else?"

"From that one, Morgenstern, you won't get it back."

"A regular Sigmund Freud you are, such a judge of character."

"Character has nothing to do with, Morgenstern. Even the Bible says don't lend money. Or borrow it, either."

"Oh ho, Vogel, now you're an expert on the Bible. Have you ever actually seen a copy? I can lend you a nice edition."

"You can laugh, but I don't like the looks of him. You won't get it back."

"You can be so sure, Vogel?"

"From that one? Yes. Besides" – Vogel swatted at his cheek – "with money, you never get it back."

During the following weeks, my father had little reason to think of his cousin, as he was finding himself increasingly preoccupied with someone else. Not long before the meeting in the Automat, he had attended a gathering of the cutters union at which Marcantonio, the city's Communist councilman, gave a speech. Afterwards, a klezmer band took the stage, and my father, although he didn't dance, *wouldn't* dance, stayed to have a drink and a bite, to watch the swirling skirts of the girls on the dance floor, before heading to the office to write his story. A man he knew, not that much older than he was, a rabble-rouser in the union named

Shalley, was there in the company of two attractive young women, and my father approached them with a wink.

"Shalley, you're more of a man than I am if you can handle two women at one time."

Shalley was ordinarily a sour man with little good to say on any subject, but tonight, in the glow of Marcantonio's speech and the growing sentiment for a strike, he seemed almost merry. He had escaped from a prison in Russia, killing a guard, my father had heard, and had been expelled from both Britain and France for his activities, making him no mere trifler.

"And two more at home, Morgenstern, just as pretty," Shalley said slyly.

"You mean these are your daughters?" my father said, with genuine surprise. Shalley was the most ordinary looking of men, but the girls, especially one, my father thought, were lovely, with flashing eyes and long, wavy hair, one of them a redhead, the other a brunette.

"Sure, they're my daughters, who else's daughters should they be?"

One of them, the brunette, surprised him further by extending her hand. "I'm Berte," she said. "This is my sister Mars."

My father shook the woman's hand and exchanged a glance with her that he felt all the way into his shoulder.

"Here," Shalley said, wrenching his daughter free from my father's grip, "dance with one of them." With that, he took her in his arms and went spinning off to the circular rhythm of the clarinet, leaving my father standing dumbstruck with the other young woman, the redhead.

"I'm sorry, I, I don't dance," my father stammered. "Let me buy you a drink."

"Come on, one dance won't kill you," the young woman said. Her mouth was very red and she smiled in a wry, lopsided manner.

"No, really, I don't dance," my father said. "I'd kill you." He looked over the woman's shoulder in the direction that Shalley and his other daughter had spun. "I'm sorry, what did she say her name was?"

"Berte," the sister said, laughing. *"She'll* get you to dance."

A few weeks after they met in the Automat, my father had a telephone call from his cousin inviting him to dinner. Reuben and his small family had taken up residence in a furnished apartment in Brooklyn, a few blocks from Flatbush Avenue, an area my father was familiar with because his brother Izzy had his dental supply shop not too far away. On the appointed evening, he left work at a little after four, bought a bottle of good red wine at a liquor store on East Broadway, and strolled slowly toward the subway, enjoying the pleasant early spring air, damp with the melting of a late snow. Even on the dirty, slushy streets of the Lower East Side, redolent with the smells of cooking cabbage and beets and fish, and crowded with people hurrying home for supper, the coming of spring could be sensed, and my father had reason to feel pleased with himself. He took a Lexington Avenue subway to 14th Street, where he transferred to the IRT for the trip under the East River into Brooklyn. When he emerged into the air again, it was already dark and the temperature had dropped a few degrees, forcing him to raise the collar of his raincoat.

Once off Flatbush, the streets, with their trees still bare, were deserted, the buildings narrow, like men standing with their shoulders hunched. He found the address his cousin had provided, a three-story walkup on Utica Avenue, with no difficulty, and climbed the stairs to the top floor. Reuben opened the door at the first knock, almost as if he had been standing close by, awaiting my father's arrival. "Morgenstern, come in, come in," he boomed, too heartily, my father thought. "Wine? That's too kind. Let me take your coat. Come, meet the wife."

My father was ushered into the fragrant kitchen and into the presence of a petite, very attractive young woman with blond hair twisted into a neat bun, and a noticeable bust beneath her modest white shirtwaist and apron. She was standing by the stove, upon which a pot was steaming, a large stirring spoon in her hand. "Morgenstern, my wife, Rachel. Rachel, this is my famous cousin, Harry Morgenstern, our generous benefactor."

"Hardly famous," my father said, surprised to find himself blushing. He offered his hand to the woman, as he had to my mother, but she lowered her eyes shyly and held up the stirring spoon by way of excuse. The aroma of cooking onions brought saliva flooding to his tongue.

"Famous enough," Reuben said, "and certainly our benefactor."

After the usual pleasantries, the two men retired to the shabby living room, its furniture threadbare and sprung, while the cousin's wife returned to her cooking. The walls were bare of decoration, there was no telephone and there were no toys or articles of children's clothing littering the floor. A bottle of whisky, rye cheaper than my father would ever buy, was produced, and Reuben, who was tieless and in shirtsleeves, poured shots for my father and himself.

"*Lechayyim,*" he said, raising his glass.

"*Lechayyim,*" my father repeated, glancing around the dimly lit room.

Through the meal that followed, served on a cloth-covered table in the warm, humid kitchen, there was no sign of and no mention of the couple's child. The furrier job that my father had helped his cousin find had not turned out well and he was again unemployed, but the table conversation was light, filled with talk of the looming strike in the garment trade and anecdotes of life in Montreal, which seemed not all that unlike New York. These latter were related by Reuben in English, in an accent my father realized was as much influenced by French as by Yiddish. The wine he'd brought went well with the fatty pot roast with potatoes and onions Rachel had prepared, which she served with a salad of wilted lettuce and onions tossed with sweetened vinegar, and slices of dark bread, still warm from the oven. Rachel contributed little to the conversation, but she followed it closely with an alert pair of eyes that were a startling shade of green, and, as the meal progressed, her shyness seemed to fade, favouring my father several times with a bold, direct glance that, had she not been married, and had he not been interested in the woman he'd met at the dance, would have thrilled him.

"An excellent meal," my father said, finishing his wine and placing a hand over his glass as Reuben proffered the bottle, a few more mouthfuls remaining in the bottom. "I'm curious, Rachel. How is it that your child is so well behaved? When I visit my brother Izzy, his children are all over me. I haven't heard a peep from yours all evening. You have a little girl or a little boy?"

Rachel seemed momentarily confused by my father's question, her face reddening, and her husband quickly interjected: "Oh, our son is with a neighbour. Just for the evening. Yes, we have a son. He's our pride, but he's no better behaved than your brother's children, of that I can assure you. When we have company, we find it's better to have the boy elsewhere."

There was a look in his cousin's eye that immediately recalled for my father Vogel's comment the night they'd met Reuben at the Automat, and for the first time he felt he knew what his friend had meant. He'd already assumed it would be a long time before he saw his fifty dollars again, but that didn't particularly concern him.

"I didn't mean that I minded my nephew and niece," my father said, turning to his cousin's wife, who was gathering up plates.

"No, no, I understand," Reuben said. "But adult talk is better left to adults, don't you agree? Perhaps the next time you honour us with your company."

Rachel served coffee to the two men, who took their cracked and chipped cups and saucers into the living room. No milk or sugar was offered, and my father, sitting in an uncomfortable easy chair, thought better than to request them. The sounds of Rachel moving about the kitchen, pouring a bucket of water heated on the stove into the sink, scraping dishes, punctuated the silence that fell on the room as they sipped the bitter coffee.

"We'll have to do something about finding you another job," my father said eventually.

"That's not necessary, Morgenstern, I have prospects of my own."

"As you wish."

"If it's the money I owe you...."

My father held up a hand. "Believe me, Reuben, that's the farthest thought from my mind."

"Not from mine, I can assure you."

The cousin got up and went to the kitchen door, whispering a few words to his wife in what my father took to be French. When he turned back to his guest, he was rolling down his sleeves and buttoning them. "If you'll excuse me, Morgenstern, I have an appointment right now to speak to a man about a job."

My father, taken by surprise, started to rise but his cousin waved him back into his chair. "Don't go, please. I won't be long. Finish your coffee, at least. Honour my wife with your company."

"If you put it that way, how can I refuse?" my father said, smiling.

Reuben slipped on his suit jacket, its elbows shiny, took the distinctive overcoat with the red stripe from the same doorless closet my father's coat and hat had disappeared into, and, without a further word, left the apartment.

My father, uncertain as to what was expected of him, took a sip of his coffee, then set the cup and saucer down on a rickety coffee table, which was otherwise bare. On an impulse, he rose and strode to the room's one window, which looked out on the deserted street three floors below, lit by the yellow glow of a street lamp, but, even after several minutes, there was no sign of his cousin. Gradually, he became aware that the sounds from the kitchen had ceased, and that he was not alone in the room.

He turned, smiling, starting to speak, "Ah, Rachel," but he was silenced by what he saw. His hostess stood in the kitchen doorway, completely naked, her long blond hair loosened, her green-eyed gaze directly on him, like a challenge.

"The bedroom's through that way," she said after a moment, nodding her head to the left. "Reuben won't be back for a while."

My father's eyes fastened on the woman's breasts for a moment, then he tore them away. "What, are you crazy?" he demanded.

"I'm not crazy."

"No? What are you then, if not crazy?"

Rachel gave my father a steady gaze that all but buckled his knees. But neither his will nor his legs faltered.

"I'll tell you what I am," she said. "What I am is ashamed."

She turned away quickly, giving my father an unwanted glimpse of a perfectly rounded behind before disappearing into the kitchen. The door closed and he heard her moving around behind it, heard what he was sure were muffled sobs.

His impulse was to follow her, to demand an explanation, and, if that was necessary, to comfort her. Instead, he strode to the closet, put on his coat and hat, and left the apartment without another word.

He had no expectations as he clattered down the stairs, but, when he came to the bottom landing, there was the man who claimed to be his cousin, smoking a cigarette and faintly smirking.

"You're a crazy man," my father said.

"Sure, I'm crazy. Thinking you would loan me more money, *that* would be crazy."

"Another loan?" My father was flabbergasted. "Is that what this is about? Money? You *are* crazy."

"Sure, and you would have given it to me, just like that."

"As a matter of fact, I would have," my father said, although, afterwards, he wasn't so sure.

"Just given it to me," Reuben repeated, this time with considerable bitterness, "without making me beg like you did the last time."

My father stared at the man for a moment, at his outstretched palm, then brushed past him, going through a doorway into a narrow outer hall with a filthy tile floor, then through a heavy door and onto a stoop. He stood on the top step for a moment, allowing his eyes to accustom themselves to the darkness, but he didn't want to linger, should Reuben follow him. He plunged down the steps and headed toward the subway station. Around him, Brooklyn hunched like an animal, expectant.

Towards the end of the war, when *The Day* was in its year-long strike and my father was working as a silversmith by day, driving cab at night, and he and my mother were afraid of losing the house they'd built in New Jersey, he went to his brother Henry for a loan. Years later, when he would talk about this, sitting at our kitchen table in his undershirt, drinking port from a water glass, he would mention that the sum was forty dollars – all he needed to make the difference between what he had and what he needed for that month's mortgage payment.

Henry said no. This was my uncle Henry, my *Uncle* Henry, who my father had helped to put through law school, who, when I was older, used to pull pennies out of my ears, always had a joke, and would gravely advise children to "follow your nose and you won't get lost." My father found the money elsewhere, and he did the next month and the month after, too, but eventually they did lose the house, and they moved me, still an infant, and my sisters into a converted chicken coop not far away.

My father continued to be friendly with his brother, so, if he felt any resentment, he didn't show it. Most likely, any resentment he might have felt would have been directed not at his brother but at *himself*, not at the one who turned him down but at the one who had asked. Still, it grated him that his own brother has refused him such a small sum. "*Forty dollars*," he would say to me, with vehemence. Then, finishing his glass of port: "Neither a borrower nor a lender be."

"Shakespeare," I would say.

"The Bible," he'd reply, smiling. "That was one time the Bible got it right."

A Message from the Brontës

HE CAME HOME from the fields for dinner one spring day and found the table bare, his wife curled in her chair by the fire weeping, uncontrollable sobs wracking her slender body, pearl-like tears rolling down her alabaster cheeks.

Both of them were young, newly married, little more than strangers despite the new intimacy they'd been pressed into, she sixteen, he thirty-two, exactly twice her age, but he would live into his eighties, outliving her by fifteen years, confounding him.

The marriage had been arranged, and they'd been together for barely four weeks the day he found his young wife in tears.

"My fr-fr-friend," she stammered, raising her luminescent eyes toward him. "My fr-fr-friend is d-d-dead." Her slim shoulders shook, and he had to take them in his stub-fingered, calloused hands to keep her from falling from the chair. He gazed at her in amazement. He hadn't seen a woman cry since he was a small boy and his mother's fifth son, his third younger brother, was born dead, and dealing with it was something beyond his experience and ken. And what she was talking was nonsense, of course, since he knew her to have no friends in the neighbourhood, no one who dropped in on her or whom she went to visit. All she did do, he knew, other than prepare his meals, keep the house in some semblance of cleanliness – though it would have made his mother shudder – and shrink from him in their bed at night, was read, one book after another from the bundle of them she'd brought with her along with the trunk of clothes and bedding that was her dowry.

"My f-f-fr-friend," she wailed, throwing back her head in a gesture that may have been more feigned than real, and gradually, slowly, he came to realize that the friend she was lamenting so noisily and wetly was a character in the book she'd been reading. He let go of her shoulders and reached for the book, and the increase in pitch of her wailing told him he was correct. He stared in respectful wonder at the open pages, but, since he could not himself read, they held nothing for him.

Though it was the middle of May, it was a cool, cloudy day and there was a fire in the hearth. He knelt by it, the book in his hands, and began to tear out pages, feeding them into the eager flame. "No, no," she whispered, her hands opening and closing into tiny fists which beat helplessly against her thighs. He ignored her, his own fingers busy with the unfamiliar task.

"Sh-sh-she had pneu-pneu*monia*," she sobbed, as if, somehow, that simple explanation would settle everything.

He got up and rubbed the ashes from his knees. Then, searching them out, he gathered together all the books in the house, all the ones she'd brought with her, and crouched again by the hearth to tear and feed the pages to the fire.

"T-t-too late," she whimpered, but he paid her no heed.

"No more books," he said when they were all consumed. "There'll be no more readin' in this house."

It's hard to believe – burning books! – that someone could act that way, but it was long ago, of course, in England, another world, another time, part of family lore. It's almost a fairy tale – a humble but pure serving girl, a wicked presence, a magic incantation – but it's easy to confuse who is who, which is which. All the more so because, as family lore again holds, there *were* books later, a whole matched set of the Brontës with red leather binding, though God only knows how much that must have cost, and all sorts of others as well.

And in the life the girl would grow to have, those early

weeks with her husband on the farm must have seemed like something that might have happened to someone else entirely, characters from a story she may have read, two-dimensional friends whose lives contain no more than what is revealed on the page – snatches of conversation that strike the ear just so, a pointed chin and luminescent eyes, details that attract the *writer's* eye more than the reader's, those few details that seem worth conveying in an attempt to make creatures of words spring to life – friends from a story who, for a few pages, seem so real, real enough that their passage can cause tears.

She was born Rosemary Higgins, and became Rosemary Wilcocks, one ordinary existence and identity transformed to another set with the simple stroke of the vicar's pen.

She was sixteen, the youngest daughter in a family of four girls and three sons, two of the little boys behind her. She had gone to school until the age of twelve, when it seemed no longer fitting or economic to continue wasting both her time and that of the schoolmistress, according to her father, who had apprenticed as a baker in London before setting up his own shop in the town where he'd been born. There were two bakeries in the town and only enough business, really, for one and a half, or perhaps one large one, so while bread was abundant – "Thank God for that," Rosemary's mother used to say – other things were scarce. At sixteen, the girl knew her manners, and many other things, could sew and cook as well as she'd ever be able to, could read – her recitations from Coleridge and Tennyson were a delight to her father, who had developed a taste for such things in London – and had a voice sweet as a nightingale's. This according to family lore.

He was a Wilcocks from the long line of that family to farm in the Dunnegan area of upper Yorkshire where the sheep herds have made the woollen mills famous, though he himself was a poor husbandryman and only a mediocre tiller of the soil.

He was a man of surprisingly flat imagination, with a devotion to the land that went no further than the crude delight brought by the feel of freshly turned earth in his thick hands, the flickering pleasure in his eyes produced by the first budding tinge of green across the brown fields. He was the second oldest of five sons, with four sisters as well, but had the fortune to see his mother mourn not only over the grave of the stillborn youngest but that of the oldest, dead at thirteen of a stomach ailment brought on by the eating of green apples, and that of her husband, his heart failing as he trudged in the traces behind his team. So, while the younger boys shunted off to work in the mills at Leeds and the girls took husbands with similar ambitions, Ernest Wilcocks was left with the dubious inheritance of the land his own father had barely been able to eke a living from.

Ernest toiled on, with a hired hand to help in the fields and his mother tending to the duties of the house until, in his thirty-first year, all the other children gone, she gave in to pneumonia. Then he was alone, musing in the evening by the fireside, his hands busy with some piece of harness needing mending or a tool caked with rust, but his eyes flickering restlessly from one blue-yellow spurt of flame to another, fascinated by the motion, with thought just beginning to coalesce into shape behind irises brown as the land they spent so much time contemplating. His experience with women, if any at all, would have been limited. The marriage – again, according to family lore – was more than convenient, it was logical.

The wedding was a simple one, attended only by the sisters and brothers of the young couple and their families, Ernest's aunt, who had been so instrumental in seeing the union come to pass, and a few others. Ernest made his x in the Bible and registry just below Rosemary's flowing, precise signature, and the small gathering moved from the church to the home of the baker, one of those stucco and beam cottages with wisteria trailing along the door frames that tourists from Canada and the States now find so irresistible, with the baker and his wife playing the part of beaming host and hostess, though it was Ernest Wilcocks who paid the bills. There was no honeymoon, it being April and much preparation still necessary before seeding – that was the reason given. The girl brought with her a trunk filled with crisp, fresh-smelling linens, spreads, curtains, towels and aprons, most of which she had sewn herself, though a few were borrowings from an older sister's hope chest, and a smaller trunk with her meagre collection of clothes, an armful of books, a battered rag doll.

The books! There were Brontës, Austens, Dickenses, a Thackery and an Eliot, mostly cheaply bound volumes that had come for a handful of pennies from the carts of ped-dlers, and even a handsome, illustrated *Pamela*, which had been a present, in Rosemary's last year of school, from the schoolmistress, who had hoped for better things for the girl than a baker's apron and marriage. They were battered, with cracked bindings and dog-eared pages, one of the Brontës so loosely held together that Rosemary had fashioned a ribbon to bind it. They were her world, as much as the expanse of green and brown stretching in all directions from the thatched farmhouse to which she was brought was his, the geography of their pages representing the boundaries and horizons of her life.

Much of what she knew of the world and the life lived upon it, with the exception of household skills, spun directly from those pages, giving richness to her speech and emo-tions, as well as, of course, her dreams. Marriage, then, was not something to hold fear for her, for she had, probably, a more brightly illuminated knowledge of that institution than most girls her age, nor was the farm, with its crude comforts and loneliness, a burden but, rather, a vaguely familiar setting for scenes perhaps to be recreated, scenes snatched directly from *Pride and Prejudice* or *Wuthering Heights*. They were, the books, without exaggeration, her most precious possessions, but more than that: they were the bones upon which the flesh and blood of her life depended.

But there was nothing in those books to prepare Rose-mary for her wedding night, or the nights which followed. There had been something about Heathcliffe's smell, and the look in his eyes, but the smell which radiated from Ernest Wilcocks' skin, even as they took their first tentative dance together at the wedding party, was not at all what she'd expected, nor was the look he was giving her when they retired to their room at the inn, the one concession to holiday, since the party went well into the evening and it was most of half a day's drive by oxcart to the farm, a trip that could wait until the next day. Nor had anything her mother told her – that she should be obedient, stoical, hopeful – been of any help. She only partly undressed, and shrank in the bed, goosebumps on her skin, heart pounding beneath her ribs and her breath ragged in her open mouth, while he stood on the other side of the room, as far from the bed as he could get, feeling foolish and chilly in his long underwear, but embarrassed to slip out of them and into his nightgown.

"Don't you worry none, girl," he said finally, his meaning oblique.

"I'm not afraid," Rosemary answered quickly, though she clearly was.

There was a rocking chair in the room and Ernest Wilcocks made it his bed that night, but before he went to it he blew out the candles, approached the bed where she crouched, clutching a pillow to her middle, the smell emanating from her skin as powerful and characteristic as his, leaned over her, put one hand on her shoulder and lowered his head, as if to graze her hair with his lips, and would have, likely, had her head not involuntarily jerked aside. "Tomorra'll be soon enou' fer me, miss," he said. "In yer new home, our home."

But the next day, and the days after it, made little difference. Rosemary wandered around the drafty farmhouse, most of its upstairs rooms closed off, in a daze, her eyes glassy and her lips trembling, always, it seemed to Ernest, just a caught breath away from chest-racking sobs and tears. As soon as he and the hired man, a mute who'd lost his tongue in some horrible adventure Rosemary could only imagine, would leave in the morning for the fields, she'd quickly tidy up and put something on the stove for dinner, then lose herself in one of the books, like someone trapped in a small, close room finally getting the window open for a deep breath of real air. She'd remember to rouse herself in time to take the men their meal, but then she was back in her chair by the fire or, on a fine day, on a swing left over from some distant childhoods in the apple orchard beside the house, the book propped up on her knee or, just as often, lying pages down on her breast as she gazed into the fire or upward, at the budding leaves and the great blue sky beyond.

In her mind, great romantic visions swept over the rocky, dramatic landscape that, by the noonday sun as she clambered over it with the men's meal, never seemed quite as stark as in the pages of her books. But at night, after the kitchen had been set to rights, and the mute, his only parting sound a discreet scraping of the legs of his chair, had left for the small shepherd's cottage across the barnyard where he slept, the visions returned, shivering down like fire-rotted wood crumbling in the hearth's blaze, spraying meaningless sparks against the screen, giving light but no heat unless you actually touched them. Tension rose in the room like a fog. "Three days more and we'll be fer th' seedin'," Ernest said, and Rosemary nodded, lifting her eyes from the knitting she occupied herself with when reading would have been, at the best, impolite, mumbling "That's good, that's a blessing," words as transient as the sparks or the wings of moths beating softly against the window. "If th' rain'll keep off that long," Ernest said, his voice uncertain as smoke, "that's all we need, really, then let 'er come down hard as she wants."

In their bedroom, Rosemary would bundle herself in her long, thick nightgown while Ernest was making his final visit to the privy, and she was in bed, the covers up to her chin, by the time he appeared. Ernest, for his part, would go as far as his underwear, then douse the candle before shedding them for his gown, climbing into his cold half of the bed with such care it made her think he was afraid to disturb some fragile thing lying hidden in the mattress. He put his hand on her shoulder, felt her shrink, hesitated. "It's a'right, girl, no need ter push it, when yer ready'll be soon enou' fer me." On the fourth night, he dispensed with the speech, merely laying stiffly back, his shoulders heavy and rigid against the sheets below the pillow, and felt her hand slip into his, no more than that, a small, warm token of gratitude that filled his heart with a bruised, miserable joy.

Quickly, they fell into patterns, like an old married couple, broken only once in those awful but strangely comfortable weeks when, his throat tight with purpose, one night Ernest left the candle flickering as he took off the last of his clothes, then came around to her side to sit naked on the edge of the bed, looking like nothing she'd ever encountered in the pages of the Brontës. "It t'ain't all tha' much ter be a skeered a, is it, now?" he said softly, but as he touched her hair the shadow along his thigh jerked suddenly, thickening before her amazed eyes.

She twisted under his touch and threw her head back, eyes closed, like a woman in the throes of labour. "Oh, God, do what you will, I'm not afraid, I'm ready," she cried out, in a voice sweet as a night bird's call, bringing the faint beginnings of tears, just the stinging, to Ernest's eyes, and he quickly leaned over the bedside table to blow out the candle. She wasn't ready, he knew that, and, despite his own confusion, he found himself trapped in the pattern that he himself had established, some twisted ritual of obligation and courtesy.

She *was* ready, then, they both were, for some rupture, some bursting of the dark clouds which had been menacing the fields without deliverance, the afternoon he came home early, the blood in his veins filled with courage and resolve. She had been reading, her usual afternoon occupation, curled this cloudy, cool day in the deep chair by the fire with *Haggerty Hall*, that little novella by Charlotte that has fared so poorly in modern times, all but forgotten. For hours, she'd been engrossed in the progress of Nell, even though she'd read the book a dozen times before.

Nell, if you're not familiar with the story, is an orphan who falls in deep but seemingly unrequited love with the aloof son of the mysterious benefactor who plucks her from the orphanage and gives her work as a maid at his estate, Haggerty Hall, the brooding, rambling mansion set upon the wind-swept moors. The son sets out to sea, perhaps to make his fortune, perhaps merely to prove something – Charlotte fails to make that clear – and Nell, still happy in her simple life at the Hall but consumed with misery at the thought of perhaps never seeing young Robert again, and not suspecting, as we, the readers, do, that her love is returned, spends many long evening hours on the cliffs overlooking the sea, imagining that she can see him, safe and happy on some distant wave, his face turned to the sun; and it's there, Charlotte makes clear, that she catches the small complaint that grows and grows, at least partly due to her neglect, festering itself into a pneumonia that finally kills her, even as Robert's ship is docking, his handsome face turned, not to the sun or sea, but toward the moors, toward Haggerty Hall, and, we finally come to know with certainty, toward Nell, the rose of his heart he fully expects, within days, to pluck.

It was just a few pages before this point, before Nell has actually expired but all that is to follow is clearly foreshadowed, that the restraint holding back Rosemary's tears crumpled and the book, its final movements so well known to her, slid down into her lap, then onto the floor as her body trembled with sobs and the hands she pressed to her face came away wet with tears, tears which, even in her misery, she was lucid enough to know were as much for herself as they were for the fleshless, lifeless girl in the book.

It was just then, in one of those coincidences that are inexcusable in literature but pepper the passing moments of real life, that Ernest arrived home, pushing open the door of the farmhouse to find it cool and filled with a sound he didn't immediately recognize. He stood in the doorway, unheard, for a moment, and observed his wife in her misery while his mind struggled to absorb and understand what he saw. There was nothing he had done or said, he knew, that might have brought this on; the pain, therefore, must arise from somewhere within the sufferer herself. He took a tentative step into the room, a floorboard beneath his foot telegraphing his presence with a ragged cry.

"My fr-fr-friend," Rosemary stammered, raising her small pointed chin and swiveling her head toward him, her eyes almost blind with tears. Through that wet blur, she couldn't make out Ernest's face, only his shape, round-shouldered and dark in his rough smock, but she had no difficulty in knowing it was him. "My friend is d-d-dead."

Ernest stepped closer, shaking his head in bewilderment. The tears were not something he felt must be contained, so he made no effort to comfort her, instead focusing his attention on attempting to understand their cause.

"My friend," Rosemary wailed, her head jerking back in a gesture of hysteria, and, if it was clear to her who she meant, it could not have been for him since, as far as he knew, she had no friends, not here on the farm, miles away from the bakery, her family and whatever other echoes there might be of the life she'd given up to join him, no friend-ships at all beyond the yet-to-be-developed relationship with him, and he dared not allow himself to make that confusion. He came abreast of the chair and stood gazing down at that dear face, his own lips trembling with a pain he couldn't fathom, his hands moving with a volition of their own toward her cheeks, fingers splayed, touching gently, and he was alarmed but didn't step back when she covered his hands with hers, pressing them tight against her face, then threw her arms around his waist, pressing her face into his belly, just above the belt, the sobs still convulsing her upper body rippling through him like sensual vibrations.

"Sh-she had pneu-pneumonia," Rosemary whimpered after a while to his uncomprehending attention. "She waited and waited, but he d-d-didn't come back and th-then she caught pneu-pneumonia and died and it was t-t-too late."

Gradually, with the kind of slow but unstoppable deter-mination of ice melting in spring, it came to him that the friend whose passing had caused her so much grief was a character in the book he was staring down at, spine-broken at his feet, its pages splayed like cards in a scattered deck. He stepped back, pulling himself out of her grasp, and bent painfully over to scoop up the book, his back still sore from where the long harness dug into it as he guided the team of horses down the endless furrows of black soil. He scruti-nized the open pages with suspicion, but, since he could not read himself and his experience with books went no further than the Bible his mother had kept, unread but often handled, on the table beside her bed until the day she died, the lines of print seemed like no more than insects, about to swarm off the page and onto his hands, and, in a sudden revulsion, he threw the book aside.

The fire had gone out while Rosemary sat transfixed with the final days of Nell's life. Ernest prodded the embers with the poker as the hazy fibres of an idea began to spin together in his mind, finding an orange glow deep in the grey, then a flurry of sparks. He knelt by the hearth and took the book in his hands, tearing out first one page, then, emboldened, two others, crumpling and stuffing them into the embers, prodding with the poker and leaning forward to blow until the sparks flew again and one of the pages, like a tuft of dry grass, exploded into flame. Then he was tearing pages from the book with a single-minded fury, stuffing them into the fire and ignoring the drumming of small fists on his bowed back, the cries of protestations, "no, no, no," that seemed to come to him through ether, from a far distance. When he'd crumpled the last of the pages, he tossed the collapsed binding in after them, stirring the fire again with the poker, and stacked on new logs until it was blazing.

"T-t-too late," Rosemary sobbed, but the violence had slipped out of her shoulders and she lay back, huddling in the big, thick-armed chair like a child, hugging herself as she watched the flames dance, her voice a soft murmur. She must have known what would happen, where the string she had torn loose would lead, and she had armed herself against it, shielding her eyes with an invisible skin so, though they remained open, they refused to see. She watched him now, without any reaction or sign that what she saw registered on her consciousness, as he rose and brushed ashes from his knees, as he gathered up from the shelf above the table, from the chair on her side of the bed, and from her trunk, still not completely unpacked, all the books in the house, all the ones she had brought with her, even the precious Richardson, and crouched again by the fire to tear and feed the pages, in huge clumps, into it. "Too late," she murmured again, to herself, but it was only words, spoken without meaning, for, without either of their knowledge, something had entered the room that was just about to make itself known.

"No more books," Ernest said when they were all consumed, the final pages turning like black fingers clutching themselves into crumbling fists. "No more books. There'll be no more readin' in this house. Hear, girl?"

Then he gathered her in his arms and carried her up the stairs, holding her lightly as he might an armload of hay, and laid her gently on the bed, on top of the covers where there was no place to hide. He thought she would just lie there as he undressed her, but as soon as his hands began to work on the buttons of her dress she sat up and threw herself into his embrace, much as she had downstairs when she'd pressed her face into his belly. Clearly, he thought, something was happening. Her mouth found his and, to the best of their ability and knowledge, they kissed, a stumbling kiss with lips and teeth and tongues in the way, and a heat rose from them real as the radiating glow from the fire downstairs. When his clothes were all off, finally, she gazed with amazement at the thing between his legs, so different now than the other time she'd seen it, alive and strong, sleek and graceful, beautiful – *golden* – and she reached out, like an awed child, one small hand, fingers trembling, to touch it. Then they were embracing again, entangled, and she felt a battering against her softness, like the wings of moths against the window, then a piercing, something sharp and sweet as the blaze of sunrise in her just-opened eyes, and she cried out in pain at the same moment that he made a smaller noise, little more than a gasp of surprise.

There was no pleasure in it for her, other than that sweet pain, and what there was for him, just that moment's sudden flashing, could not have been much more than release, but they lay locked together for a long time afterwards, smiling into each other's hair, engrossed in their own thoughts, not yet speaking, not yet knowing, if they ever would, what to say. She felt him stirring in her and she jerked her head slightly, then smiled and nodded her head to signify "nothing" when he arched his head back with questioning eyes. *In her*, like two parts of something whole, that small prize of flesh turning within her like a gift, a joining too mysterious and secret for words, a mystery too sacred even for books, whose authors could only point, hoping the reader would find the way.

The Man I Am

ONE LEAFY SPRING day when I was thirteen, I stood on a streetcorner talking to a boy named Burton Sachs and he told me a story about a man whose penis was bitten off by his girlfriend when she sneezed.

Think of all the millions of moments in a lifetime, the thousands of conversations, events, sightings, smells, thoughts, and then think of the handful of memories we carry around with us. We can spiel off – with relative accuracy – dozens of things we did, saw, heard yesterday, but the further back we go the more difficult it gets, the fuzzier. That year I was thirteen – it was 1955, in Toronto – I did all the things one supposes a boy in my circumstances would: got up every morning, ate breakfast, went to school, did whatever it was we did there, talked to my friends, played games and sports, had dinner with my family, did homework, listened to the radio, read, lay awake in bed counting shadows on the ceiling, dreaming. But most of it is a blur, as is your thirteenth year, and our eighth and twenty-third. A few moments stand out, important moments that, by the weight of their importance, have made impressions on the wet sand of memory. There are others that can be dredged up, if we direct our minds to them. And a few linger for inexplicable reasons: memories of a smell encountered upon entering a room, of a moment of fear that pulled the skin of your scrotum tight as that of a fresh peach, of a smile from a certain girl, caught with the side of the eye from across a classroom. And so, over the years, that moment with Burton is fixed in time and space with the same certainty of memories with more purpose: the time I flooded the kitchen, the hollow feeling when I left home, a certain kiss, my mother's horrible death in the fire.

I haven't seen Burton Sachs since we were boys together but I recall his name with certainty because of a game I used to play, turning people's names around. His read out as *Notrub Shcas*, a pleasing, punny sound I'd be as unlikely to forget as "kemo sabe" or "shazam." The year I'm thinking of was the last before high school, when my life began its abrupt transition toward adulthood, and, judging from the canopy of pea-green leaves waving above us as we talked, it was spring, April or May. We are standing – I *think* – on the corner of Dufferin and Dupont, which was several blocks from my home, and I believe Burton lives nearby, perhaps in the brick apartment building on the corner. It's not a building I'm familiar with, and yet I can see it clearly: the brick faded to the colour of sand, a concrete arch over the entrance with small rectangular anchors painted a vivid blue, open windows, six stories' worth, framed by fluttering white curtains. In fact – since the memory does play tricks – what I'm seeing may not be the building where we're standing at all but the one where my friend Hal lives, and where our dentist, Dr. Shatz, lives and keeps his office, a few blocks away on Davenport Road, a building I've been in hundreds of times. Hal is nowhere in sight this afternoon, nor is Larry, the two of them the friends I would most likely have been with any time after school that year, trading comic books, playing catch or singing *a cappella* versions of "Sh-Boom" or "Stranded in the Jungle."

There is no real reason why I should be with Burton – he's not a particular friend and I can summon up no other single recollection of him, just the general, hazy memory of him as one of the faceless, interchangeable boys in my class at Dufferin School. A boy called Alfred stands out because of his offensive smell. Mark Somebody because of his dazzling black hairdo, glistening with Vitalis, the part marching its way across his scalp like a line of albino warrior ants. Peter, the one Negro boy in the class. One or two others. But not Burton, except for his backward name and this moment, the story he is telling me now, his eyelids fluttering with excitement, the flutter and the story itself rolling on unbidden through the years.

"Can you imagine the blood?" he is saying, and I believe it is this image which most enthralls him, a rich vision of blood pumping out of the cleanly severed stump – the way water gushed from fire hydrants we kids would pry open in the hottest days of summer – that he could almost smell, and, indeed, his short, slightly puggish nose is wrinkling at the thought. "And never, ever being able to do it," he says, the immensity of that loss sweeping over him and straightening his features. "Never ever."

"But why didn't he pull it out?" I ask. The question is ingenuous. I am, in all ways, fascinated, perplexed and preoccupied with sex, but I am, perhaps because of my mother's strictness, her protectiveness, a bit behind my peers. I know all about intercourse, though I'm several years away from my first experience with it, and I know about what we call blow jobs, but the notion of teeth so close, so menacing, makes me edgy, certain I would be more cautious.

Burton laughs, not so much at me as with genuine delight at my simpleness. He is a big boy, but not a bully, with a tousle of dark brown hair worn, like mine, clipped close on the sides, a cowlick in the front which now, as he frequently does, he brushes back with his hand. "Are you kidding? Ain't you ever done it? The harder she blows, the better it feels. He musta thought he was gonna come like all hell busting loose."

Traffic is passing, its noise spraying against us like rainwater from the gutter. There are schoolbooks in my hand, so I know it's afternoon and I'm on my way home. Burton has a magazine in a brown paper bag, a girlie magazine, not *Playboy* but one like it, and he's showing me pictures, holding the magazine close to his chest and standing sideways. There are – I believe – pictures of girls at a pool party, the tops of their bathing suits off, their breasts flopping like wine sacks as they leap into the water. Burton is saying something, but the memory fades here, the mind's needle stuck endlessly in the groove of this moment, the phrase leading to it repeating again and again. Exit Notrub Shcas. It's not *he* I remember so well, but the story he tells, his delight in its telling, the pumping blood, its scent in his nostrils, the involuntary tightening of my shoulder blades, as if a fingertip had been zipped up my spine or a piece of chalk scraped across a blackboard, at the thought of teeth.

The obligation of memory – its demand – is that we make sense of what sticks, or try to. Over the years, I must have thought of that moment with Burton hundreds of times, but I cannot say why. I am not perverse by nature, my sex life is normal, I have no peculiar attraction to violence. When I put my mind to it, I can summon up dozens of other sex-related memories of childhood, but this particular one needs no summoning up; it arises on its own, much the way I often find myself thinking of the premonition – there is no other word for it – of my father's death I had when I was eight.

He was on a night shift, leaving for work just as I was being readied for bed, and often he would come to say goodnight and tuck me in already wearing his frayed leather jacket. After the light was put out and the door shut, I would crawl out of bed and hurry to the window, sidling against the curtain until the pool of light from the open front door spilled out across the sidewalk. Then I'd pull back, so just my nose was against the edge, and watch as he moved across my line of vision, then out of it again. I'd fall to my knees at the window, craning my neck to watch him back the car out of the garage and pull away. Then, secure in the knowledge that he was safely on his way, I could sleep. But this night – it was in February and a soft, feathery snow had been falling since before school let out – I cried when he turned off the light. I didn't know why, just didn't want him to go and told him so. "Don't be silly, Martin, you know I have to go to work," he said, coming back to the bed to lean over me and kiss the top of my head. But I was cold, and I didn't get out of bed that night to watch, and I never saw him again.

I think of that often – not his death, but the way I seemed to know – and usually without warning. Looking up from a book, or settling behind the wheel of the car, just before I turn the key, there it will be, that shivering moment, as fresh and real now as ever. But that doesn't surprise me.

I live in the west now. I don't get back to Toronto often and, when I do, I always have mixed feelings. The city has become so big, so frantic. Still, it breathes a vitality, an excitement I don't find where I live. Two weeks ago, I was there on business and I was struck once again by how much I like visiting, but how little I would like living there again. On the second day, I went to dinner with a friend who works at the *Star*. She moved to Toronto because it seemed her career demanded it, but now she's an editor and feels as stifled and stuck as she was ten years ago in Saskatoon. She was telling me some of this on the streetcar home. I had met her at her office, and we had a drink in a bar up the street on Yonge that hurt my eyes with its glitter. We had to stand for the first few stops, jostling against each other in the crowded streetcar, one of the bright red new ones. Then we found a double seat toward the back, and my friend was so engrossed in her story, about a piece she'd wanted to run but was killed by her superior, that we missed her stop and had to walk back a few blocks through the slushy snow.

"God, I don't know where my head is today," she said, laughing, her hand on my arm.

"In mine," I said.

"It's okay, I have to stop at the store anyway and there's one on this side that's better than where I usually go."

We went into a Mini-Mart, and my friend collected milk and bread and a composite log, one of the kind that makes coloured flames and burns for hours. I picked out several pastries, a butter tart for each of us and an eclair for her daughter, who is the same age as my eldest son, and I was paying for them when I was attracted by the voices.

"I never even done it."

"Don't give me that, I know you did."

They were loud enough to make me turn, and when I had my change I wandered closer, pretending to be looking at the magazines in the rack. The boy was about fifteen, husky, wearing shiny grey pants with fatigue pockets and a cheap bomber jacket. His skin was black and shiny as the plastic housing of the electronic cash register. The policeman was tall and broad, but starting to sag, like a house in which beams and posts are rotting. He had one of those bland, expressionless faces affected by bureaucrats that make them so hard to remember when you're trying to find them a second time, but his hat was tilted slightly to the side, almost rakishly, revealing salt-and-pepper hair swept back fifties-style and sideburns long as police regulations likely allow. There were three stripes on the arm of his jacket and a tag marked "supervisor" below his chin to the left of the zipper.

"What you mean, someone *saw* me?" the boy was saying. "I been in here all this time." He was playing an arcade game, standing with legs apart in front of it, torso bent slightly forward, eyes fixed on the flashing lights, trying to be as cool as he could.

"Sure, sure," the cop said. "You been in here since the break of day. You ain't been to school?"

"School's out *hours* ago, man. Why'n't you leave me alone, I ain't done nuthin'."

"I *know* what you done. What I'm telling you is, I don't want to hear about you doing it again. You hear me, boy?"

The kid snapped his head up and around, the hairs on the back of his neck bristling. "Wha' you buggin' me for. I didn't do nuthin'. Tell me who says I did."

"The people you was bothering."

"Aw, man, *who* was I botherin'? I don't see nobody looks bothered. Show me these people."

"I don't have to show you squat. I'm *telling* you, I know you did it and you ain't gonna do it again, understand me?"

I guess I was staring at them, and when the cop looked up, he flashed me a sour, crooked smile and began to push the kid toward the door.

"Hey, man, I ain't done playin'," the kid complained.

"You done enough," the cop said. "C'm'on, get outta here before I lose patience with you."

"Hey, man, this is still a free country, ain't it? I got a goddamn quarter in there."

The argument kept lapping back at itself as they edged toward the door, the cop shoving, the kid resisting but not enough not to be moved, and I went back to the counter where my friend was getting her change. She'd been listening too and we looked at each other, twisting our lips in identical awkward half smiles. The man behind the counter, an East Indian wearing a dirty white shirt, shrugged and looked away. I put the small pastry bag in her bigger one and collected it in my arms, holding it the way schoolgirls hold their books shielding their breasts.

When we stepped out the door, the argument was still going on, and my friend gave the policeman a sharp look. The cop grinned at her like a boy caught stealing apples. "Kids," he said, shaking his head, as if that word, in the vastness of its singleness, would explain everything. Then, waving the boy off and starting to move away, he said over his shoulder: "G'wan, get outta here. G'wan home and eat your watermelon."

"Aw, man," the kid said. "That all? Ain't you gonna call me nigger? Go ahead, man, say it."

"That wasn't called for at all," my friend said. We had stopped, and she was staring at the cop as if sizing him up for a punch or kick.

"Lady, you don't know what this kid is like," the cop said. There was no embarrassment in his voice, no apology.

"It doesn't matter what he's like," my friend said. "There was no call for you to say a thing like that."

"You should hear the language that comes out of him."

"I *have* been hearing it. I haven't heard him make a racist remark to you. And even if he did, that wouldn't justify *you* doing it."

The cop glared at her and shook his head, and I could almost hear the things he'd be saying later at the station, about this busy-body lady who took the side of this delinquent he'd been reprimanding, how you couldn't rely on public support anymore and damned if it wasn't getting to where the job was hardly worth it.

"And you're a supervisor," my friend said.

"That's right," he grinned, feeling vindicated.

"You should be setting an example, not waiting for one."

He shook his head and turned his back, walking away. The kid, who had listened to the exchange, melted into the shadows. My friend looked around and saw me standing on the corner, frozen to the spot, still holding the grocery bag like a shield.

Finally, there is Peter.

There was a class photo once, showing us all, me and Hal side by side, grinning like fools, smelly Alfred and slick Mark, Notrub and the others whose faces and names I can't remember. Girls too: skinny Sandra, whose father was our postman; blonde Linda, with breasts and hips already and always so stuck up; Sheila, the girl who put her knee between my legs when we necked during post office at the party after graduation. Girls I never saw again, because we moved that summer, and haven't thought of since. Those are the faces and names I remember, those and Peter. If I had the picture in front of me, I probably would remember others, names of a few, something of perhaps all of them – that is to say, I would look at the face of a certain chubby boy and remember the funny golashes he wore; at the cherubic face of a girl, and the feel of her hand in mine as we lined up for assembly would come back to me. These are the gems memory gives up if it's mined, like slivers of gold sluiced along with gravel into a pan.

The picture, framed and with signatures and funny sayings on the back, was in a trunk in the attic of my mother's house in Brampton, along with my high school yearbook, my swimming medals and a lot of old sweaters, but the last time I saw it – remember seeing it – was the summer before the fire, when I was home from university on holiday. Within the tin armour of that trunk, and behind its glass shield, the photograph may have survived, but my sister and I agreed there was no point in scavenging among the ashes and charred beams for mementos, and the bulldozers were sent in. After the funeral, I never went back to the site.

Even without the photograph's aid, I remember Peter vividly. He was the first black person I ever knew, though I'd seen others. This I *don't* remember, but my mother used to tell the story of the two of us standing in line at the Bay downtown once behind a Negro woman, a little boy about my size in tow, and, down there at the level of our mothers' knees, three or four years old, we found ourselves inspecting each other, gazing with wonder. I reached out – my mother used to say, always laughing as she retold the story – and stroked his face with my finger, then held up the finger for examination. Then, puzzled, looked up into my mother's amused eyes and asked: "Choc'late?"

I used the word again when I met Peter, my first day at Dufferin School. We had moved to the two-storey house on Concord Avenue after my father's death, and he was one of the classmates I inherited when I entered grade four. At supper that day, I mentioned there was "a chocolate boy" in my class.

"Don't use that word," my mother scolded me, with a sort of half smile-frown.

"Why not? You do."

"That's different, Martin. I use it when I tell that funny story, that's all, I don't really use it. And there's a difference between what you might say at home, where there's no one to take offence, and what you would say in public."

"This *is* home," I insisted, reluctant to give up, though I knew she was right.

"I know, dear, and I know you don't say it to be mean. But I don't want you to get into the habit. I don't want you ever to say anything that would hurt someone."

As far as I can remember, there was no hurt for Peter at our school. He was one of half a dozen or so blacks of all ages, some of them related, who drifted through the life of the school like punctuation points, part of its grammar of sameness, but different nonetheless. The only other one I

197

remember was a large, ebony-skinned girl, called Sharon, with enormous blue lips, who spoke with an accent so opaque as to be almost unintelligible. She, we all knew, was an African, plucked, we liked to believe, directly from some naked jungle village and deposited inexplicably in our midst. Her father was a janitor for the school board, not in our school but in one nearby, and he was arrested on a charge of molesting a girl in a washroom. The charge was dropped and he and his daughter disappeared. Sharon was so totally different from all of us and from anyone within our experience that I don't think we connected her in our thoughts with the other blacks in the school, anymore than the frequently erratic behavior of Mrs. O'Hara, the horrible woman with the huge red nose who owned our house and lived below us, would ever be construed as some general discredit to the white race, or the Irish. Our blacks were Negroes; Sharon was an African. In fact, though, I have no idea what Peter was, African, West Indian, home-grown or what.

We were friendly but not friends. He was in my class in grade four and six and again in grade eight, but we were not thrown together, except once. In those days, I lived for hockey, but Peter, rail thin and gangly, played basketball. In the spring and summer, we played baseball together, though: softball at school, hardball catch on the streets, pick-up games at the park. We had between us the same kind of easy locker room comradeship I had with lots of other boys. I know this out of the general pool of memory's knowledge, not because of any particular incident which has stuck with me. The one sharp memory of Peter I do have – the one unearthed in Toronto the other day – is of a very different kind.

It was spring, probably within weeks of that afternoon I stood on the corner with Notrub Shcas. In the memory, I am wearing dungarees, a striped polo shirt and sneakers. Peter and I both have our gloves under our arms and we're walking toward the house I live in, laughing. He is taller than I am and skinnier, dressed exactly the same, except his polo shirt is white, greyed from repeated washings and smudged with dirt from this afternoon's game. His skin is the colour of coffee with a teaspoon of milk, and his hair is short and without a part, clinging to his scalp like a burr.

We are talking about comic books, and that's why we're heading toward my place now. I had been reading *Mad* – the old comic version – since it first came out and I had most of them. Today, at gym, while we were climbing the ropes, Mr. Burke, the phys ed teacher, scolded Peter for being lazy and he replied with a shrug and a "What, me worry?" that broke us all up. In the locker room, we were talking, and it turned out he had a passion for *Mad* too. I want to show him my collection, find out if perhaps he has any of the ones I'm missing, and if he'd be willing to trade for some spares I have. We are engrossed in our conversation, and Peter is absently tossing the scuffed hardball a few inches into the air and catching it with a pink-palmed hand. We are already halfway up the porch steps, and I have not yet noticed her, when Mrs. O'Hara speaks.

"Where the bloody 'ell you boys think yer goin'?"

We stop short, and I look up sharply, but more in annoyance than shock. We had lived in the house, on the second floor, for four years, and I was used to Mrs. O'Hara's moods, which ranged from grouchy to furious. She was always carping about something, either the weather or the state of the neighbourhood or the stupidity of politicians, and, though she owned our house and several others in the row, she was quick to plead poverty if there was any repair to be made. She was dedicated to a campaign against noise and disorder, which pitched her constantly at war with the neighbourhood children, myself included. My mother had several times warned the woman to leave me alone.

"Just upstairs, Mrs. O'Hara," I say, starting up the next step and veering to the right to dodge around her.

"Not with this'n, you ain't," she says, and sticks out an arm made shapeless by the ragged sleeve of the thick wool sweater she is bundled in. The sweater, stained and ragged, had once been navy blue, but its colour now is more like that of a choppy sea.

I think I said "Huh?" but it may have been something more expressive.

"Not this nigger in this house, young mister."

I stared at her with disbelief for a few beats – I knew the word, of course, but had never heard it used against another person – before I turned to Peter, who had taken a step backward and was below me. As I watched, his eyes, which had already narrowed, turned a shade darker and tears sprang up in them.

"G'wan, get out of here, nigger, 'fore I get me broom," Mrs. O'Hara said to him. "And you, Martin, don't you be tryin' to sneak yer dirty friends through this door again or I'll have you and yer mother and yer snotty sister out on the street."

I was speechless – not frightened or upset, because the enormity of what was happening had not yet sunk in, merely speechless, so outside of my experience was it – and when Peter turned and ran down the walkway, I followed him without uttering a word. I don't know what would have happened – most likely him racing to the corner and pausing for breath, me catching up and standing awkwardly beside him trying to think of comforting words, him shrugging off my hand and sulking on toward home alone while I stood helpless trying to make sense of what had happened – but just at that moment, in one of those peculiar shiftings of circumstance that, with more force, can define history, my mother, who worked in an insurance office on Dupont and always left promptly at five to be home in time to make dinner, appeared.

She was walking up the street with her pocketbook swinging from her shoulder, a grocery bag in her arm, wearing a green dress and a matching green and white scarf, and her steps quickened when she saw Peter and I racing toward her. "Peter, wait up, it's my mother," I called, and we both stopped. My mother looked from Peter's face to mine, and I realized, when I saw her expression, that tears were streaming down my own cheeks.

"She called Peter a nigger," I sobbed. "She won't let us in the house." I didn't have to say who "she" was.

My mother knelt down, dropping what she'd been carrying, and put her arms around us both, Peter stiff and un-yielding, his tears already dry and sniffed back, me wanting only to bury myself deep within the safety there. "It's all right, Martin," she said. "Peter? I'm Martin's mother. I'm pleased to meet you. I apologize for our landlady's rudeness. She's a hateful woman. I hope you can forget what she said."

"I guess," Peter said, shrugging.

My mother stood up and collected her bags. She must have been forty, still a fine looking woman without the extra weight that bothered her so much later on, and I don't know enough about her childhood and young womanhood to know what had made her into the woman she was, what had prepared her for this late afternoon in spring in 1955. For what it's worth, she'd been raised Lutheran but wasn't much of anything now, though I know she believed in God and maybe even in Jesus, as an idea if not as someone who was once a real person, and she'd voted Liberal since she was old enough, though the last time she would vote, four years later, I know she went CCF because she told me so. She looked across the fence to the porch, where Mrs. O'Hara still stood, watching us. "Martin, dear, will you carry the groceries? Come along, Peter, we'll go upstairs. Perhaps you'd like to stay for dinner?"

Taking each of us by a hand, she marched to the walkway and turned in. Mrs. O'Hara took a step forward, like a sentry challenging an intruder. "Don't you say a word, Mrs. O'Hara," my mother said.

"An' why not? It's my house, ain't it? That lease of yer'n yer so fond a quotin' from don't say I can't speak me mind."

My mother stopped at the bottom of the steps and glared up at the woman. "It does say anyone can visit us. Anyone. And don't you ever dare to tell my son one of his friends can't come up to our suite."

"I'll not have that black devil in me house," Mrs. O'Hara said defiantly, her nose gleaming like a beacon. "That dirty nig...."

My mother let go of our hands and sprang up the steps. Mrs. O'Hara lurched back clumsily and my mother stopped just short of slapping her. They stood in a frozen tableau for a moment, the older woman pinned against the glass door, glaring at each other.

"Don't you say it," my mother hissed. "Don't you ever say it, now or ever." She drew back a few inches, her shoulders relaxing, and a sly look swept across Mrs. O'Hara's bloated face.

"Don't say nigger? That's a bloody laugh."

My mother reached down and picked up the flower pot at her foot. It was about the size of a football, and just that colour as well, and it contained petunias, three or four brave blue faces with vivid white tongues. "You witch, I'll kill you," she hissed. Mrs. O'Hara moved with surprising speed, ducking out of the way as the pot came crashing down against the wall where her head had been, and through the door, slamming it behind her, into the safety of the hallway, shrieking an unintelligible sound of pure fright. "I'll kill you," my mother screamed after her, but then she immediately turned away, her eyes filled with tears, and she bent down and gathered Peter and me in her arms. We huddled like that for what must have been minutes, and it's not clear to me now, fixing that space of time in my mind, whether she was holding us or we were holding her.

The police were called, I remember that, but not by who, or anything of what happened. I know we weren't evicted, although the relationship between us and Mrs. O'Hara, already poor, deteriorated. She and my mother never exchanged another word, and it fell on my sister to deliver the rent. That summer, we moved to Brampton. I have no memory of ever discussing the incident with Peter, or even of seeing him again. With the class picture burned, he exists now only in this remembered moment.

My mother, who was as good a woman as you could have asked for, lost her husband early, and died a horrible death, gasping for breath, smothered by smoke. It would give me some satisfaction, I suppose, to report that Mrs. O'Hara died horribly, too, of cancer, perhaps, but I have no knowledge of her after we moved. As for me, I have grown into what most people would describe as a decent man. I am still an athlete, and I have shouldered opposing players into the boards and to the ice, but I've always been a clean player. My marriage failed, but I don't believe that was my fault. My children, who I see quite often, love me, and, I believe, respect me. That moment with Peter, which I have thought about quite a bit in recent days, receded from my mind in the excitement of the end of the school year, examinations, graduation, parties, then our move, starting high school, making new friends, being on the hockey team, then swimming. I have to say I have not thought about it for twenty years or more, but it came flooding back to me with the force of an accident on the highway that lingers vividly in the mind as I stood frozen to the ground outside the Mini-Mart watching my friend scold the indifferent policeman. I was too busy for the next couple of days, attending to my business, to think of it, but on the airplane coming home I allowed it to slip forward in my mind to where I could turn it over and over, like a coin being examined under a light. I studied it and probed it, looked at myself in it, my mother, even Peter, who was, after all, only an accidental player, and Mrs. O'Hara, of course, and I think of it still, at moments like this, when it seems to be important to try to understand how I came to be transported from the boy I was then to the man I am today.

Acknowledgements

Some of these stories have appeared in the following magazines and anthologies: "A Book of Great Worth," originally in *The Windsor Review*, subsequently in *Due West: Thirty Great Stories from Alberta, Saskatchewan and Manitoba* (NeWest/Coteau/ Turnstone, 1996) and *96: Best Canadian Stories* (Oberon Press, 1996); "Feathers and Blood," in *Out of Place* (Coteau Books, 1991); "Goodbye to All That," in an earlier version, in *Descant*; "The Man I Am" and "River Rats" in *The New Quarterly;* "Night Is Coming" and "Pennies on the Tracks" in *Dalhousie Review*.

Long Distance Calls was winner of a Saskatchewan Writers Guild literary award for fiction manuscripts.

Words from "The Boy in the Bubble" by Paul Simon © 1986 Paul Simon/Paul Simon Music (BMI), used by permission of the publisher; words from "White Rabbit" by Grace Slick © 1966, renewed 1994, Irving Music, Inc. (BMI), all rights reserved, international copyright secured, used by permission of the publisher.

Author's Notes:

Writers are scavengers, magpies. We cannibalize our own lives and the lives of the people around us. The stories in this collection are indebted to my mother and father, and a number of friends, including Bob Beal, Anne Boody, Tom Fensch, Michael Henderson, Eric Horsting, the late Charlie Niehuis, Bill Perry, Pat Preston (and her kids) and Mary Veronica Whiteley-Dawson. Thanks (and apologies) to them all.

– D.M.

About the Artist

Alex Colville is one of Canada's most respected visual artists. Works such as *"To Prince Edward Island"* are recognized and appreciated throughout Canada and around the world.

A painter, draughtsman, printmaker, and muralist, he was born in Toronto in 1920, moved with his family to Nova Scotia in 1929, and graduated from Mount Allison University in New Brunswick. In 1942, he joined the Canadian Army and served in Europe as a member of the War Art program. After the war, he returned to Mount Allison University to teach art and art history and remained there until 1963.

Colville served as Chancellor of Acadia University in Nova Scotia from 1981 to 1991. He is an Officer of the Order of Canada.

Dave Margoshes is a fiction writer, poet, and journalist living in Regina, Saskatchewan. His work includes two short story collections, *Nine Lives* and *Small Regrets* (both Thistledown Press), and two collections of poetry, *Walking at Brighton* (Thistledown Press) and *Northwest Passage* (Oberon Press). He is also an editor and creative writing teacher, and was Winnipeg's writer-in-residence in 1995/96.

He won the 1996 Stephen Leacock Award for Poetry.

His stories and poetry have appeared in numerous anthologies, including three times in the *Best Canadian Stories* series.

Margoshes has worked for a number of newspapers including the New York *Daily News*, San Francisco *Chronicle*, Calgary *Herald* and Vancouver *Sun*.